Phil Campion, author of *Born Fearless* and *Desert Fire*, is a veteran of military operations in just about every conflict-prone corner of the world, both as a soldier in the regular Armed Forces, an elite operator and as a mercenary. He lives with his partner, Wendy, and their children and continues to work as an operator on the private military circuit.

LEFT FOR DEAD. BACK FOR REVENGE.
THE EXPLOSIVE NEW STEVE RANGE AND BLACKSTONE SIX THRILLER

KILLING RANGE

PHIL CAMPION

Quercus

First published in Great Britain in 2013 by
Quercus Editions Ltd

55 Baker Street
Seventh Floor, South Block
London
W1U 8EW

PBO ISBN 978 0 85738 445 4
EBOOK ISBN 978 0 85738 443 0

10 9 8 7 6 5 4 3 2

Text designed and typeset by Ellipsis Digital Limited, Glasgow
Printed and bound in Great Britain by Clays Ltd, St Ives plc

For Danny Kay,
who has been gone for a while now,
but will never be forgotten.

Acknowledgements

Special thanks to the following: Richard Milner, David North, Josh Ireland, Patrick Carpenter, Jane Harris, Caroline Proud, Dave Murphy, Ron Beard and all at my redoubtable publisher, Quercus. My literary agent, Annabel Merullo, and Laura Williams, her assistant. My film agent, the formidable Luke Speed. Publicist Digby Halby, and all at the aptly-named Flint PR. Very special thanks are also due to London-based SecureBio for the Chemical, Biological, Radiological and Nuclear (CBRN) defence advice and technical support, without which the CBRN aspects of this book would no doubt be far less realistic and far less on the nail. Thanks also to Julie Davies, Hamish de Bretton-Gordon, Jamie Napier and Steve Heaney MC, for reading the early drafts and for timely and apposite critiques of the story.

CHAPTER ONE

The sun beat down from a merciless sky as Range began
the walk. The bag felt strangely heavy in his sweat-soaked
palm. But what did he expect? Five million dollars was one
hell of a lot of responsibility to carry around.

The glare from the burning African blue sky seared into
his eyes. It was made all the worse by the fact that in every
direction around him the flat, featureless rock and sand
threw back the sun's rays like a force field. In the distance
he could just make out the thin, stick-like figures moving
towards him, their indistinct forms shimmering and
dancing in the heat.

One was the girl. That he knew from studying their position through a sniper's scope, just a few minutes before
each side had started to make the walk. The other was the
so-called Somali 'negotiator'; in other words, a gutless,

piratical bastard who preyed on the weak – innocent hostages like this girl – as a way to make a living.

To his rear Range had a handful of crack operators watching his back – some of the very best – but a fat lot of good they would be now, with him alone and isolated out here. The instructions from the Somali negotiator had been simple and impossible to misinterpret, leaving little, if any, scope for effective back-up.

'You come alone, with the money; I come alone, with the girl,' Amir had told him, speaking over an echoing satphone link. 'You leave your people with their vehicles; I leave mine with ours. You walk five hundred yards north; I walk five hundred yards south. We meet. I hand over the girl; you hand over the money. We turn around and walk back again.'

Range had told him that he understood.

'One more thing,' Amir had added. 'You come unarmed. I see a weapon, the deal's off. We get to keep the girl – maybe for ever.'

By the tone of his voice and the easy professionalism with which he treated this trade in human lives, Range figured Amir had done this countless times before. Word was that Amir al-Jihadi was a freelancer; he negotiated for whichever group of Somali pirates had the best and most lucrative kidnap and ransom deal going. He worked for no single group and had allegiances to no one. He took his cut – rumoured to be a cool 15 per cent – and moved on to the next victim.

Range could feel the sweat pouring off his exposed neck, trickling down the small of his back and pooling in his pants. He felt like he'd pissed himself; like he'd pissed himself with fear. He hadn't. He was just a big, taut, shaven-headed bloke in the very heart of the white man's graveyard that was this part of Africa. But the last thing Range wanted was for Amir to think that he was somehow fearful.

He took a long look around himself, as his boots crunched through the loose gravel and sand. There was nothing to mark this out as being an international border. Where northern Kenya met southern Somalia was a lawless wasteland, one wherein heavily armed tribes, warlords and rival clans battled for control. Yet in amongst all of this barren, sun-baked emptiness people like Amir and his kind were making serious amounts of money.

Range did a quick bit of mental arithmetic. Amir's 15 per cent of five million amounted to a cool $750,000. It was a shedload more than Range and his men were making on this job. Hell, they'd struggle to make that in a lifetime working as private military operators. They were on Blackstone Six's top rates for this contract: one thousand dollars a day, plus expenses. For a two-week tasking like this one Range would walk away with $14,000 – *that's if he walked away at all*.

Fourteen grand against Amir's $750,000: not for the first time Range wondered if he wasn't working for the wrong side. Range liked to tell people that his only loyalty was to his bank balance. That was only partly true. Sure, money was important, but in truth his first loyalty was to the blokes he soldiered with in Blackstone Six, and prior to that, those he'd served with when in the military.

After that came a cascading series of loyalties, and right now a big part of his allegiances lay with that girl who was making her way towards him across the burning sand. A few days back Range had gone to meet her father, in his plush, high-security mansion in Geneva. He'd seen the photographs of a striking-looking daughter. He'd heard the pain and desperation in the father's voice, as he'd asked – practically begged – Range to take the job of doing the handover with her kidnappers.

Few men could listen to a proud father begging for his only daughter's safe return and remain untouched. So in truth, there was a big part of Range that was here for the father, as much as being here for the girl.

It probably explained why he was here now, getting his balls fried off in this godforsaken, sun-blasted oven, each step taking him closer to the showdown. He figured Amir had set the rendezvous time for two o'clock in the afternoon deliberately: it was the very hottest part of the day, and the worst time for a man like Range to be out under the fierce sun.

The two sides approached each other.

They came face-to-face in the very heart of the heat and the emptiness.

They stopped.

Range stood on the one side, the girl and Amir on the other, maybe ten feet separating them. Range noticed that the tall, wiry Somalian had one hand in the small of the girl's back, and he could see the butt of the pistol he held there.

Range may have come unarmed: Amir certainly hadn't.

Range lowered the bag of cash to the dust at his feet.

Silence.

A dry wind blew a sand devil across the space between them.

Amir stared at Range, his eyes like narrow slits as he searched him for the telltale bulge of a weapon. Range was carrying nothing. His mission was to get the girl, and shooting Amir wasn't going to help in achieving that. In any case, if he did have to kill him he'd far prefer to do so slowly and with his bare hands.

The visual search completed, Amir returned his gaze to Range's face. The silence drew out between them. Range figured there was little point in indulging in any more macho posturing – like who could hold the other's stare longest under this blistering sun. They were here for a purpose. Might as well get on with it.

Range nodded at the girl. 'Let's get this done.'

Amir cracked a smile, white teeth flashing in the sunlight. but it wasn't matched with any warmth in his eyes.

'The money. First you show me the money. Then, if it is all there – all five million of it – I hand over the girl.'

Range bent down and unzipped the bag. He pulled it apart, revealing the bundles of tightly-packed bank notes within. They'd agreed to make the payment in Euros, for the €500 was the largest denomination bank note in the world. The same amount of money in dollars would have made up five times the volume, requiring several bags to carry it, so for simple reasons of portability and space, the €500 was fast becoming the bank note of choice for drugs dealers, mafias and kidnappers the world over.

'How do I know it is all there?' Amir demanded.

Range went down on one knee and began flicking through the bundles, counting off each one and adding up the amount as he went. 'Three million seven hundred and fifty thousand Euros,' he finished. 'That makes five million dollars, or it did when I last checked.'

'And they are not the fakes?'

'As I think you know, the father of Isabelle de Saint-Sébastien is a very wealthy man. You think he would try unloading fakes on you lot, and risk losing his only daughter?'

At the very mention of her father's name Range had seen the girl stiffen. In part he'd used it deliberately, and he'd been hoping for just such a reaction. He'd yet to get a look at her face, to check on her identity. Amir had led her forward draped from head to toe in Islamic dress, and her face was completely veiled.

'Monsieur de Saint-Sébastien may not be willing to risk it,' Amir remarked. 'But there are no guarantees that you and your men would not, are there, Mr Range?'

Range noted that Amir's French was far better than his own, which was all but non-existent. Plus the English he spoke sounded suave and sophisticated, and Range didn't doubt he'd had some of the best education money could buy. Most likely Amir had been sent to a top private school in England, more was the irony.

'The money's genuine,' Range grated. 'You'll just have to trust me on that.'

'Mr Range, we have very strong links to the local tribes – the Turkana and Shomali – who control this region. You have a very long drive ahead of you, on a near-deserted bush road.' Amir let the silence lie between them. The menace was clear. 'If we examine this money and there is any suspicion in our mind that it might be fake, one call to the chiefs of those tribes and they will set out in force to hunt you down. We pay them well, as you can imagine. Conversely, it doesn't pay to mess with us.'

Range stared unflinchingly into the other man's eyes. 'Like I said, the money's genuine. Now, let's get this done.'

Amir waved the girl forward with a flick of his pistol. As she took the first, faltering steps he moved forward and reached to take the bag, switching the pistol's position to cover Range.

Range's grip tightened around the bag's handles. 'Not

yet; not a fucking chance. You get the money when you've shown me the girl.'

Amir took a step back. 'You think she is not the one? What, you think we would hand over a good Somali girl instead of . . . *of her*?' He laughed. The laughter was cruel, and it lent Amir's face a hyena-like look. 'After what they have done to her, do you really think any of us would want to *keep her*?'

Range fought the urge to grab Amir by his scrawny neck and beat the living daylights out of him; slowly, methodically, and savouring every moment of pain until the bastard was pleading for mercy. But one false move and the girl's life would be forfeited, and very likely his own too.

The operators who had Range's back would have deadly accurate sniper rifles trained on the handover, but he felt certain the other side – Amir's lot – would be doing likewise. They had the money to buy the best weaponry and hire the best operators. It was the only way such a handover ever worked: mutually assured destruction, unless both sides played by the rules.

'Like I said, I need to see the girl,' Range repeated. His voice sounded unnaturally low, like an animal growl. It was the effect the suppressed aggression that was coursing through his veins was having on his vocal chords. He'd noticed how similar situations in the past had lowered his voice several octaves. 'You get the money when I've seen her and made a positive ID.'

Amir shrugged. He returned the pistol to menace the girl's back, and half turned his face away to avert his gaze. 'Show your face to the white man,' he ordered. 'Then veil again, before I have to lay my eyes on your corrupting . . .'

'I just need to get a look at you, love,' Range cut Amir off. 'Then we can get this done, and get on our way.'

A deathly white hand flicked out from under the dark robe, and reached for the veil. Range knew she'd been kept locked away, secreted and well hidden from prying eyes. It didn't look as if her skin had seen any sunlight for an age now. She reached up and twitched the black face-covering to one side.

Range had been steeling himself for what was coming, yet still he couldn't help it: he gave a sharp, pained intake of breath as he stared into her ravaged features. It was her all right – Isabelle de Saint-Sébastien – but she was barely recognisable as the happy, healthy, striking woman he'd seen photos of in Geneva. He was trying not to betray the consternation he was feeling, but still his mind was reeling. Her eyes were sunken pits, her gaze dead and empty, her cheeks cadaverous and shadowed, her lips scabbed and peeling.

Christ, what the hell had they done to her?

Range forced himself to speak. 'Hello, Isabelle. My name is Steve Range. This is almost over now. We'll soon have you away from all of this and home.'

He saw the barest flicker of recognition in her eyes, before the hand darted up and the veil was flicked into place again. Range's gaze swivelled back to Amir. He fixed the man's features – hyena smile and all – in his memory in such a way that he knew he'd never forget. If ever he came across Amir al-Jihadi in a situation where he could get to him, he knew for sure that the Somalian wouldn't be walking away from such an encounter.

Range picked up the bag and held it out to him. 'Take the money.' With the other he gestured for Isabelle to walk towards him.

He saw Amir give her a last jab in the back, which sent her stumbling forwards, as the tall Somalian stooped to pick up the cash. Range felt an almost irresistible urge to smash his fist into the back of Amir's head and in one blow stove in the guy's skull. The fierce anger that was burning through him would give added force to the blow, and he knew he could fell the bastard with one massive hit. But he kept a firm hold on himself and stayed his hand.

A moment later Amir straightened up with the bag clutched in one hand. He stepped back a few paces, paused and placed the money at his feet. Then he pulled back the pistol's breech and flashed it at Range, just to show he had a round chambered.

'As you can see, it is fully armed,' he announced, 'but I do not intend to kill you. The girl even less.' His hand patted the bulging bag of cash. 'It would be bad for business. Those paying ransoms have to have some security that the person they are paying for will be delivered. I pride myself on successful delivery. When a fine deal like this one is completed, it bodes well for the future of our business.' He raised the pistol. 'But rest assured, if you try to deviate from the agreed plan – which is to walk the girl directly back to your car – I shall use this.'

Range didn't bother to reply. He turned on his heel, took the girl gently by the arm, and together they began to walk back the way he had come.

They continued in silence for several paces. Range glanced at the figure at his side. He didn't know how to put this . . .

'You okay?' he ventured. 'You good to make the walk? It's about another five hundred yards, if you can manage it? You need water or anything?' Then, the real point of what he wanted to say, for he couldn't imagine how she could see properly to find her way, 'You're good to remove the veil now.'

He saw the hunched shoulders flinch imperceptibly, as if the girl was trying to fight back her tears. 'I'd rather stay like this,' she murmured. Her voice was barely audible above the lonely hiss of the desert wind. 'For now, anyway.'

Her accent was a lot like her father's; they spoke a refined English, but with a strong French lilt to it. The de Saint-Sébastien family was a long-established Geneva dynasty hailing from the French-speaking half of the country. Isabelle's father was one of the wealthiest businessmen in that city, one that was truly paved in gold.

11

Range knew what it was that had brought Isabelle to such a godforsaken place as this. Her father had told him as much. She was a trained doctor, but somewhat guilt-ridden at her family's considerable wealth. She'd volunteered to work for a medical aid charity, one that sent doctors and nurses into some of the harshest parts of the developing world. Fine motives maybe, but her father had been dead against it from the start. Yet Isabelle was a feisty, young twenty-six-year-old, and she had thought she knew best.

Range figured it'd be a while now before she volunteered her services again on a mission of mercy. Maybe even a lifetime.

They walked on in an uncomfortable silence, Range doing his best to support her but sensing her instinctive revulsion at a man's touch. He could barely believe that she was only twenty-six. From that one glance he'd got of her face he'd have put her at twice that age. As they moved, Range became aware of a not particularly pleasant odour coming off her. It was a mixture of scents: that of an unwashed body, fresh sweat and the unmistakable smell of pure fear.

'Isabelle, there's nothing to worry about any more,' Range told her, gently. 'There's nothing to be afraid of. You know that, don't you? Your father sent us to pay the ransom and to get you out of here. Once we're at the vehicle, we'll drive you to a fine hotel and from there, when you're ready, we'll get you to the airport. You'll have armed guards with you all the way, right until we get you home. Your father will fly in to meet you, or wait for you at Geneva – whichever you prefer.'

There was no answer from the slight, veiled figure moving through the sands beside him.

Range fished into his pocket and pulled out a small piece of jewellery. It was a child's necklace – a gold chain carrying a tiny angel whose wings were encased in shimmering diamonds. He had been intending to keep this for the road journey ahead, or maybe for when they were back in the hotel, but he felt a driving need to get through to her somehow, to lift the veil of submission and terror behind which her kidnappers had imprisoned her.

Range was about to pass it across to her when he stopped himself. He prided himself on his professionalism, and this job was far from over yet. Getting Isabelle to accept and embrace her freedom and to climb out of her tomb of fear – all of that could wait. It could wait until they were in a place of real safety – and that sure as hell wasn't here. All he needed her to do right now was to keep it together for long enough to reach the vehicle, placing one foot in front of the other.

Range went to slip the diamond necklace back into his pocket. But something, the movement maybe, or the glittering of the gemstones, drew the girl's eyes. Range hadn't realised quite how much she could see from behind the veil, which from the outside appeared like an impenetrable barrier.

'What is that, Mr Range?' she ventured. 'I'd like to see it, if I may? I think I almost recognise it . . .'

Range passed the necklace across and fed it into the girl's palm. There was no point in trying to hide it any more. That would only cause suspicion between them, and Range needed her to trust him implicitly.

'Your father asked me to give you this.'

He saw her flick up the veil and glance down at what he had placed in her hand. And then her shoulders seemed to collapse in on themselves, and the girl all but tumbled to the sands as the wailing cries rose up from deep inside her. Range caught her just before she fell, and held her for a moment as her body began to heave with wracking sobs.

'It's all right. You're safe now,' he comforted her. 'We'll get you home to your father soon.'

And then he heard it: from behind them, there was the screaming whine of a 4x4 being driven at high speed across the desert sands.

CHAPTER TWO

Range pulled Isabelle sharply down onto the hard dirt. A few hundred yards to the north of them he could see the dust storm thrown up by the approaching vehicle. There was little point in running: they couldn't outrun a speeding 4x4. And there was nowhere much to hide in such flat, open terrain. All they could do was try to make themselves as small a target as possible.

He forced the two of them deeper into the sand, trying to shield Isabelle with his bulk, to protect her from whatever was coming. But he could feel her struggling desperately beneath him, and he knew for sure what horrific memories she had to be reliving right now.

'Keep down!' he hissed. 'Keep down! They're coming back!'

Yet beneath him Isabelle scratched and fought like a wild cat. Nothing he said seemed to calm her. It was like the devil himself had been released inside her. He felt her spit at him, then nails raking across his exposed face. He'd had enough of this shit. *Christ, no one was paying him enough for this kind of crap.* He grabbed her arms, forced them down to her sides, then pinned her legs to stop them from kicking out at his groin.

'Miss de Saint-Sébastien,' he growled, 'I am not – repeat NOT – trying to rape you. I'm trying to save your fucking life. So lie still and stop yelling, or those fuckers who kidnapped you are going to come find us again. I'm sorry for what you went through with those . . . people. But right now we're the good guys, and we're all that you've got.'

He felt the wired tension in her limbs lessen a little. Maybe his words were getting through. Keeping a tight hold on her, Range spoke into the tiny radio mouthpiece he had wired into his shirt collar.

'There's a vehicle coming up fast from behind! Stop it before it can get anywhere fucking near us.'

'Affirm. We have you visual. Stay down. Standby.'

The voice was that of The Kiwi, an ace on the sniper rifle and one of Range's most trusted operators. Typically, he sounded calm and easy, like today was just any other day. Range wished it felt like that from where he was lying, with Isabelle still struggling and the kidnapper's wagon bearing down on them fast. Lying low like this they'd be very hard to see or to shoot, but one false move by the girl and he knew they'd be spotted. And still she hadn't completely given up fighting to be free of him.

He spoke to her with real urgency. 'I gave you your father's necklace, remember? Your father trusted me. *You have to trust me.* We have to lie very, very still, for it's all about to go noisy. I've got a team of soldiers – the good guys – at our vehicle, and they're about to take out Amir and his lot. Bullets will start flying above us, but if we stay down we'll be safe. *Trust me.*'

He heard a faint whimper of acquiescence from below him, felt the last shreds of resistance fade; sensed the silent sobs which now took hold of her, replacing the terror, the revulsion and the burning outrage.

'Stay with me,' he urged her. 'We'll get through this. We're going to be okay.'

Before setting out on the walk Range had set his radio receiver to permanent send. That way, The Kiwi and the others had been able to monitor every moment of the hostage handover. He spoke into it again now, having to raise his voice to drown out the noise of the oncoming vehicle.

'Fire warning shots. Get someone on the satphone to speak to Amir. Tell him this isn't what we agreed. Tell him to back the fuck off. Tell him you'll nail him otherwise.'

'Affirm. Firing warning shots. Standby.'

The last thing Range wanted right now was to waste a load of the kidnappers. Foremost in his mind was the thought of the long drive through the open bush that lay ahead of them, and he hadn't forgotten Amir's warnings about the local Turkana and Shomali tribes. If they had to fight their way through hundreds of heavily-armed desert warriors, it was all too easy to guess who would win that battle. . .

An instant after The Kiwi's message Range heard the distinctive *tzzzzpphht* as a high-velocity sniper round tore through the air above them, followed an instant later by the bark of the weapon firing. With the bullet travelling faster than the speed of sound, you'd hear it pass overhead a fraction of an instant before the noise of its firing reached your ears.

Range watched for where it hit, and saw the distinctive plume of sand kick up in the path of the speeding vehicle. The 4x4 swerved and a second round went tearing past, this one kicking up the dirt right beneath the front wheels. The vehicle slowed, and Range noticed a tall figure running for the passenger door. It was Amir, and he had the bag of money clutched in his sweaty hands.

There was a squelch of static in the receiver that Range had wired into his ear. 'Got 'em on the satphone.' The voice was that of O'Shea, the ex-US Navy SEAL on Range's team, and his second-in-command at Blackstone Six. 'They say they've come to pick up Amir. I told 'em that wasn't how we agreed it'd be done. They say we're welcome to send the truck to pick up you guys.'

Range cursed. He should have known. Whenever did a bloody Somali stick to the rules or the plan?

'Okay, keep them covered,' Range grated. 'They do anything other than pick up Amir and execute a rapid about-turn, you put a bullet into their tyres to stop them. And if they keep coming forwards on foot, slot them. And presuming they *do* get the hell out of here, you can send the bloody wagon for me and the girl.'

'Affirm,' The Kiwi replied. 'Stay down.'

'Mate, I'm not bloody going anywhere.'

Some twenty minutes later Range and the girl had been scooped up by their own vehicle and they were on their way, moving south through the harsh desert scrub. The Kiwi was at the wheel, with Range, O'Shea and Tak – their giant of a Fijian operator – riding shotgun, weapons at the ready. Range didn't think that Amir would have double-crossed them, alerting the tribes to hunt them down. He was making too much money out of the kidnapping business to risk that. But even so, northern Kenya was lawless, borderless and plagued by banditry. Each of his operators had their eyes scanning the terrain all around them, their weapons cradled in their laps and very much made ready.

The dirt track they were travelling on snaked its way unpredictably through the scrub, and no matter how carefully the Kiwi drove, their 4x4 Toyota threw up a massive cloud of dust behind it. Their passage had to be visible for miles around.

It made every sense to have The Kiwi at the wheel. He

was ex-New Zealand SAS, and they were renowned as being the world's best bush trackers. The New Zealand government even used its SAS to track prison escapees, those that might be trying to evade recapture by heading into the open wilderness and mountains. Right now there was no one better to navigate the maze of dirt tracks that criss-crossed the bush, and to get them to their intended destination – Nairobi, the Kenyan capital – and relative safety.

O'Shea threw an inquiring look at Range. 'She okay?' he mouthed, jabbing a thumb at the figure in the vehicle's rear.

They'd offered Isabelle the front passenger seat, but she'd declined. Instead, she'd crawled into the cramped seats at the very back, curled up across two of them, and she seemed to have fallen into the deepest of sleeps, fully robed and veiled.

'I guess she'll be like that all the way to Nairobi,' Range replied. 'All we can do is wake her for some water every hour or so, and food if she wants it, plus get her back to something like civilization.'

Range wasn't particularly surprised by how Isabelle had reacted to the events of the last hour or so. Massive trauma and shock could do that even to elite soldiers – those who were rigorously trained to deal with such extremes of human experience. For a young girl like Isabelle the last few hours – plus the months of hell before that – must have been devastating.

O'Shea took a long look at the figure curled across the

rear seats. 'I feel real sorry for her,' he remarked. 'Y'know what our instructor taught us in SEAL training? During Hell Week we ran in the surf up the beach past the Hotel Del Coronado. There were ranks of girls in bikinis catching some rays. 'Course, we couldn't help stare. Senior Chief Iossa spoke to us as we ran. "There's only one way a SEAL ever treats a woman. If you're a real SEAL, every time she leaves your side she'll feel just a little better about herself."'

Those sentiments were typical O'Shea. He might be a gun-for-hire – they all were in B6, as Blackstone Six was known in the trade – but somehow he managed to combine private soldiering with an unbending attitude of always trying to do what was right. *Honour thy country. Honour thy fellow soldier. Give no quarter to the enemy. Dishonour no woman. Leave no man behind on the battlefield.* That was pretty much the Navy SEAL creed and O'Shea stubbornly sought to perpetuate it in the kind of private soldiering he did with B6.

Range didn't particularly mind. Quite the reverse: it made O'Shea one hundred per cent loyal, rock-solid and reliable – which were qualities as rare as rocking-horse shit on the private military circuit. He wasn't necessarily Range's toughest operator – that accolade would probably be shared equally by The Kiwi and Tak – but those very qualities made O'Shea indispensable as Range's second-in-command.

'Leave a woman always feeling better about herself,' O'Shea echoed. He nodded at the sleeping figure of the girl. 'How the hell are we going to manage that with her?'

21

Range touched the angry welts where Isabelle had raked her nails across his face. 'Mate, you could always try looking on the bright side. At least she's not still trying to kill us.'

The long drive to Nairobi proved far from drama-free. Whilst Amir and his pirate kind must have got word through to the local tribes to leave their vehicle well alone, there was no way of warning off the punishing terrain. In spite of The Kiwi's superlative off-road driving abilities, twice they'd got the vehicle bogged in the soft sand and almost up to its axles.

Being on a one-vehicle move, there was no sister 4x4 to help tow out the stricken Toyota. In such circumstances freeing the wagon had to be done by brute force and skill alone. Using full-sized shovels they had strapped onto the roof rack, they'd dug the wheels free from the worst of the sand. Sand-ladders – tough lengths of flat, perforated steel – had been worked under the wheels, to give the vehicle some traction via which to haul itself onto hard ground.

The WARN winch bolted to the front bulbar had been unwound – the steel cable being looped around an ancient acacia tree that lay to the front of the stricken vehicle. Using the pull of the winch, plus the grip the tyres gained on the sand ladders, the wagon had eventually hauled itself free. But for all the time it took to get the vehicle moving they had been sitting targets, and while two men worked feverishly to free the Toyota, two had been scanning the desert terrain for any hostile forces.

It was exhausting work.

The drive was completed in one twenty-hour stint, the only stops being when they'd got bogged in, to refuel from their jerry cans, to piss, and to feed Isabelle water. They'd kept rotating drivers, keeping two guys on alert whilst the other grabbed some kip. Isabelle had refused any food or attempts at conversation, and Range figured it would take several years – plus a lot of professional help - for her to fully recover from her ordeal, that's if she ever would.

Their destination, the Windsor Country Hotel, was set well away from Nairobi City. Nairobi sits at some six thousand feet above sea level, and consequently it and the surrounding countryside is unusually lush and green for this part of Africa. Situated amidst the rolling hills, forests and lakes from which the surrounding golf greens had been fashioned, the hotel was exactly what Range and Isabelle's father had figured she'd need: an oasis of private peace and luxury, and about as far removed from the chaotic heart of Somalian piracy as you could ever get here in Africa.

The dust-covered Toyota pulled to a halt in front of the sweeping crescent of grand colonial-era buildings that formed the main part of the hotel. Before Range could dismount, a formally-attired footman was at his side, holding open the passenger door. Range got down, folded forward the seat that gave access to the rear and called Isabelle's name. A head emerged from the shadowed interior, though the veil prevented Range from knowing if she was fully awake yet.

'Isabelle, we're here. The Windsor Country Hotel. You can rest, eat, sleep and recuperate as much as you like – and when you're ready, we're out of here. Your father's chartered his private jet to collect you and fly you home. It's coming direct from Geneva.' Range glanced at his watch. 'It should be touching down at Nairobi airport any time now. We called your father en route and told him the good news. He asked me to tell you that he's overjoyed.'

She stepped out of the vehicle, but was clearly unsteady on her legs. Range went to try to help her, but she half pushed him away. She shied away from the hotel footman too.

'I'm fine,' she said. 'Really. Fine. I'd just like to go to my hotel room. Is there a female member of the staff who might show me there? Please?'

Range got the footman to rustle up a hotel maid to act as Isabelle's escort. He reached inside the rear of the Toyota and fetched a smart-looking leather overnight case. He handed it to the girl who was going to show Isabelle to her room.

'Take that,' he told her, passing her the bag and folding a fifty-dollar bill into the palm of her hand. 'It's a change of clothes, toiletries, plus a few special treats packed by her father. Be careful with her. Very careful, okay? You don't want to know what she's just been through . . . If she wants female company, get it sorted so you or one of the other hotel girls can stick with her.'

The maid half curtseyed and nodded that she understood. Range watched the two of them go – the Kenyan girl with her braids swinging freely, as she skipped across the gravel drive in her smart, tailored hotel uniform; Isabelle, dragging her exhausted feet, the dirty robes rendering her a shapeless negation of her womanhood – until they were swallowed up by the shadows of the hotel's interior.

He followed at a distance, keeping his eyes on the two figures as they made for the lift. They were halfway across the hotel lobby when an official from behind the desk called out to the dishevelled, dirty figure that was Isabelle.

'Madame! Madame! You have to sign . . .'

Range silenced the man with a gesture – his hand doing a knife-slash across the throat. *Shut it.* He strode across to the desk, and informed them that he was signing in for a team of five – *the lady included* – booked in the name of Range. He turned as the receptionist tapped his keyboard, and watched Isabelle step into the lift, the hotel maid dutifully at her side.

He noticed one of Isabelle's sandals had the heel half hanging off. She'd been in captivity for so long her footwear had started to disintegrate. No wonder she'd half lost her mind. For a moment he searched his memory, trying to figure if her parents had packed her any replacement footwear. He didn't think that they had.

He turned back to the desk. 'Right, is there a lady's boutique anywhere in the hotel? There is?' He palmed another fifty-dollar note into the clutches of the concierge. 'Get one of your lady staff to fetch a selection of shoes, all of the kind of size that might fit the lady guest who's just gone up in the lift. Take them to her room. Whatever she chooses, you're to put it on my bill. Got it?'

The concierge smiled ingratiatingly and dashed off to do Range's bidding.

Once they were checked in Range gathered his blokes in the lobby. 'Right, way I see it I made the walk to get the girl, so I get first dibs on getting some proper kip.' There were nods of agreement all around. It was fair enough, really. 'It's 1000 hours Nairobi time. I'm presuming we're not going anywhere until tomorrow. Between then and now I want two guys on watch, and two getting some rest. This isn't over until we've got her on that jet en route to Geneva.

'O'Shea and Kiwi, you take the first watch. Tak and me'll get our heads down. I figure we can afford a good six hours, so we'll relieve you around 1630. I don't suppose for one moment we've been tracked to this hotel, but you know what they say: presumption is the mother of all fuck ups. I want one of you sitting outside her door, and the other watching the hotel lobby. You see any Somalians – big, tall, gangly fuckers with dollar signs in their eyes – you wake me and Tak. Likewise, if there's anything else that strikes you as suspicious. Got it?'

The two men nodded. 'Got it.'

'You eat on watch: order room service. And if you need to take a piss break, you inform the other. Whoever's standing guard at her door gets replaced by the other bloke, if he needs to take a break. There's only one way in and out of the hotel room, and I want it guarded at all times.'

O'Shea and The Kiwi grunted their confirmation. 'One more thing,' Range added. 'I may be stating the obvious, but I figure we're also keeping watch over the girl – to protect her from herself. I'm no psychiatrist, but she strikes me as being in a pretty bad place head-wise. So keep a close eye.'

For a good six hours Range slept the sleep of the dead. He then stood a very boring watch outside the girl's door for another six, by which time he was famished. He headed for the restaurant, leaving O'Shea and The Kiwi to cover the girl. The interior of the Windsor Country Hotel was as sumptuous as the lush grounds suggested it might be. Every nook and cranny exuded money and privilege. Range had rarely stayed in such a place of timeless luxury; he certainly couldn't afford to on the kind of money he earned with B6.

Sitting on the terrace of the bar-cum-restaurant he gazed out over the breathtaking view. It was ten thirty p.m. by now, and above the lights of the distant city stretched the wide African heavens – intense, spectacular and star-bright. The stunning vista was reflected in the still surface of the lake that formed the centrepiece of the hotel grounds. The air was balmy and the rhythmical *breep-breep-breep* of the nighttime insects lulled him into a relaxed state of mind.

He'd just ordered himself a massive plate of steak and chips, plus a local Tusker beer, when there was a ringing on his cell phone. It was The Hogan, the boss of Blackstone Six, and a guy who was as near as Range had ever had to a father. Doubtless The Hogan would be calling to check how things were going.

'Range,' he answered.

'I hear it's mission accomplished,' The Hogan's rich, clubby tones echoed over the long-distance phone link. He chuckled. 'I've had a call from Geneva, offering us a rather large bonus on a job apparently very well done. Looks like I'll be able to afford to pay my bar bill at The Beaujolais after all.'

It was Range's turn to laugh. The Beaujolais was his and The Hogan's favoured watering hole, a discreet wine bar tucked away in London's West End. The Hogan was such a fixture there that he was marked as permanently 'in' on the regulars' blackboard that hung to one side of the bar. He and Range treated the place as B6's second office.

Oddly, considering the gulf in their upbringings – The Hogan was from a moneyed, public school background; Range had spent his childhood in a string of kids' homes – he and Range were very close. Range figured The Hogan saw him as the son that he'd liked to have had – rather than the two city slickers that he'd reared.

'It's not all roses, though, I'm afraid,' The Hogan continued. 'Bit of a surprise, this one. Can you get online where you are? You can? Great. Well, prepare for a bit of a shock. Log on to www.vimeo.com. It's a private website where you can upload videos. I've been alerted to one that's been posted there. You'll need the password. It's rather melodramatic I'm afraid: the people who posted the video chose "assassin's blood feud".'

'What?' Range snorted. 'What is it, some kind of teenage shoot-'em-up video game?'

'Unfortunately not. You've made a note of the password?'

Range scribbled it down on his napkin. 'I have.'

'When you've got the video up, pull up your Skype link. This call's costing me a fortune. That way I can talk you through what you're about to see. The Colonel and I have spent a good while studying it. And unfortunately, our conclusion is we're going to have to take this rather more seriously than you or I might like.'

'Fuck me, Tony, you're being a bit cryptic,' Range remarked.

At the mention of The Colonel, Range's curiosity had been truly pricked. The Colonel was B6's liaison with Her Majesty's Government, and if The Hogan had thought to get him involved there had to be something of serious import on that video.

But with a password like assassin's creed, or whatever it was, Range couldn't quite believe there was.

CHAPTER THREE

Range had his iPad perched to one side of his dinner plate. With one hand he was feeding French fries into his mouth, while with the other he tapped out the password. ASSASSIN'S BLOOD FEUD. Enter. He saw the icon spinning over the screen, showing him it was buffering and preparing to stream the video at speed.

'Connection might be slow here in Nairobi,' he remarked to The Hogan, speaking through a mouthful of chips. He was using the Skype link established via his iPad direct to The Hogan's computer screen to talk. 'It might be a bit stop-start.'

'Gives us time to talk as we go,' The Hogan replied. It never ceased to amaze Range how, over a long-distance link like this Skype-to-Skype call the connection was invariably far clearer and less plagued by time-lags than a conventional phone call. As a bonus, a Skype-to-Skype call was also absolutely free.

The other advantage of using Skype was that it was far more secure than any normal phone line. Because the link from computer to computer went via the internet, their voice data would be routed via an endless series of electronic pathways, and hence it was all but impossible to monitor. That was why the intelligence services hated Skype so much, and why terrorists, criminals and kidnappers like Amir and his lot so favoured it.

Indeed, about the only traceable evidence of a Skype-to-Skype call was the electronic signature that it left on the laptop or iPad. From that, any half-decent agency could trace a user's Skype contacts, which would be a first step to breaking any terrorist or criminal network. The seriously bad guys – people like Amir and his ilk – would smash up their laptop every six months or so, as the only safe way of destroying that electronic record. Then they'd buy a new one. On the kind of money that Amir was making, he sure could afford it.

'Okay, it's started playing,' Range announced, speaking more loudly due to the horribly distorted Arabic music that was blaring out from the video. He pushed the icon on his iPad screen several times, turning down the volume. He could see one or two of his fellow diners eyeing him disapprovingly. He didn't blame them; the terrace of the Windsor Country Hotel was hardly the place to blare out the Arab Jihadi beat.

A figure emerged on the screen. It was a still photo of an elderly man dressed in what Range recognised as the robes of the Tuareg – the famed nomads of the Sahara Desert. Some eighteen months back Range had led a mission into the Empty Quarter, in southern Libya, to snatch the last surviving son of the late Colonel Gaddafi. Sultan Gaddafi had been held captive by the Tuareg, plus the terrorist outfit they'd thrown their lot in with, Al-Qaeda in the Islamic Maghreb (AQIM) – 'Maghreb' being the Arabic word for 'west', or 'the place where the sun sets', which referred to the north-west African desert.

A sentence flashed onto the iPad's screen, at first in Arabic but with a translation fading up below it in English. It read: 'Henceforth the blood feud is declared on behalf of Moussa ag Ajjer, by those sons that survive him. May it last until the feud is paid in blood.'

'It gets a bit repetitive,' The Hogan remarked drily, via the Skype link, 'but it's worth bearing with it.'

Range grunted an acknowledgement. The sentence remained on the screen as the Jihadi beat wailed. *Get on with it*, he found himself thinking. The screen faded and another took its place. The camera was zoomed in to frame a younger man dressed similarly in indigo-blue robes. He was sat cross-legged before a pair of distinctive Tuareg swords – the metre-long, straight *takoba*, which was worn encased in an ornate leather scabbard.

As the figure started to speak, punctuating his words

32

with a fist that pounded the butt of an AK-47 assault rifle cradled in his lap, Range had a good idea of what was coming. The first subtitles flashed up in English. 'In the name of Almighty Allah, let all who hear and see this know that I, son of the late Tuareg chief Moussa ag Ajjer, invoke the blood feud against all those who soldiered against my father, and their wives, children, fathers and mothers and grandparents even until . . .'

'Yeah, Tony, I get the drift,' Range snorted. He killed the sound on the video, allowing the subtitles to continue to flash across the screen. 'So it's the son of Moussa ag Ajjer, the Tuareg leader we killed on the Gaddafi mission, swearing a blood feud against me and the other lads for as long as he shall live, and for his sons and their sons to continue until we are all very, very dead. Is that it? 'Cause if it is I'll get back to my steak and cold Tusker.'

The Hogan let out his signature chuckle. 'Well, that's the half of it, yes. We were alerted to the video's existence by a private message that was delivered to the British Embassy in Tripoli. They clearly very much wanted you to see this. I think you need to warn the others on the mission, if for no other reason than you might want to consider your families' safety.'

'Not an issue,' Range remarked. 'I don't have a family, do I? Or have you forgotten?'

Range had never had any parents – apart from the ones who had abandoned him at birth, leaving him to a life in the children's homes. In fact, he had no mother or father, brother or sister or even any kids to worry about.

'But it might well be an issue for the others,' The Hogan remarked.

'It might,' Range conceded. 'But let's be frank about it, Tony mate, when are that lot ever likely to be in Finchley or Florida to have a pop at any of the lads' grandparents?'

'I know, it does seem like a remote risk. But either way we think you should warn all who were on the mission.'

'All who returned alive, you mean? We lost a couple of good blokes, remember?'

The Hogan coughed uncomfortably. 'Well, as it happens that's just it. That's the reason why The Colonel and I have spent so long studying the video. You see, it appears as if one of those men we thought we'd lost wasn't actually killed after all.'

Range shook his head, taking a long gulp on his beer. 'Sorry, mate, you've lost me. Randy got whacked during the first attack. We lost big Jock on the exfil.'

'It appears not,' The Hogan replied. 'Fast forward the video: it's all just a lot of ranting and raving from old Moussa's son about how they're going to kill you all anyway. Start playing it again about ten minutes from the end.'

'Got it.' Range dragged the cursor along the video's time line, bringing it to a stop at the ten-minutes-from-the-end mark. There were a few more seconds of ranting in Arabic, before the Tuareg chief's son turned and ushered another figure centre stage. As the man squatted down beside him, turning to face the camera, Range practically choked on the lump of steak that he'd just shoved in his mouth.

'What the fuck?' he spluttered. His hand shot out and punched pause. He stared into the face that was frozen on the screen, dumbfounded. The figure was dressed in similar robes to the Tuareg beside him, but that was where the similarity ended. 'No fucking way. It can't be. Tony, mate, we left him in the middle of the desert very, very, very fucking dead.'

'It appears not. I was about as shocked as you when I first saw him. We've had the video analysed by the very best in the business, Range, and it seems that it's genuine. We don't know how, and trust me we're as mystified as you are, but somehow Randy seems to have survived the Gaddafi mission . . .'

'No fucking way,' Range cut in. 'No way. The Kiwi's the best medic in the business. The Kiwi told us the guy was dead. There's no way it can be genuine.'

'Steve, I'm afraid it is. And not only that – it's Al-Qaeda in the Islamic Maghreb who somehow seem to have rescued Randy. And not only rescued him, but from what appears to be on that video they've turned him to their cause. It's why I've risked interrupting your present mission, Range. What you're doing there is hugely important, and you've got to see it through to the end. But once you do, there's this little matter that needs attending to.'

'FUUCK!' Range slammed his fist onto the wooden tabletop. His plate jumped, the crockery tumbling to the floor.

He uttered a string of curses half under his breath. A figure stepped forward and hurried towards him. It was the chef d'hôte – the head waiter.

'Sir. Sir. Please sir, if I might suggest to keep the voice down . . . ?'

Range was about to fire a few choice expletives at him when he suddenly remembered where he was. He glanced around at the sea of faces staring at him in open hostility – fellow diners who clearly hadn't appreciated his outburst and the language.

He glanced at the waiter. 'Yeah, sorry. Sorry. Just had some bad news is all.'

'I understand, sir, and I am sorry. It does happen to all of us from time to time. But if you will just please keep your voice down?'

'Yeah. No problem. Understood.'

At The Hogan's urging Range spooled through the last ten minutes of the video. It consisted of Randy, another ex-SEAL who'd been part of B6's Gaddafi team, apparently ranting and raving in Arabic about how he was going to hunt down Range and his men – 'gutless infidels who deserved only the worst the world has to offer' – and kill every last one of them, until the blood feud was finished.

Range knew all about blood feuds. He'd come across the

concept first in Afghanistan. It was pretty simple really. You killed one of my family: now, in revenge, I'm going to kill you and all of yours. In some tribes the feud lasted for generations, being handed down from father to son. Clearly, this Tuareg lot was one of those tribes. Nothing so surprising there; no, the real shocker was Randy.

Range didn't have the slightest clue how he could possibly be alive. They'd taken the Fort of the Mount, an isolated hunk of rock in the midst of the Libyan Sahara, but in doing so Randy – the rangy, tough Afro-American on his team – had got hit by a shedload of shrapnel. It had peppered his torso, causing horrific injuries. The Kiwi – a first-class Special Forces' medic – had patched up the guy as best he could, but without getting to a hospital Randy hadn't stood a chance. With no blood transfusion and no surgery possible, he'd died from loss of blood and organ failure.

Or at least, so they had all thought.

They'd left the Fort of the Mount badly shot up and without the ability to carry Randy's body out of there. O'Shea had all but refused to leave him: *leave no man behind on the battlefield*. Tak had practically mutinied at the idea. But eventually Range had prevailed. They'd wrapped Randy's body in one of their black silk parachutes – the means via which they'd been dropped in to assault the fort – and buried his body under a cairn of rocks. And when the mission was finally over they'd mourned his passing the way they did with all fallen warriors.

And now this.

'I got to go to my room,' Range blurted out. 'Tony, I need some headspace. This is doing my head in. I've got to watch that video properly, in private, if I'm to believe this shit is really true. They can't have turned him. Not Randy. It isn't possible. Maybe he's slipped something into the video to signal to us they haven't?'

'We thought exactly the same thing. We searched it in detail, Range. Scanned every frame. There's nothing we can detect. But maybe there's something you can pick up on that we've missed. Get O'Shea on it. He knew Randy better than anyone. And whilst you're at it, don't take your eye off the present mission or the girl.'

'Yeah. No. Trust me, we won't. I'll Skype you again when I've got something.'

'Understood. I'll leave my Skype link open.' The Hogan paused, 'Range, you know how we run things at B6: we never leave a job unfinished. This development with Randy, it's not good. I'm not underestimating that. But we've still got a job to do. So get that girl onto that jet . . .'

'Don't worry,' Range snapped. 'I risked my bloody life for her today. Saw how they'd fucked her up. No one's leaving until she's safely out of here. But just as soon as she is, we're heading home. And then, fuck knows how, but we've got to go get Randy back again.'

'Even if he's turned?'

'He's not turned,' Range growled. 'Trust me. Not Randy.

You remember why we nicknamed him Randy? That good-looking, cool bastard was such a hit with the women with his laid-back American charm . . . Randy was the only name for him. You trying to tell me he's signed up to AQIM's no booze, no women, prayers five times a day and jihad mantra? He's the last person ever in the world would do that.'

The Hogan chuckled. 'You do get to have the four wives.'

'That'd last Randy about a week. Anyhow, Tony, I've got to go. I've got to study that video real hard.'

'One last thing,' The Hogan added. 'We've got a fix on where we figure Randy's located. It's need-to-know, but suffice to say we've got a source of HUMINT embedded with AQIM. Anyhow, it seems AQIM have rented a walled compound on the outskirts of Tripoli. It's some kind of forward mounting base, from where they're about to get operational on a mission, but at least it means they're not slap bang in the midst of the Sahara, where it's hard as hell to get to them.'

'So if we're going after Randy, we've got to hit them whilst they're at that compound?'

'Something like that, yes. We figure from our source they've got another week or so before they start filtering out to cause whatever mayhem they're planning.'

'In that case pull the A Team back together. I've got O'Shea, The Kiwi and Tak here. Take it they're in. Get the rest of the lads on standby for what's coming. You and The Colonel can work out how many blokes and what kit we need to take down that compound, and how we do it without killing Randy in the process.'

'We'll do our best,' The Hogan confirmed. 'Get the girl gone as soon as she's ready, and get yourselves back here.'

Range rolled over the cover on his iPad and called for the bill. He scribbled his signature, threw a fifty-dollar note onto the silver plate and hurried inside. The head waiter was left staring at the tip in surprise. The Englishman had looked to be having such a horrific time of it. He'd left his food half-eaten, his beer pretty much untouched. He'd been expecting no tip at all.

These foreigners. There just was no telling how they were going to behave from one moment to the next. Only that morning he'd heard how an otherwise quite beautiful and wealthy white woman had arrived at the hotel dressed from head to toe in a set of dirty and stinking Islamic robes. Apparently, she'd spent the whole day resting, bathing herself, washing her hair or having the female beauticians at the hotel tend to her every need. After some twelve hours of such treatment she'd emerged looking ravishing and dressed like a queen. She'd given strict instructions to the hotel staff to burn the Islamic robe and veil in which she'd arrived. She'd even made sure they presented her with a bag full of whatever ashes remained. And for all of that time she'd had one of the white men sat outside her door standing guard.

He shook his head in bemusement, as he snaffled up the

fifty-dollar bill and slipped it into his pocket. These foreigners. There was no understanding them.

From his room Range radioed O'Shea, and got Tak to take his place outside Isabelle's door. All four of them needed to see the video, of course. It was of crucial import to them all, and he didn't doubt for one second that all would want in on Randy's rescue mission. But Range remained convinced that Randy couldn't have been turned, and that the secret to unlocking that enigma lay somehow in that video – and for that reason he needed O'Shea. O'Shea was Randy's closest friend and a fellow Navy SEAL, and he needed him to watch that video and scrutinise it closely.

There was a tapping at the door. Range strode across, unbolted it, peered outside and let O'Shea in. The stocky American was a good five inches shorter than Range, but he'd been an ultra-marathon runner in his youth, and he was rumoured to have unbreakable stamina. Range had seen him in action over some of the toughest terrain imaginable, and he wouldn't want to be the man's enemy.

He gestured to the desk in his room. 'Take a seat, mate. Beer?'

O'Shea shook his head. 'I got hours left of watch still to do.'

Range grabbed him a can of beer from the mini-bar, plus one for himself. He handed it to O'Shea. 'Trust me, mate, you're going to need it.'

Range got O'Shea seated before the iPad, explained what

he was about to show him and pressed play. This time, Range watched the video all the way through, his eyes glued to every frame, searching desperately for something of significance. Once they got to the point when Randy made an appearance, if anything O'Shea's reactions were even more violent and outspoken than his own had been.

O'Shea had never wanted to leave Randy behind in the first place. He'd fought Range every step of the way. He'd despised The Kiwi for the cold way in which he'd announced that Randy was dead, so what did it matter to a dead man where they left him? And he'd railed against Range when he argued that it was fine to leave a dead man, if so doing was the only way they could achieve their mission.

But to O'Shea's great credit he brought none of that up now. By rights, he could have torn into Range, telling him the obvious: that if he'd had his way they'd have brought Randy home, and he'd very likely be alive and at liberty right now. Instead, he listened to Range explain the lengths to which The Hogan had gone to verify the video, and prove that it was genuine, after which all he had to say was this.

'Then it's simple. If Randy's alive we got to go in and bust him out of there. We left him behind once, buddy. No way are we going to do so a second time. No way.'

'Agreed. But tell me: is there any chance that Randy's been turned?'

'Fuck, Randy? No fucking way. You'd have more chance

of screwing the Pope. No fucking way has Randy ever been turned by those assholes.'

Range suggested they watch the video again, each checking for anything that might be a clue to Randy's real allegiances and intentions. If he hadn't been turned, he must have realised the vital importance of embedding something in that video to act as a signal to his brother warriors. Randy was speaking in Arabic, so it was unlikely to be a verbal clue, for AQIM were sure to pick up on that. But maybe there was something visual.

They played the last bit of the video over and over. Finally, O'Shea punched pause. 'Can you play that bit again, and in particular as he shakes about his weapon.'

Range did as asked. Randy held up his AK-47 to the camera and brandished it angrily. 'I was a US Navy SEAL,' he mouthed in Arabic, 'I fought for the infidel. But not any more. Now I have been reborn as a true warrior of Allah.'

O'Shea tapped the space bar icon, to pause the video again. 'See how he's got his two mags taped together,' O'Shea remarked. 'It's supposed to allow for an ultra-fast mag-change?'

'Yeah. It's kind of ally, especially with the AK.'

'Ally?'

'British squaddie-speak for cool.'

'Right, well it's something you never do as a Navy SEAL. Never. It's a total no-no. You keep your spare mags in your chest rig. That's just how it is. We had it drummed into us in training. So why would Randy start doing that now?'

43

'Who knows? Who knows what kind of bloke comes out the end of his own dying. Maybe his memory's completely shot. Who knows?'

O'Shea studied the screen some more. 'Can you zoom in on that image, particularly on the butt of his weapon?'

Range tapped some icons and the image started to magnify, pulling the weapon into closer focus.

O'Shea jabbed a finger at the screen. 'There! See how he's got something scrawled across the butt of his AK-47. It's like he's showing it off to the camera or something.'

Range increased the magnification. 'Yeah. It reads: US SEAL ZAP: 5CR3WPL34534MEM1QA.'

'It's kinda like his ZAP number,' O'Shea volunteered. 'Y'know, the unique number you read out when you call in a Medevac, if your buddy goes down injured in the field.'

'We got the same,' Range confirmed. 'ZAP number signals the soldier's blood group, any drugs he's taking, next of kin, that kind of thing.'

'Exactly. Only there's one problem. No Navy SEAL ever had a ZAP number looked anything remotely like that.'

'What?'

'Take mine. ZAP: DPO-987651. It starts with your initials and is nine characters long. Randy's ZAP number should start with JFR – for Joe Frank Reiner, his real name. Plus no one ever had a ZAP number that was eighteen characters long.'

'So what the fuck does it mean?'

'Search me.' O'Shea read it out in full. '5CR3W-PL34534MEM1QA. Search me. It's gibberish.'

Range stared at the strange combination of letters and numbers for a few long seconds. As he did so, the figures seemed to swim before his eyes, and then momentarily re-form to make a legible sentence. For a second he thought he had it, but then it was lost again.

It was a good ten years since Range had soldiered with The Regiment, as the SAS was informally known. O'Shea had been out of the SEALs for a similar amount of time. Modern military communications kit tended to scramble messages automatically, so the old skills of using Morse and codebooks were barely taught any more. Code-making and code-breaking wasn't really part of modern-day Special Forces' soldiering, or the kind of work they did as private operators with B6.

'5CR3WPL34534MEM1QA,' O'Shea repeated. 'There's a message in there somewhere. Gotta be. We just gotta find it.'

Range scribbled down the code – if code it was – on the hotel notepad, ripped off the page and handed it to O'Shea. 'Here, take this. We'll have to keep working it through, but for now at least best get back to your watch. I'll cut around to the others and tell them the basics of what's happened – that bloody Randy's come back to life and we've got to go bust him free.'

'Got it,' O'Shea confirmed. 'And buddy, let's be clear – there ain't no way we're leaving him behind again.'

CHAPTER FOUR

Range couldn't sleep, and it was hours until his turn for watch. He headed for the hotel's Library Bar, a place of dark wood and deep, snoozy armchairs, a room that was steeped in history. Faded sepia photos of white men in formal attire adorned the walls, posing with their big-game kills. He found himself a secluded table, ordered a Tusker with a whisky chaser, and fired up his iPad.

He'd taken a screen grab of the zoomed-in image – the close-up on Randy's rifle butt. '5CR3WPL34534MEM1QA.' What the hell did it mean?

The drinks arrived. Range took a long pull on his beer. Much that he was trying to ignore it, there was a part of him felt guilty as shit over what had happened. They'd left Randy behind – believing him to be dead – at Range's insistence. He still believed if they'd taken his body with them the mission would have been blown, but that didn't help much with how he was feeling right now.

There was a buzz in his earpiece. A message was incoming. 'The girl's left her room.' It was O'Shea. Isabelle had been living off room service all day long, and she'd had a string of female staff in and out of there. This was the first time she'd actually emerged. 'She says she's heading out to get some air,' O'Shea added, 'but I can't exactly follow her every step she takes . . .'

'Stay by the door,' Range confirmed. 'Watch for her return. The Kiwi's scanning the lobby and I'm in the bar. We should be able to keep eyes-on.'

'There's one other thing,' O'Shea added. 'You're not looking for a dirty old hag dressed in rags any more. The reverse. The transformation's something like a freakin' miracle.'

'Got it. Out.'

The Kiwi would have been listening in, so Range knew he'd be alerted that Isabelle was on her way down.

He turned back to his iPad. He pulled up the video clip, the one of Randy waving about his AK-47 in front of him. It was almost as if they'd got him to write his ZAP number there on purpose, so they could parade it in front of the camera. Displaying his ZAP number was as good a way as any for this AQIM lot to boast and brag, Range figured: *See, we've recruited a genuine US Navy SEAL to our cause*.

There was no way for the AQIM leadership to know it

wasn't a genuine SEAL ZAP number. That in turn meant Randy had had the freedom to write just about anything he wanted. It couldn't be a blatant 'AL-QAEDA SUCKS' – there were those amongst AQIM who spoke good English – so Randy would have known that within his supposed ZAP number he would have to embed a message in some kind of complex but breakable code.

He'd have felt secure in the fact that only a fellow SEAL could see the jumble of letters and numbers and know they weren't a genuine SEAL ZAP. And he'd have known for sure that O'Shea would be amongst the first to watch the footage, and to get wise to that fact. So in theory all they had to do now was unscramble the seemingly random jumble of letters and numbers.

Range stared at the screen, wracking his brain. '5CR3W-PL34534MEM1QA.' What in God's name did it mean?

Range heard a faint cough behind him. He turned to see a figure standing there, half in the shadow of one of the miniature palm trees that dotted the bar. It was Isabelle, but if he hadn't had the warning from O'Shea he might never have known. Sure, he'd been shown the father's photos back in Geneva, but those had been blown out of his memory by what he'd seen of Isabelle when making the handover at the border.

The transformation was almost unbelievable. The young woman that stood before him had dark, almost raven hair that fell past her shoulders, framing a face white like ala-

baster, and eyes that were a deep emerald-green. Her deli-
cate features still carried the telltale signs of what she had
suffered, but if anything that only made her appear more
arresting. Like a beautiful but wounded bird, Range thought
to himself. He wanted to scoop her up and protect and heal
her – not that now was the time or the place for any of that.

He realised that he was staring. He gestured at the table.
'Sorry. Isabelle. Care to join me?'

She smiled. It was the first time that he'd seen her smile.
It was like the breaking of dawn.

'Thank you. That would be nice.'

She took the chair opposite. He rolled over the iPad cover,
and signalled to the waiter. They ordered drinks – him
another beer and whisky, her a glass of fine champagne.

'I am free,' she told him, softly. 'I feel the need to cele-
brate. Thanks to you, I can.'

Range tried to mutter something about it all being in a
day's work, but she waved him into silence.

She took the glass and raised it, her eyes meeting his.
'To freedom, and to liberty. You never know how sweet it
is until it is taken from you.'

'Freedom,' Range echoed.

'You can ask me, you know,' Isabelle remarked, quietly.

She waved a hand vaguely at her dress and her features.
The dirty black robes and veil had been well and truly dis-
pensed with. Instead, she was draped in a cream dress
embroidered with what appeared to be tiny gemstones, one

49

that looked as if it had cost more than Amir would earn from a whole string of kidnap and ransom deals. She was like Angelina Jolie, but with bucket loads of breeding and class.

'Erm . . . the transformation,' Range stammered. 'I mean, it's like the proverbial ugly duckling to the swan.' He regretted it almost as soon as he'd said it. How bloody stupid . . .

But Isabelle was actually laughing. 'Yes, I suppose it is. From what you saw of me at the border . . . It is amazing what you can do with money, and with an unlimited supply of talented beauticians, and in a fine hotel such as this one.'

'A twenty-four-seven make-over,' Range quipped. He figured he might as well capitalise on the apparent transformation in her mood and demeanour. 'Does that mean you won't be taking your nails to my face again any time soon?' There were still a series of angry red nail marks scored across Range's features.

Isabelle's hand went to her mouth. 'I am sorry. That was me? I don't remember. But no, I don't think I shall be attacking you again, at least not this evening.'

'That's a relief. In my line of business a bloke's got to look after his finer assets . . .'

'And you believe your face to be one of them,' she smiled.

Range grinned. 'Don't you? But seriously, Isabelle, I'm glad to see you so . . . recovered.'

She nodded an acknowledgement at the compliment.

'And you, Mr Range, how are you this evening? If you don't mind me saying, I caught you staring into your computer screen like you had just seen a ghost or something?'

Range shrugged. 'I guess in a way I have.'

'Do you care to share it with me?'

For a long second Range didn't answer. Randy's coming back to life apparently as an AQIM terrorist had nothing to do with the present mission, or with her. But there was no problem with showing her just the code, and seeing what she might make of it. She'd bring a fresh perspective to the conundrum, and there was no telling how a woman's mind might see things. Range never had been able to fathom the fairer sex, even after several decades of trying.

He scribbled the code onto a napkin and pushed it across the table to her. 'I think you know my line of business by now?'

Isabelle gave a faint bob of the head. 'I'd be a fool not to, Mr Range.'

'Steve. It's probably better Steve. Like I'm calling you Isabelle . . .'

'Steve.'

'Right. Take a look at that. It's some form of a code. One of our fellow operators has kind of shown it to us, and clearly wants us to crack it. It's pretty bloody important we do, 'n' all. But I've wracked my brains and can't seem to figure it.'

Isabelle studied the code for a good minute or more. 'It

has to be a visual play on letters and numbers,' she mused. She glanced at Range. 'Sometimes, you know, it is better to stop trying to concentrate so hard – to wrack your brain as you say – on the puzzle. You let the left side of your brain take over, and allow the figures to find their own way into your mind.'

She gazed at the apparently random sequence of figures. 'The first thing that strikes me is this,' she announced, softly. 'In the centre of the code are three figures: 4ME. To me that says a word: "For Me." You know, like people commonly use in a text message? So maybe we needed to break it down into groups of numbers and letters that somehow form words.'

'Let's try working on the basis that the numbers might somehow correspond to letters. If we move to the figures prior to 4ME: we have PL3453. So if a 3 became an 'E', and a 4 is . . . an "A"? Then 5 equates to an "S", and so on. PL3453 makes "Please".'

'So whatever he's saying has a "Please" and a "For me" in it?' ventured Range.

Isabelle bobbed her head in agreement. A strand of hair fell across her face, and she brushed it aside as she concentrated hard. 'Now, the five figures that start the code: 5CR3W. That I think is quite easy. With 5 being an "S" and 3 being an "E" that reads . . .'

'Screw,' volunteered Range.

'It does,' she confirmed. 'So far we have "Screw please

for me . . ." Not perhaps the most eloquent of phrases, but maybe it is starting to mean something. Now, the last word: M1QA. If the 1 is an "I", that spells MIQA? Does "miqa" mean anything . . .?'

Range shook his head. 'Nope.'

'How about "please screw for me miqa"?'

'Nope, not unless Miqa's some woman he's never told us about.'

'I'm sure you get to meet many . . . women in your line of business.' Isabelle's eyes were smiling. 'So, perhaps there is an added layer of encoding in these last four figures,' she mused. 'The most common form of coding is an anagram – basically mixing up the normal sequence of letters. Mr Range – Steve – I can borrow your pen?'

He passed her the hotel biro that he'd taken from his room. 'We start by rearranging the figures in possible combinations, focusing on those that make obvious words,' she explained. 'Shout if anything suddenly becomes meaningful to you.'

Isabelle began to scribble. As she drafted out the possible combinations the list grew longer and longer and soon she was on the rear side of the napkin. Range felt his eyes swimming as he tried to keep his concentration. Basically, he was a fighter and a leader of men, not really a cerebral kind of a bloke. His mind drifted, and it was only the gentle touch on his arm that brought his focus back to what she was doing.

'You are still concentrating, aren't you, Steve?' she teased him. 'Or if not maybe you will miss something?'

Range ran his eye down the dozens of combinations she'd added whilst his mind had been wandering. He almost missed it. Then his gaze flipped back to the one, four-letter word that jumped out at him. Between 'QAIM' and 'IQAM' was written: 'AQIM'.

He jabbed a finger at it. 'That's it! AQIM! Al-Qaeda in the Islamic Maghreb. AQIM. That's it!'

'AQIM. Al-Qaeda. This is some . . . terrorist group?'

Range nodded. 'It is. You get to meet the nicest kind of people in our line of work.'

'So, if you put it all together what your friend is saying is: "please screw for me AQIM." Or, in its more grammatical order: "Please screw Al-Qaeda in the Islamic Maghreb for me."' Isabelle smiled, happily. 'We have solved the riddle, I think. It still isn't very elegant, perhaps, but as coded messages go . . .'

'It's pure fucking genius,' Range completed the sentence for her. 'Forgive the language. Or rather – you're pure genius for cracking it.' He eyed her for a second. 'So tell me, when you're not volunteering in Africa what d'you really do for a living? Your father had you working as a doctor, but I'd figure the FIS is more your kind of thing?'

'The who?'

'The Federal Intelligence Service – the FIS. The Swiss

intelligence agency. It's got a similar kind of a name in German and French, but they're gibberish to me.'

She laughed. 'Not the FIS. No. Back in Geneva I am a medical doctor. Well, not even that. I am still training to be a medical doctor.'

Range called for a bottle of champagne. The code was at once complex and simplicity itself, but it was disguising it as the ZAP number that was the real touch of genius. No doubt about it, Randy hadn't been turned. Far from it. He was just acting out his part, knowing that once his buddies saw the video and knew he was alive they'd be coming for him – and especially when they deciphered the ZAP code.

Part of Range was tempted to call the others in, so they could learn that the code was cracked and what it meant. But they still had a job to do, and much as things were relaxed and comfortable right now, it was never over until it was over. They had to maintain their vigilance until they'd got the girl loaded onto the private jet. Even more so now, for they owed her big time – Isabelle having cracked the code.

Range made do with a message over the radio: 'I've cracked the code, or rather we have. No way has Randy been turned. His supposed ZAP number reads: "Please screw AQIM for me." Please screw AQIM for me – it's classic Randy! In fact, it's fucking priceless!'

Range could hear the others whooping over the net. He was tempted to give a couple of cheers alongside them, but at the same time he knew he had to keep a lid on this thing.

'Right, don't let it go to your heads. Stay on task. I've got the girl – sorry, Isabelle – with me right now, and it's largely thanks to her that we've cracked it. So we've got double the reason to get her home to her family in comfort and in safety. Stay alert and on task until me and Tak take over, around 0300 hours.'

Range signed off and turned back to Isabelle. He tilted the champagne bottle towards her empty glass. 'Top up? Right now this is a double celebration: to your freedom, and cracking that code.'

'You know, I haven't had any alcohol for months now, so I am feeling already a little woozy.' She smiled. 'But, another glass, why not? We have to raise a toast to solving this thing. It would be wrong not to.'

'So what's with the code-cracking genius, anyway?' Range asked.

Isabelle gave a slight shrug. A distance had crept into her eyes, as if she was reliving memories of long ago. 'You know, my father and I were never very close when I was a child. I was sent away to school, you see. And on the rare occasions when I was at home he used to get me to do all these cross-words and puzzles. I think he did it as a way of avoiding any real intimacy between us – father and daughter. But as a result I am sometimes not so bad at solving these things.'

'You were a lonely child?' Range prompted.

'Not lonely, no. Not lonely. I had friends. But perhaps deprived of everything a small girl could wish for from her parents. In truth, I didn't really have a relationship with them as a small child. I think they are trying to make up for that now . . .'

'Reminds me of my childhood,' Range remarked. He was never one to hide where he had come from, no matter whose company he was in. He told Isabelle a little about his own upbringing, and the fact he had no parents – or at least that he'd been abandoned at birth and had no idea who they were. The shared lack of a family life as children – hers by dint of wealth and privilege; his by dint of poverty and deprivation – seemed to draw them closer together.

'So, why all the euphoria?' Isabelle asked, when Range had finished speaking. 'What does this code mean?'

He gazed at her in silence for several long moments. She'd cracked the code. More than that, over the time that they'd been talking this young woman had somehow disarmed him. And there was a part of him that felt like unburdening his betrayal – for that's what it felt like he had done; betrayed Randy – onto someone, so why not her? And for sure, it would help her keep her mind off whatever horrors she had suffered at the hands of her kidnappers.

'Well, it's pretty way out leftfield kind of stuff,' Range ventured.

'Try me.'

'Okay. So, eighteen months ago I led a team into the Libyan desert . . .' Range gave what he intended to be a quick overview of the Gaddafi mission, their leaving Randy for dead at Range's behest, and his surprise reappearance looking very much alive. He rounded off by telling Isabelle about the video, and the code that had been embedded in the so-called ZAP number scrawled on the butt of his rifle.

She gestured at the iPad. 'Do you mind? Could I see?' Range reached for it, pulled up the image and angled the screen so they both could look. 'A normal ZAP number starts with the guy's initials, and is nine characters long. This does neither. O'Shea, the American, is a fellow former Navy SEAL, just like Randy was – is. He's the one who first realised it wasn't a real ZAP. AQIM – that's the group that Randy supposedly threw in his lot with – have sworn a blood feud against us, hence sending the video.'

Isabelle threw Range a look. 'Somehow, Mr Range – Steve – I don't think Randy has thrown in his lot with these sorts. Not if he is anything like you are, or the rest of the men on your team.'

It was well into the early hours by the time Isabelle was ready to return to her room. With the Library Bar closing at eleven p.m., they'd had to relocate to the hotel's Kingfisher Bar, which was open all hours. It was a modern creation of burnished steel and chrome, and it didn't have anything like the cosy, easy ambience of the Library. But they'd stayed for several drinks and chatted away like old friends, before Isabelle had decided she would like to go to her room.

It was about the time that Range needed to take over on watch, so he offered to escort her. He necked a couple of strong coffees, signed the bar tab and led her to the lift. It was busy, so they decided to take the stairs. The hotel was a low-rise affair, so it was only a short climb.

Range gestured for her to go first, being the true gentleman that he wasn't. As she climbed ahead of him he let his eyes feast upon every curve of her body, which the dress sculpted perfectly. It was no fucking wonder her kidnappers had kept her cloaked in shapeless, stinking black robes. In anything else she was fucking dynamite.

Range was well aware that there was another reason why he hadn't wanted to call the others to the bar, to share in the code-breaking euphoria. He'd built up a certain intimacy with Isabelle over that iPad screen. It wasn't so often he got to spend time alone with a beautiful, elegant, captivating twenty-six-year-old. Sure, he was almost old enough to be her father. And sure, there was no way he would ever let anything happen under such circumstances – that's if she would ever entertain it, which he very much doubted. But it didn't detract from the fact that it had been a very enjoyable evening.

Range relieved O'Shea at her room, and the wiry American headed down to catch a bite to eat and a late beer in the bar.

Isabelle paused outside her door. 'Thank you, Mr Range. Steve. This evening has been more fun than I have had in . . . well, it feels like a lifetime.'

Steve smiled. 'Likewise.'

There was a moment's awkwardness between them, and then Range leaned forward, kissed her briefly on both cheeks, French style, before lowering himself into his chair.

'You can sleep perfectly soundly and for as long as you need,' he told her. 'I'll be here, or one of the other lads will.'

'Thank you.' She turned the door handle, then paused. 'You know, I think after tonight I will be ready to leave tomorrow. Your company has cheered me. It has made me happy, and especially solving the Randy puzzle! I think I am ready to go home.'

'I'll put a call through to your father and let him know.' Range had the cell phone number of the pilot, who was on standby. He'd call him too, and set a take-off time for around midday.

'Goodnight, Mr Range.'

'Goodnight, Isabelle. Sleep well. And sweet dreams.'

Range figured he'd been sat there for a good hour when he heard the door crack open a little. He'd been rubbernecking, his head falling to his chest as he dropped off momentarily, only to jerk himself awake again. He welcomed any distraction.

Isabelle's head appeared around the door. She was dressed in a thick hotel gown. 'Well, I couldn't sleep . . . So I thought I would check on you, as you are watching over me.'

Range shrugged. 'I'm all right. Bored out of my brain, to tell you the truth. But hey, what's new? Occupational hazard.'

'It is? I thought being a soldier was all about excitement and drama and action, no?'

'Far from it. War: long periods of boredom interspersed with the odd bit of sheer terror and bloody mayhem.'

She laughed. She flicked her eyes up to meet his. 'You know, you would be much more comfortable perhaps with your chair inside my room? Or maybe sitting on one of the comfy armchairs?'

For a second Range let his hard, slate-grey eyes stare into hers. God, but this was so fucking tempting. He knew for certain that if his chair went inside that room, there was zero chance that he was staying out of her bed. But he also knew that this was absolutely crossing the line. The golden rule of such jobs was that you never dipped your pen in the company ink. He had to resist. She was also vulnerable, damaged, traumatised and all the rest of it, so he would be massively taking advantage. But he couldn't deny it: he actually liked this girl very, very much.

This wasn't just lust. Or not exclusively so, anyway. He'd felt a real connection with her. Maybe this was all to do with the fact that he'd rescued her, and so he was her saviour, and she in turn felt she had to somehow show she was grateful. But for some reason he felt relaxed and easy in her company. Yet he knew that he couldn't cross the threshold. He also had to think about the others in his team. He knew they'd find out, and that they'd crucify him for it – as well he would deserve.

His first loyalty was to the blokes and the mission, it had to be. 'Isabelle, don't think that isn't the most tempting offer I have ever had, because it is. But right now, right here at this very moment, it isn't right and I can't. You do understand, don't you?'

She smiled, a little reluctantly. 'Steve, I do. You are a man of integrity.' But in spite of the words, she wasn't trying to hide her disappointment. 'I was going to say sleep well, but you won't be sleeping, will you? If you need anything, you only have to knock at my door.'

How Range managed to last the rest of his watch without taking her up on the offer God only knew. He had to keep reminding himself over and over how deeply unprofessional it would be to sleep with the client, especially in such circumstances as these. The first thing he did when O'Shea came to relieve him was to go and find the hotel gym. He ran hard for thirty minutes then violently pumped iron, in an effort to burn all the tension – and frustration – out of his system.

The rest of the morning flew by. They had to check out of the hotel by nine a.m. sharp to make Kenya's Jomo Kenyatta Airport for eleven a.m. It being a private flight, security and check-in were a mere formality, but the plan was to have Isabelle in the air en route to Geneva by midday, and Range liked to stick to a schedule. They headed to the airport in the Toyota, with Range driving and Isabelle looking crisp and stunning in the front passenger seat.

All through the journey she chatted away as if nothing had happened the night before, which of course it hadn't. More was the pity, Range told himself, ruefully. There was no hiding the fact that he had a serious crush on this woman, but he figured hers had been only a passing infatuation with the man who had saved her.

No worries. He'd get the job done, move on and put it all down to experience, or so he tried to tell himself. *Who was he kidding?*

They pulled into the secluded car park adjacent to the terminal that handled private flights coming into and out of the country. Kenya being such a massive landmass with so many remote areas, there were a lot of private light aircraft that flew across its airspace. But there were very, very few private jets of the de Saint-Sébastien ilk flying intercontinental itineraries.

Range was about to whisk Isabelle through departures when a distinctive figure appeared. He was tall but stooping, with pepper-grey hair and dressed in an exquisite suit with knife-edge creases. It was Isabelle's father, Jean-Pierre de Saint-Sébastien, and as he caught sight of the burly figure of Range with his daughter by his side, he broke into a wide smile.

'Mr Range,' he barked, thrusting out his hand in greeting.

'I see your reputation for bringing your people home alive extends even to getting my daughter through a chaotic African airport!'

'Sir,' Range confirmed. He felt a flush of relief now that he hadn't gone ahead and seduced his daughter.

Jean-Pierre de Saint-Sébastien stopped and stared at Isabelle, seeming all but overcome with emotion. 'And Izzy . . . Little Isabelle. So beautiful. I flew in just to surprise you. You are ready to come home?'

There was a moment's silence as she stared into her father's face. Then: 'Yes, Papa, I am.'

A part of Range was expecting raw emotion and tears. Instead, the father stepped forward a little stiffly and enfolded his daughter in what could only be described as a formal kind of a hug. As for Isabelle, she seemed oddly reserved with him. But Range wasn't so surprised either; he knew how these born-to-wealth gentry types tended to function. He'd come across enough of them in the military.

Father and daughter embraced briefly, before he seemed to take over from where Range had left off and steered Isabelle towards the departure gate. For a moment he saw her resist, and she turned back towards Range.

She took a few steps towards him. 'Thank you, for everything.'

'Not at all, thank you – and especially for solving the ZAP code.'

She laughed, teeth flashing brightly from behind her

64

dark head of hair. 'Well, you really have my father to thank for that. He is the one who taught me so much puzzle solving.'

The old man arched one eyebrow. 'A little mystery it seems? No doubt, Isabelle, you can reveal all on the flight to Geneva.'

They turned to go, before the old man stopped himself. 'Aha, and before I forget.' He delved into his pocket and handed an envelope to Range. 'A little something to say thank you. First Class tickets via BA to London. Open-ended. I'm not having that cheapskate Tony Hogan fly you home cattle class. And so, thank you so very much, and enjoy the flights.'

Range kept watch as the two figures were ushered through the 'VIP Only' channel, and out to the waiting Gulfstream. That done, he gathered his team together from where they'd been staking out the terminal building, just in case of any last-minute surprises.

Having checked out flight availability – First Class was rarely full – they made for the vehicle. Their schedule now was simple: back to the hotel, get checked out and wrapped up for the BA flight direct to London that evening.

'O'Shea, you drive,' Range told him.

He wanted a few minutes' peace to himself. As they pulled into the busy traffic on the airport road Range leafed through the envelope. Along with the First Class flight tickets there was a thick wad of one-hundred-dollar bills.

It looked as if they'd earned themselves a nice little bonus. But oddly, Range didn't feel as if he had. His overriding sense right now was one of loss – the loss of the girl. He'd barely known her for forty-eight hours, yet he was hopelessly what . . . in love?

He shook his head angrily. He needed to snap the fuck out of this. Within twenty-four hours they would be back in London and preparing for the next job – the mission to rescue Randy. And this time they'd be going up against a lot more than a few Somali pirates. He needed to get his mind off the girl and onto the job in hand.

Range heard a bleeping on his mobile. There was a text message. He clicked it open.

Mr Range. Steve. I should like to see you again. Very much. You probably think this is just a kidnap victim's infatuation with her rescuer. It is not. I have grown to like you very much over the last few hours. This is my Geneva mobile number. Kindly, Mr O'Shea gave me yours. Please call me when you are able to. Isabelle. X.

Range dropped the phone on the dash and swivelled his head around to eyeball O'Shea. 'O'Shea, you fucker . . .'

It was then that the catcalls and whistles began, as all three of his fellow operators ripped into him.

CHAPTER FIVE

'So, everything went entirely to plan with the Kenya job?'
The Hogan was speaking to Range and his Kenya team, plus
a handful of other B6 operators seated before him. They
were gathered in Blackstone Six's Mayfair office waiting
for The Colonel to arrive, so they could get down to some
proper business.

The Kiwi snorted derisively. 'Yeah, you could say that –
all apart from Range seducing the client's daughter.'

Range ran his hand through his short-cropped hair,
shaking his head in mock despair. 'No one seduced anyone.
If nothing else, it would have been "very bad for business"
– to coin Amir the pirate's phrase.'

O'Shea jerked a thumb in Range's direction. 'He'll be off
to use the bathroom soon, only he'll be checking for text
messages from *Isabelle*.'

Range shook his head again, but stayed quiet. Sometimes, you just had to shut the fuck up and take it.

'Where I come from, you never hit on the Big Chief's daughter,' Tak rumbled. 'Not if you want to live to a grand old age.'

Range eyed the three of them. Piss-taking bastards. Still, had Isabelle taken a shine to one of the others he'd be doing exactly the same right now. And truth was he *had* been exchanging one or two text messages with the client's daughter. And once they brought Randy home, he fully intended to hop on a flight to Geneva and go visit her.

There was a tap on the door and the distinctive figure of The Colonel strode in. Like The Hogan he was in his late fifties; he acted as B6's liaison between the Secret Intelligence Service (SIS, otherwise known as MI6), Her Majesty's Government and their foremost allies. Much of B6's work was purely private – like the hostage handover mission they'd just done – but increasingly they were getting tasked with missions that governments wanted doing, but which needed to be kept very much off the books.

The Colonel's role was thus a vital one, and after several years of working with him Range trusted the man almost as much as he did The Hogan. Mostly, Blackstone Six was staffed with ex-military operators from the CANUKUS – Canada, Australia, New Zealand, UK and US – Special Forces, so it was a perfect conduit via which to run such deniable contracts. And occasionally, the needs of private business and Government were in such close alignment that a B6 mission might be contracted by two distinct parties.

The Colonel ran his eye around those gathered in the room. 'So, gentlemen: tell me, who cracked the ZAP code?'

'You don't want to know,' The Kiwi muttered. 'Range and his love child. Talk about young enough to be his daughter . . .'

The Colonel raised one eyebrow inquiringly. 'Someone care to explain?'

Range gestured helplessly. 'Isabelle de Saint-Sébastien, the Somalia kidnap victim, happens to have a very smart head on her shoulders. You might want to offer her a job, before she gets snapped up by one of your rivals.'

'I suspect we might not be able to afford her,' said The Colonel. 'Anyhow, whoever managed it – well done. Now, to business.' He turned to The Hogan. 'Tony, you have those slides I emailed you?'

The Hogan tapped a few keys on his laptop and an image appeared on a screen mounted on the far wall.

'Tripoli,' The Colonel announced. 'Aerial photo of. I presume you know the city fairly well, from your last – erm, the Sultan Gaddafi – mission?'

There was a series of muttered affirmatives.

'This is the airport here, and the port here,' The Colonel continued, 'plus the main thoroughfare, here. There's not a great deal more you need to know. You'll be coming into the target from outside the city – that's if you're good with the plan that Tony and I have formulated. Best to avoid getting tangled up in the chaos of the city if at all possible. Even so, study this and any maps of Tripoli carefully, just in case you have to do an exfil via an unexpected route.

'Now, to the west of the city lies our target. Tony, if you flip to the next slide?' A new image appeared, showing a close-up aerial photo of a compound. 'What you're seeing here is AQIM's forward mounting base: this is the stepping-stone between their deep desert hideouts and terrorist operations worldwide. It sits on the outskirts of Tripoli. Basically, east of here lies the city suburbs. West and south are open bush and desert. We figure they chose this location because it is private, yet gives easy access to Tripoli airport and the docks.

'We believe they are planning to launch a series of terrorist atrocities from here, and access to travel hubs – docks, airports – is key. Unfortunately, we have little idea of their targets or timescale. We have recruited a HUMINT source inside AQIM, but their leaders are smart. Very. They don't seem to let on about the specifics of a mission – where, when, how – until the team undertaking it has departed. In fact, we were hoping as part of your coming mission you might garner some intelligence that might lead us to their objectives.

'One thing we are clear on, though: a terrorist spectacular is imminent. For that reason, your mission has to proceed with the utmost urgency. As far as we know, Randy is still at this location: but how much longer he may remain there, before he is . . . deployed, is anyone's guess.'

The Colonel glanced around the assembled men. 'We believe the AQIM leadership are ninety per cent convinced Randy has fully bought into their cause, but they still don't trust him completely. It is some eighteen months since they apparently brought Randy back from the dead. As far as we can tell, they still keep him closely watched and guarded.

'The eight of you in this room are the ones Tony and I could pull together in the short time available,' The Colonel continued. 'Your coming mission has the backing of HMG, because we believe key targets of AQIM include British inter-ests overseas: oil installations, mine sites, embassies. As yet we have no knowledge that they are planning attacks on the UK mainland, but nothing should be ruled out with these people.'

The atmosphere in the room had changed completely now. It was deadly serious. Range eyed the others who were gathered, most of whom were veterans of the Gaddafi mis-sion. One was Tiny, a guy who'd earned the nickname due to his imposing physique. He was maybe an inch taller than Tak, though not quite as broad in the beam. Tiny was the proverbial barn door to Tak's brick shithouse.

Tiny wasn't necessarily the sharpest tool in the box. He was a tattooed, flat-nosed street fighter, with a face like a sack of claw hammers, but Range knew he could rely on him to lead from the front when the bullets started to fly.

He'd proved as much during the intense and bloody combat they'd experienced assaulting the desert fortress on the Gaddafi mission. Tiny had voted with Range and The Kiwi to leave Randy behind – believing him to be dead – but he hadn't exactly danced for joy at the prospect.

Like the rest of them, Tiny had scores to settle in Libya, and Range was glad he was free to take the mission. Next to Tiny sat Ghost and Sticky, two blokes who were ex-1 PARA. The Parachute Regiment's 1 PARA formed the British Army's Special Forces Support Group (SFSG) – elite soldiers who went in alongside the SAS and SBS (Special Boat Service – the sister regiment to the SAS) to provide sheer grunt and firepower in support of operations. It was obvious how Ghost had earned his nickname: he had white-blond hair and almost albino skin; but as to 'Sticky', Range didn't care to speculate how he'd earned that moniker.

Each of them had been on the Gaddafi mission, so they too had a burning reason to be here. As opposed to the SAS and SBS, SFSG wasn't Tier One Special Forces, but Range knew the capabilities of both men, and he didn't give much of a shit about any such elitist crap. He took every man as an individual and judged him on his ability to fight, and on that basis Sticky and Ghost were about as good as it got.

The last member of the eight-man team was the new addition. Joe was ex-SBS, and his real name was Mitch. He'd been nicknamed after Joe's Dive Shack, a business he'd set up with several fellow SBS operators. Joe's Dive Shack had failed spectacularly – those guys were fighters, not business people – and Mitch had got saddled with the piss-taking nickname 'Dive Shack Joe' ever after, or just Joe for short.

At six-foot-two Joe was about the same height as Range, but he had more of an athlete's built, as opposed to Range's street-fighter physique. He had massive shoulders and arm muscles, built up over the years doing deep-dive missions from submarines, or climbing ropes and ladders to assault a ship or an oil rig. He wore his sandy hair longish, like The Kiwi, and he was another cool, laid-back operator. He was also a man of few words, and Range knew of his reputation as a steely-eyed bringer of death when the red mist of combat went down.

They'd needed an eighth man to make up the numbers, and Joe was also the Arabic-speaker on the coming mission. Joe had made no bones about why he wanted in. First, he needed the money that B6 would pay him, for after the dive business went kaput he'd been saddled with a lot of debt. Secondly, and more importantly, Joe relished the idea of having a good pop at Al-Qaeda in the Islamic Maghreb.

'Next slide please,' The Colonel announced, dragging Range's attention back to the briefing. An image appeared of a wider map of Libya. 'This is a deniable operation, obviously. That being said, you have full backing of HMG – who is funding this – plus our armed forces.' The Colonel indicated a point on the map in the open desert to the southwest of Tripoli. 'There is a small British base – here, at Wadi

Idhan. It's hidden away and isolated. I think some of you may already know it?'

'We do,' Range confirmed. 'We transited through it during the exfil from the Gaddafi mission.'

'To be clear, it's a UKSF base,' The Colonel added, 'and it is very, very discreet. This will be your forward mounting base for operations – not that you will be spending very long there, if you agree to our plan of attack. That plan is predicated on maximum stealth, coupled with speed, aggression and lethality. And it's been designed to marry up all of that with bringing Randy out alive, plus one other individual who is very much sought after.'

'Next slide.' An image appeared that was immediately recognisable to Range. It was a grab from the AQIM video he'd first seen back in Nairobi. 'Most of you will recognise this man: Moussa ag Ajjer Junior – named after his late-lamented father. Moussa is now the operational commander of AQIM in the Horn of Africa – a region encompassing Kenya, Somalia, Sudan and a few other nations. We believe they are planning a terrorist hit somewhere in that area, and Moussa is to lead it. Memorise his face. Along with Randy, we'd like him brought out alive.'

'Next slide.' A schematic diagram appeared on the screen, showing the Tripoli compound and the immediate terrain surrounding it. 'Plan of attack. And remember, speed of operations is the critical factor here. You fly out to the Wadi Idhan base in a C130. Since you were last there the runway has been extended to take transport aircraft of that size. You arm up at Wadi Idhan. You'll be going in with silenced weaponry, and all of that will be provided to you there. From Wadi Idhan you do the infiltration to target via two Chinooks. Each helo will carry one Toyota 4x4, which will be very much a local vehicle.

'Now, you will need to dress like locals and the vehicles will also look the part. This is critical: there can be no suggestion after the event that this attack was carried out by Westerners or, God forbid, by British forces. You'll see why shortly. The Chinooks drop you here, well out of range of any at the target building who might otherwise hear you. You drive in via this dirt track, which we understand is perfectly navigable. Your aim is to hit the target at around 0300 – so during the dead hours. You will work your timings back from there.

'Your route will take you past several settlements. There is no way to avoid them, I am afraid. We assume their occupants will be sleeping at that time of the night. Either way, you work on the presumption that if anyone does see you, they will conclude you are a local militia passing through. This is Libya post-Gaddafi: it is lawless and rife with conflict. Tribes fighting tribes; militia fighting militia. You are posing as local militia, but you will need to treat everyone as a potential enemy.

'Slide.' A sharp photograph appeared on the screen. It showed a metal canister set against a white background.

Around the canister was scrawled some Arabic writing. 'As I'm sure you know, the late Colonel Gaddafi had an extensive chemical weapons programme. Much of his stock was old, but much remains usable. This is a canister of Sarin. Sarin is one of the G Agents developed by the Germans in World War Two: it is less highly toxic than the later V Agents, like VX. However, it remains a potent chemical agent: from first ingestion it is highly debilitating, and it doesn't take long to kill a man.'

The Colonel eyed the men in the room. 'With the fall of Gaddafi much of his chemical arsenal is unaccounted for. Some has doubtless fallen into the hands of the militias and worse. Your assault plan is predicated upon that fact, and that those who discover the aftermath assume it is the work of rivals settling old scores.

'You are a force of eight,' The Colonel continued. 'AQIM, we suspect, has three dozen fighters stationed in that compound. Not all of them will be as highly trained or capable as Randy – and I am not suggesting for one moment that he has been turned, especially not after the ZAP code was decoded. Even so, you will be up against thirty-five very tough and determined fighters. You will use some of the late Colonel Gaddafi's Sarin to even up the odds a little.'

The Colonel went on to explain things in more detail. The assault force would hit the compound in conditions of total darkness and surprise. Canisters of the nerve gas would be hurled through doors and windows, knocking out the defenders and killing them. Range and his men would head into the building immediately following the gas, wearing NBC suits and masks, so as to drag out Randy and their secondary target, Moussa ag Ajjer, as quickly as possible.

'Sarin degrades relatively quickly. Gaddafi's stockpiles may be too old to be effective. You will be using recently manufactured Sarin that we have acquired, but in canisters marked up in a similar way to those supplied by the then Soviets to Gaddafi. You will be going in twenty-four hours from now, so tomorrow night. The MET forecast is for an overcast sky, so it should be pitch black. The target building generally seems to have security lights running all night. You'll start the assault by killing those. This needs to be an unseen, silent attack, and you should be in and out without anyone noticing.

'That being so, no one in Libya will have any reason to believe this attack wasn't carried out by a rival militia, or even a rogue element of the new Libyan security services, intent on purging AQIM from the country. As you know, AQIM are no friends of the new and struggling Libyan democratic regime.

'Questions?' The Colonel prompted. 'And it goes without saying that you should feel free to modify and develop the plan of attack to suit the conditions as you encounter them on the ground.'

'So we grab Randy, drag him out and get a nerve gas antidote into him?' queried Range.

'You do. You'll need to administer injections of ComboPen – a blend of the nerve agent antidotes Atropine, Pralidoxime and Avizafone – as soon as possible. You've all had extensive NBC training: but mug up on it, and quickly.'

'So how long do we have?' Range asked.

'Sarin kills a man within a matter of minutes of first inhalation or ingestion. Even if you get the antidote into a victim, a man's body can be damaged beyond repair. Any longer than fifteen minutes, and he'll suffer permanent nerve damage. That's how long you have to get in, get Randy out, administer the antidotes and decontaminate him.'

'So, it's the same with that wanker Moussa ag Ajjer?'

'It is, although Randy is obviously the key priority. And frankly, if this Moussa chap comes through all this just a little bit the worse for wear, so much the better. All we need is for him to be able to talk.'

'Why the need to use the nerve agent?' O'Shea queried. 'Why not treat it like we would any normal killing house? A standard CQB assault? We go in with flash-bangs and silenced MP5s, and clear it room by room that way.'

Range had figured the use of a nerve agent wouldn't sit comfortably with his American second-in-command. Though a SEAL would give no quarter in battle, he was still supposed to kill the enemy in a way that conformed to the SEAL's code of honour. Gassing the fuckers fell a long way short of that.

'Several reasons,' The Colonel answered. 'One: the use of

flash-bangs will alert the surrounding population. You're immediately compromised. Two, there are thirty-five of the hostiles and eight of you: I am not underestimating the capabilities of any man in this room, but clearly those are deeply unfavourable odds. Three: Randy is under more or less permanent guard. If AQIM realise an assault is underway, we believe they will kill him. The use of Sarin is silent, stealthy and utterly debilitating: it gives you the greatest chance of achieving your main objectives. It isn't pretty or nice. No one's pretending that it is. But rest assured, the kind of terrorist spectaculars that AQIM are planning are going to be far less pleasant.'

'It doesn't matter how they die – dead's still dead,' The Kiwi announced. His snake-green eyes flicked across to O'Shea momentarily. 'There is no issue with using the Sarin. Sometimes it takes a smaller evil to stop a greater one.'

There was a long beat between the two men. Whilst O'Shea and The Kiwi respected each other as operators, they had never seen eye to eye. It was an open secret that O'Shea blamed The Kiwi above all others for leaving Randy behind on the Gaddafi mission. As for The Kiwi, he didn't much seem to give a shit: in his mind, he'd done what was best for the mission and his fellow operators. QED.

'You say you have a HUMINT source in with AQIM,' Joe, the newcomer to the team, volunteered. 'If we use gas, presumably we're going to kill him. That's a waste of a valuable intel asset, isn't it?'

'Good point,' acknowledged The Colonel. 'Except that our HUMINT source happens to be back in AQIM's desert base, deep in the Empty Quarter.' The Colonel glanced at his watch. 'Gentlemen, time is running. Any more?'

'One,' O'Shea volunteered. 'Maybe gas is the only way to do this . . . But does anyone have any goddamn idea how Randy's still alive?'

The Hogan coughed. 'Ah, yes, the elephant in the room as it were . . .'

'None whatsoever.' The Colonel's eyes sought out The Kiwi. 'Mike, you care to . . . ?'

'During the battle for the Fort of the Mount, Randy took massive internal injuries from grenade shrapnel,' The Kiwi related, matter-of-factly. 'He was in a coma for the last few hours, and only major surgery might – I repeat might – have saved him. He was clinically dead by the time we left him. So by rights, it's impossible for him to be alive.'

The Kiwi paused. 'But I've thought long and hard about this since seeing him on that video. I'm no expert, but it's just possible that when we wrapped him in that mass of silk, we somehow mummified or embalmed him. Maybe his body functions had shut down to a level I couldn't detect, but those who found him – AQIM as we now know – managed to revive him. But it's all pretty much conjecture . . .'

'So, in short, no one has a clue how he's still alive?' O'Shea pressed.

'Indeed, it remains something of a mystery to all,' The Colonel confirmed.

'Only one way to find out,' announced Range. 'We go in, get Randy out and we ask him.'

The Colonel tilted his head at Range. 'So, we're agreed: this is the way to do it?'

'Seems like a plan to me,' Range confirmed. He turned to his men. 'You all good with this?'

There were a series of affirmatives from around the room. Only O'Shea seemed less than convinced.

As the briefing broke up Range felt The Kiwi draw him to one side. A lot of people figured The Kiwi to be a cold, hard, heartless bastard. They could be forgiven for doing so. He didn't show his emotions much, if at all. He was the opposite of men like O'Shea, who wore their heart on their sleeve. But Range valued The Kiwi possibly above any other man in his unit. He'd soldiered with him for longer than any other, and if ever he had to go on the run behind enemy lines, he'd choose The Kiwi as his running mate every single time.

The Kiwi was a hard, fast and merciless killer. He was an expert at Krav Maga, the Israeli martial art which is a blend of kung fu and the most vicious kind of street fighting. He was a natural with most weapons, but his real speciality was the sniper rifle. Most of all, The Kiwi had a superb brain in his head, and was a lateral thinker par excellence. If anyone could think outside the box, The Kiwi could, which was why Range always paid special attention to whatever the man had to say.

'Mate, you ever wondered if it's a double-cross?' The Kiwi ventured.

'Like how?'

'Like the ZAP code. Just because it's written on Randy's rifle doesn't make it true.'

'You've lost me, mate.'

The Kiwi's eyes narrowed imperceptibly. 'There's no point avoiding the truth: we left Randy for dead. Abandoned him. Those are the facts. Now he resurfaces a year and some later, in an AQIM video in which they're vowing a blood feud against us lot. Sure, he's got a message written on his rifle butt, apparently in code. It pretty much invites us to go in and rescue him. How could we not, if after all that's happened he's stayed loyal to his brother warriors – to us? But what about if this is all part of the feud? What about if they're all in on it? They knew we'd decipher it and be left with no option but to go get him.'

'You mean, like it's a come-on?'

'You got it.'

'Never thought about it.'

'Well, think about it,' The Kiwi grated. 'If it was you we'd left for dead, and AQIM came and found you, nursed you back to health, saved your life and made you one of their number, where would your allegiances lie? Fucking think about it, mate.'

'I am. Who fucking knows?'

'Exactly. My point exactly.'

'Yeah, but Randy's a SEAL, remember? They aren't like us. They've got their code of conduct and morals and all that honour-God-country shit.'

'We still left him for dead and abandoned him.'

'So what do we do about it?'

'All we can do is keep a very close eye on Randy when we go in to get him.'

'And once we pull him out of there?'

'We keep watching him, for as long as it takes.'

'So it's TNF all over, then?' Range queried. TNF was an old saying shared across the SAS family of regiments. It stood for Trust No Fucker.

The Kiwi gave a thin smile. 'TNF it is, mate.'

CHAPTER SIX

Range felt his mobile vibrate. It was amazing how you could get a signal even here, in such a god forsaken stretch of the Libyan Desert. By rights he shouldn't have had the phone with him. Mobiles were easy to track and intercept, so it was bad security and tradecraft, but ever since Kenya things had been moving lightning fast, and he'd barely had the time to shit, let alone sanitise himself properly.

He checked. Text message. Isabelle. *Good luck with your Randy mission. Stay safe. And please call me when you are back. We need to talk. xxx*

It struck Range as being an odd phrase: *we need to talk*. There had been a few like that recently – less personal, and almost bordering on the desperate. Range wondered what might lie behind it? Just how messed up was Isabelle, post-

Somalia? Not for the first time he worried what exactly he might be getting himself into here.

But he forced such thoughts to the back of his mind: plenty of time for all of that when they'd got Randy home. He stuffed the mobile phone into the bag of crap he'd be leaving behind at the Wadi Idhan base, and turned to pack the last of his assault gear.

Some twenty minutes later Range was squatted on one of the fold-down canvas seats that ran along the Chinook's hold. His four-man stick – Fire Team Alpha – consisted of himself, The Kiwi, Tiny and the new guy, Joe. O'Shea's lot – Team Bravo – was likewise preparing to get airborne in the second Chinook, with Tak, Sticky and Ghost under his command. Each helo was loaded with a battered white Toyota pick-up, fully fuelled, and with a pile of kit secured under a tarpaulin in the vehicle's rear.

There was nothing that marked those Toyotas out as being any different from the thousands of other 4x4s that plied the Libyan Desert. Likewise, Range and his men had dressed themselves in local Arab dish-dash-style robes. Most were dirty-grey or off-white, and stained and mud-spattered. Those who were lacking a suntan had dirtied up any exposed skin, and an Arab-style *Shemagh* – a checked headscarf – wrapped around hair and the lower half of the face topped off the local dress.

The only thing that might mark them out as foreigners

was their footwear: they needed proper boots for an assault such as the one that was coming, not flimsy sandals. But that shouldn't pose a problem: they'd ride to the target in the helos and then the pick-ups, so the lower half of their bodies wouldn't be visible until the moment of the attack.

Range heard the turbines spool up to speed above him, and then the giant, twin-bladed Chinook lifted off, the pilot banking it around onto the right bearing. As the aircraft gathered speed he could see his men checking and re-checking their weapons. They'd each been issued with the AK-74 – the more modern version of the Soviet-era AK-47 – complete with a folding stock, and a stubby silencer bolted to the muzzle. AK-47/74s were ubiquitous across most of Africa, and they were the only weapons to be seen with around here.

They'd loaded the mags with subsonic ammo, which provided enough power to stop a man but almost zero muzzle noise. They'd be accurate up to a maximum of two hundred metres, but at the kind of distance they'd be engaging the enemy that was range enough. It was silence and stealth that they'd put at a premium, and about the only noise the weapon made when it fired was the action slamming home. They'd got the AK-74s zeroed in at the Wadi Idhan ranges, during the few hours that they'd spent there.

They thundered onwards across the desert, the aircrew operating on black light – showing no lights at all, and navigating on night-vision goggles. The pilot was flying at treetop level and throwing the massive, ghostly machine around like it was a Formula One racing car. The effect in the dark and echoing hold would have been puke-inducing, were Range and his men not so used to such a ride.

Libya wasn't a war zone any more. Not quite, anyway. But after a mixed bunch of so-called freedom fighters had toppled Colonel Gaddafi's regime, their coalition of convenience had faltered. Scores of militias, each with a rival tribal or religious affiliation, were vying for power – and thanks to the British, French and Americans arming them during the war to topple Gaddafi, they were now very seriously tooled up.

The Zintan Brigade. The 17th February Militia. The Shariah Brigade. The names of the rival militias were about as confusing as trying to work out who controlled what territory. Zintan seemed to have grabbed the airports. The 17th February Militia had taken control of Benghazi, one of Libya's most wealthy coastal cities. The Shariah Brigade were terrorists in all but name. And as to the capital, Tripoli, it was anyone's guess which militia controlled which areas.

Range's men were heading into the unknown, and especially as they had no eyes-on the intended landing zone (LZ), and no one on the ground to guide them in. The Colonel's words rang in Range's ears: *This is Libya post-Gaddafi: it is lawless and rife with conflict. Tribes fighting tribes; militia fighting militia . . . you will need to treat everyone as a potential enemy.* They were going in blind and all but defenceless –

apart from the gunners hunched over their miniguns at the helo's open doors.

For a good thirty minutes the pair of helicopters tore ahead at approaching their maximum speed of 250 kph. The terrain flashed past in shadows and pockets of darkness a few dozen feet below the porthole-like windows. There was a momentary dull glint of water as the lead Chinook flashed over a waterway – one of the irrigation ditches that watered the rich farmland to the south of Tripoli.

Range stared at it for a second, his mind wandering to thoughts about whether The Kiwi's warning about Randy might prove true. Until they hit that building there was just no way of knowing.

He heard a whine from behind him and the Chinook's ramp started to lower. He glanced at the loadmaster – the guy whose job it was to orchestrate all that went on in the helo's hold. He flashed ten fingers at Range: ten minutes to their arrival at the LZ. The noise in the Chinook's hold was deafening, as the cold night air swirled and roared over the open ramp and the twin rotor blades hammered away above them.

Range glanced at his men. From each he got a silent nod and a calm thumbs-up. These guys were absolute pros – the best – and he didn't detect the slightest hint of nerves from any of them. Sure, they were outnumbered more than five-to-one, but he figured the Sarin made the odds just about even. No one relished using the gas, but sometimes, as The Kiwi had argued, *you used a lesser evil to fight a greater one*.

The loadie flashed five fingers in front of their faces: five minutes to the LZ. It was time for Range and The Kiwi to mount up the Toyota. It was a twin-cab version, so there was more than enough room for the four of them to ride up front, but Tiny and Joe would dash out first – one providing cover as the other helped guide the vehicle down the helo's open ramp.

The desert night was bitter and there was little point suffering the road journey that lay ahead riding in the open rear, so all four of them would be up front in the cab. They'd also be less visible to any watching eyes, which was an added bonus. But they'd keep their windows rolled down, so they could listen out and put down fire from the vehicles if the need arose.

Not a man amongst them was carrying anything that might reveal his identity. Wallets, photos of family, ID cards, papers of any sort – all of it had been dumped at their Wadi Idhan base. That way, if anyone was captured or killed during the coming assault, there was nothing that would reveal his nationality or the force from which he hailed.

As the Chinook decelerated from speed, the rear of the aircraft dropping fast towards the earth, Range felt his last meal – British Army boil-in-the bag pasta, wolfed down in the Wadi Idhan hangar – threatening to launch itself out of his stomach. The pilot was 'flaring out' in preparation to land. He'd touch down with the open ramp for just the barest of seconds as the Toyota nosed out of the Chinook's rear and got its wheels onto the sand. They'd reversed the vehicle into the hold, to make the exit all the more fast and manageable.

The first tendrils of choking dust swirled in through the open ramp as the helo descended, the rotors whipping up a heavy brownout of a sand storm. Range, The Kiwi, Tiny and Joe pulled on their sand-goggles – protective eyewear looking a little like a welder's glasses – and wrapped their Shemaghs even tighter around their faces. A dull thud rang out from below, as the rear ramp made contact with the hard terrain.

The loadie gave the signal: 'Go! Go! Go!' An instant later The Kiwi had the Toyota in motion, nosing down the open ramp and powering into the blinding, dust-choked darkness. Range turned around to shout some kind of confirmation that they were gone, but the pilot wasn't hanging around to hear.

The pitch of the rotors rose to a fearsome scream as the Chinook lifted above them, then the pilot put the helo's nose down, banked southwards and powered away. Within moments the dark form was swallowed up by the empty night, the only sign of its passing being the blinding pall of dust it had left in its wake, plus the beat of the rotor-blades fading to nothing on the cold air.

Range and his men hunched over their weapons, as they

waited for the visibility to clear. First priority now was to get away from the LZ, for the Chinooks' arrival had been a very noisy and noticeable affair. But there was no point going anywhere until they could see to drive.

The first thing that became visible was the other vehicle, its blocky silhouette bleeding through the thinning cloud of dust. They sat and waited until it was clear enough to move. On Range's word The Kiwi led off, with Tiny and Joe scanning their arcs in case anyone had detected their arrival and might be homing in on them. As soon as they were underway O'Shea's vehicle fell in line behind.

They'd been dropped in a patch of desert some five hundred metres to the west of the dirt track – the route that would take them northwards into Tripoli. The Kiwi pushed ahead for three hundred yards, using his natural night vision and with the vehicle showing no lights. It was easy enough driving, the terrain being hard-packed gravel and sand.

Once they were a good distance from the LZ he pulled the wagon to a halt, O'Shea's vehicle drawing up alongside them. The men listened hard for several seconds. The noise of the Chinooks had faded away to nothing: in place of the deafening roar and the confusion, there was now a deep and residing stillness such as you only ever seemed to find in the vastness of the open desert. Both vehicles were enveloped in its empty silence.

For five minutes they waited. Listened. Scanned their arcs with eagle eyes. If someone had seen the Chinooks land, it was now they were most likely to put in an appearance. But there was nothing that Range could detect. No noise. No movement. Seemingly no life at all out there. All around was utter quiet and stillness.

He leaned across to O'Shea, speaking through the open window. 'All-good?' he whispered.

'Good to go,' O'Shea confirmed.

As far as they could tell their infil had gone undetected, and it was time to press on with the mission.

The Kiwi flicked on the headlamps – the light was blinding after the thick darkness. It felt odd to be making a night drive through the desert and doing so on full lights, but the priority here was to act and look like locals, and this was exactly how they'd do things from here on in.

The two vehicles pulled out, dust dancing in the powerful beams of their headlamps, and they moved onto the dirt track that would take them north into Tripoli.

Range glanced at the faintly luminous dial of his watch. 0245: Fifteen minutes before they hit the target. Just as The Colonel had predicted, the drive across country had been a pretty straightforward affair. It was a basic enough dirt track, but the powerful Toyotas had eaten up the sandy terrain. For the last few miles Range had kept a close watch on the map and GPS, bringing them to within a few hundred yards of the target building.

They'd drawn the vehicles into the cover of a patch of

scrubby waste ground, from where they were shielded from prying eyes. They planned to make the final approach silently on foot, and by now Range could feel the adrenalin of the coming attack kicking into his veins. It was time to get moving.

He spoke into the tiny Cougar radio receiver he had taped to his throat. 'Suit up.'

The NBC suits they were using were a Special Forces variant, one made by the German company, Blücher, of a lightweight material similar in feel to Gore-Tex. They were far superior to the heavier, more cumbersome suits used by many conventional forces. Even so, they were hot and claustrophobic, which was why they'd left the suiting-up to the very last moment, and Range was more than a little glad they were going in during the dead of the night when the air temperature was at its coolest.

All around him figures began to struggle into their NBC gear. The threat from a nerve agent like Sarin was two fold: one, breathing it in; two, ingesting it via a living, porous membrane like the skin. The Blücher suits were designed to protect the body from any droplets or spray that might remain in the air. Once used, the suits were contaminated and best discarded – which was exactly what they were planning to do with these. It was the mask that shielded the face and eyes, and which also prevented the lungs from breathing any of the Sarin in.

More than any of his men, Range figured he had reason

93

to hate the respirators. The years spent locked up in kids' homes had left him with a phobia of enclosed spaces, plus a general hatred of anything that made him feel in any way trapped. But he steeled himself, threw his head forward, pulled apart the mask and dragged the thing over his skull and down over his head, making sure that the rubber formed an airtight seal with the skin of his neck. Then he tightened the retaining straps and felt the mask pull in closer around the contours of his face.

They were using C50 gas masks, again kit used by British Special Forces. With its single eyepiece, high protection and close-fitting design, the mask was a superlative piece of gear. Range and his men had had to fit the masks to their face-size back at the Wadi Idhan base, from a selection provided by those stationed there. Without knowing Randy's face size or whether he was clean-shaven or not, they'd opted to bring escape hoods for him and the terrorist leader The Colonel wanted captured. These hoods were a universal size, but they still provided total protection for at least fifteen minutes in high concentrations of gas.

The one other thing that Range had made sure of back at Wadi Idhan was that all of his men had got a proper shave. Just the barest hint of any stubble could interfere with the masks' seal and let the gas seep in. He placed his hand over the mask's filter, his palm making an airtight seal. He breathed in hard, sucking the mask tighter onto his face, so making doubly sure the seal was airtight. That done he dragged in a few deep gasps of air through the filter, hearing the rasp and suck of his own breathing roaring in his ears.

The mask was all-good.

'Alpha One, mic check,' announced Range, his voice sounding weirdly muted and nasal inside the mask.

With the radio mic taped onto his neck and the tiny receiver tucked into his ear, the Cougar should work fine even from within the confines of the NBC mask. But Range wanted all his men to radio-check the Cougars before the assault went in.

'Alpha Two, check,' The Kiwi confirmed.

Alpha Three and Four – Tiny and Joe – confirmed likewise.

'Bravo One, check,' O'Shea confirmed, followed by the rest of the men in his team.

Their comms kit was good to go.

Range pulled the hood of his NBC smock over the mask, the elastic sealing around the front. That done, he dragged on the weird rubber over-boots, so they encased his combat boots completely, and then he laced them up tight around his ankles. Last but not least he pulled on the thin, white, cotton under-gloves, and covered them with the heavy rubber over-gloves.

His world was now reduced to whatever he could see via the scuba-diver-like eyepiece in the gas mask. The dual filter sat to the front and the left side of the mask, in an effort to prevent it from impeding the view. But still Range felt like the bloody Michelin man, and already he could sense the heat and the stuffiness starting to build inside the suit. It was all the more reason to get going with the assault and get it done.

At Range's signal they moved through the darkened terrain like unseen shadows flitting through the thick darkness. They slipped across the patch of waste ground until they were directly opposite the target building. All that separated them from it was a stretch of rough dirt highway some thirty yards across.

From the cover of the bush Range stared at what was AQIM's forward mounting base here in Libya. As per The Colonel's briefing, it was bathed in a halo of harsh light, and they obviously kept the security lights on all through the night hours. That's why none of his team was using any night-vision gear. The security lights would white-out night-vision goggles, completely blinding the user. The assault was all going to be done with the Mark 1 human eyeball.

In spite of the desert chill, it was hot and sticky inside the bulky suit and Range could feel the beads of sweat trickling down his neck. He wiped the eyepiece of the mask, so he could see properly. Several windows were lit up on the third floor of the target building, which was all that was visible above the high perimeter wall. Every now and then he could see a figure pass back and forth across one of them. Someone was awake and active in there, but that was only as he had expected. AQIM were sure to have sentries.

He scanned the building's perimeter. To one side there were a couple of pick-up trucks. They were parked up for the night and deserted but still they needed immobilizing, just in case anyone survived the gas and tried to make a getaway. He flicked his eyes up to the top of the building. It had a flat roof, which meant there could be sentries up there. It was the obvious place from which to keep watch.

For a full three minutes he kept his eyes glued to the roof. There was no movement that he could detect and it looked to be deserted. O'Shea's team were tasked to cover all doors and windows, as Range's lot went in and hurled around the Sarin. But if there was access onto that roof, it was the one exit point from the building that he and his men couldn't keep covered.

He spoke into his throat mic: 'Bravo, you're a go. Keep eyes-on the roof. Plus immobilise those vehicles as you pass.'

'Affirm: keeping eyes-on the roof, plus taking out SUVs. Standby.' O'Shea's reply was barely audible through the alien suck and blow of his breathing.

Range watched the hunched figure of the ex-SEAL as he led his team in a dash across the open road. O'Shea paused at the rear of the lead vehicle. It took barely seconds for him to set a booby trap, using a grenade rigged to a motion-sensitive trigger. If anyone tried to drive the Toyota

anywhere, the movement alone would be enough to detonate the grenade.

He did the same with the other wagon. Barely thirty seconds later he confirmed he was in position at the rear of
the compound's perimeter wall. O'Shea had gathered his
men around the main power line that led into the building.
From there he would use a handy little gizmo to send a
massive surge of current through the power line, so blowing
all the fuses and light fittings in the target building. Even
if AQIM had a back-up generator it would be of zero use,
for the entire electrical circuitry of the place would have
been fried.

Range glanced across at The Kiwi, Tiny and Joe. He placed
the palm of his hand on top of his head – the signal for 'on
me'. He rose to his feet and scuttled across to the front of
the building, feeling like the abominable snowman trussed
up in all his NBC gear. His pulse pounded in his head as he
ran. If there was one moment when the mission was most
likely to get blown, it was as they crossed the open road
and went over the perimeter wall.

He rounded the corner and flattened himself against the
wall to one side of the front gate. A split second later the
others were at his side. There were no cries of alarm or
gunshots from the compound, so it seemed as if they'd
made it across unseen. He could feel the radio pick-up
pressing into his neck. It was so sensitive it would transmit
even the faintest whisper.

'Alpha, in position,' he breathed.

'Affirm,' came the whispered reply from O'Shea. 'Going dark.'

A split second later there was a fizzing and popping of light bulbs from all across the compound, and the entire complex went suddenly very black. At exactly that moment The Kiwi and Joe lifted the aluminium scaling ladder that they'd carried with them and set it against the perimeter wall.

In spite of its height the ladder still barely reached the apex of the wall. The lithe form of The Kiwi went first, like a rat up a drainpipe, and Joe's powerful figure followed directly on his heels. Range went next, with Tiny taking up the rear. Once all four of them were perched on top of the wall, they hauled the ladder after and dropped it down the far side, before making their way down.

It had taken barely sixty seconds to get over and onto the ground inside the compound, but already Range could hear muffled voices coming from the building, as those inside woke up to the fact that the lights had died. In an instant the front door swung open and a figure strode out. Range and the others froze. They watched the man move across to a galvanized iron shed in the far corner of the compound. That had to be where the back-up generator was situated.

As the figure disappeared inside, Range dashed forward, the others on his shoulder. He flattened himself to one side of the doorway, with Tiny beside him, The Kiwi and Joe doing likewise on the other. Range whipped out a Sarin canister from one of the chest pouches in his NBC smock. At the same time Tiny unhooked an axe from his belt. Range glanced across at The Kiwi and Joe. The Kiwi gave a thumbs-up. They, too, were ready.

Range glanced down at the canister and grabbed the pin holding the retainer clip. Once he pulled it the canister was primed to pump out its deadly gas cloud. This was the point of no return. Gently, he eased it free. Only his fingers held the retainer clip closed now. Once he released his grip, the clip would fly free, and there would be five seconds before the gas started pumping.

'Alpha, in position,' Range breathed into his Cougar.

'Bravo, in position,' O'Shea replied. He had one guy watching the building's rear entrance, another on the front gate, and two stood back from the sides scanning the windows.

'Going in,' Range confirmed.

Tiny swung the axe through the glass at their side. The noise of the shattering pane was drowned out by Arabic cursing, as those inside crashed about in the darkness. Tiny dragged the axe out again, and Range heaved the canister in through the broken window, the clip flying free as it went.

Range began counting silently, in his head. 'One. Two. Three . . . '

He could hear a faint hissing from inside the building, as the canister started to gush out its deadly gas. Suddenly, there was a gasping and choking from inside the room. There were a series of strangled screams as the nerve agent began to take hold. Range heard bodies smashing into furniture. A figure started vomiting violently, another thrashing about as he fought to breathe.

From behind there was a cough and a roar, as the generator kicked into life. The figure emerged from the shed to check if the lights had come back on – which, of course, they hadn't. In that instant The Kiwi raised his AK-74 from where it hung on his chest harness and fired off a double tap – *pzzzt, pzzzt, pzzzt* – two rounds tearing into the man's torso and a third ripping into his head. The bullets threw him backwards, and he crashed into the shadow of the shed.

'Could have been fucking Randy,' Range hissed a warning.

'It wasn't,' The Kiwi hissed back.

Ten. Eleven. Twelve . . . The voice continued counting out the seconds in Range's head.

For an instant he was struck by a terrible thought of what it must be like inside that building. Darkness. Total confusion. Then the first breath of the Sarin. A moment's terror and panic as each man tried to make sense of what was happening in the pitch dark. And then the gas had got them, burning down their windpipes and choking their lungs.

Range knew what nerve gas did to people, what a horrible way it was to die. He tried to blank the images from his mind. He tried to tell himself that they were AQIM scum, and that they had it coming. But somewhere in there was Randy – the man he had left behind – and every single second now was precious. Range had no idea if Randy was on the ground floor or not, but either way they had to get in there and find him.

Seventeen. Eighteen. Nineteen. Twenty! Range stepped away from the building, raised his leg and smashed the NBC over-boot into the door. The cheap wood splintered, the door cannoning inwards on its hinges, and then he was kicking his way into the dark interior. He had his AK-74 at the shoulder, and using the torch attached to the weapon he swept the room with its beam.

The air was thick with an oily white fog that danced in the light. Bodies writhed on the floor, clawing at their faces as if they wanted to rip their own throats out. No one seemed to notice him. Their eyes were blinded by the searing gas, their lungs on fire as it burned its way into their bodies.

Range moved further into the room, checking each man as he went. He vaulted over a figure heaving and writhing on the floor and pushed onwards. He used his boot to roll guys over who'd curled into a foetus, taking a good look at their features. None were Randy.

Everywhere he looked the room was wreathed in Sarin fumes. At his feet were bodies twitching and convulsing in their death throes. His torch beam probed the darkness, the light catching in a slurry of vomit. A body lay next to it. Range could see that the figure had shit and pissed himself. The nerve gas had wrecked his bodily functions. The stench would have been sickening, but nothing could make it through his mask.

He forced himself to keep going, to blank out the horror, and to remain focused on the job in hand: *find Randy*. For several seconds he moved through the eerie, suffocating cloud, one lit a ghostly white by the canister that was gushing out the last of its gas, and then he was at the rear of the room.

He paused. The stairs lay up ahead. He sensed Tiny at his shoulder, and then The Kiwi and Joe were bunched up on the far side of the stairwell. Range felt in his smock and pulled out a second Sarin canister. He ripped out the pin and held down the retainer clip, ready to hurl it up the stairs. And then a spike of claustrophobia hit him like a vicious punch to the gut, and he felt himself double over and freeze.

It was crucial to keep the momentum going when engaged in such an assault, and especially when one of your own guys might have been hit by the gas. But a wave of panic and nausea had swept up from the pit of Range's stomach and now it possessed him. He felt like he was drowning in the dark sea of his phobia and was unable to go forward, or even to hurl the canister that was gripped in his hand.

All he could think was: *I've got to fucking get out of here.*

CHAPTER SEVEN

The Kiwi started yelling over the radio net: 'Throw the fucker! Randy's up there somewhere! Go! Go! Go! Go! Go!'

The Kiwi's voice broke the spell. It took a massive effort of will to rip through the fear that had taken hold of him, but somehow Range managed it. He raised his arm and hurled the Sarin far into the shadows at the top of the staircase. An instant later he was pounding upwards, leading the charge.

With The Kiwi right behind him he thundered to the top of the concrete staircase, sweeping the area above with his weapon. Tiny and Joe followed, tight on his heels. They could almost have done this with their eyes closed: during the years they'd spent serving with elite units, clearing buildings was one of the most heavily rehearsed of all of their drills. It was fast, instinctive and natural.

Two doors led off the top of the staircase; one to the front and one to the rear of the building. Range went left, letting fly the retainer clip on a third canister of Sarin. Tiny hit the door, his boot crashing through the wood and shunting it wide open. The second he did so Range tossed the canister inside.

As the gas began to pump into the room, a ghostly figure stumbled towards the doorway, cursing in Arabic. He raised an AK-47, but as he did so Tiny let rip: *pzzzt, pzzzt, pzzzt!* Three silenced bullets at point-blank range. For a split second the fighter's eyes bulged outwards. Then his face caved in where Tiny had shot him, and he keeled over and hit the floor.

A horrible choking and gasping came from the room behind him. Range did a rapid body-check for Randy, and not finding him he left the gas to deal with those who remained. The first floor was cleared from end to end, and still there was no sign of their man.

They paused for a second at the bottom of the stairs leading to the next level. Range and The Kiwi were soaked in sweat and their breath was coming in heaving rasps, but each grabbed a Sarin canister and prepared to press on. *They had to keep the momentum going.*

On Range's signal they hurled the canisters up the stairwell, into the hallway high above. Range really didn't want any shooting up there, for the simple reason that Randy had to be on that level, for it was the last there was. Instead, they'd go for nerve gas overkill. He grabbed another Sarin canister and they hammered up the stairs.

When they reached the top of the stairwell the entire floor seemed to be deserted. They spread out to search. After a few seconds Range heard a burst of static in his earpiece, and The Kiwi came on the air.

'Stairway at the rear leads to the roof. Roof looks occupied.'

Range turned and hurried in that direction, thick gas swirling all around him as he went. He found The Kiwi and Joe at the bottom of a flight of metal steps. Above, a trap door lay open to the sky. Range had studied the roof of the building for a good few minutes prior to the assault going in, and it had seemed clear. But from what he could see now there was a route leading up there, and it looked well used.

With barely a moment's hesitation he started to climb. Randy *had* to be up there, plus he couldn't wait to get the fuck out of that building and into the open air. As his head neared the trap door he switched off the torch beam on his weapon. He reckoned there was enough light to see and to kill by up there, and the torch would simply make him an easy target.

He brought the weapon to his shoulder. With one hand he held onto the steps and with the other he kept his gun in the aim. There would be no point using the gas up here. It was little use in the open air. Slowly he crept up the last few steps, The Kiwi joining him on the ladder below. His head emerged into the open, and he tried to stay as light on his feet as possible, all the while scanning around him for signs of the enemy.

There were good patches of cover up here: a heap of concrete blocks to his left with an old bicycle leaning against it; a stack of oil drums to the right; lines of washing right in front of him, over a pile of wooden planking. With just his head and shoulders visible above the roofline he kept scanning for the enemy . . . or for Randy. Someone had gone through that trap door, so they had to be up here somewhere.

For several seconds he stayed like that, silently listening and watching. Finally, he placed one hand on the roof and vaulted onto it. As he rolled away from the trap door, he heard a crash. The bicycle had tumbled over, as a figure raised a weapon. A moment later there was a deafening burst of gunfire.

Range came to his feet in a crouch, his weapon in the aim. Bullets were tearing all around him and ricocheting off the hard concrete surface of the roof. He sighted on the muzzle flash just above the pile of concrete, and squeezed off three silenced rounds: *pzzzt, pzzzt, pzzzt!* In this game it was all about being first on the draw with deadly accurate fire, and his adversary's had been a fraction wide of the mark.

Range changed position so as to present a less easy target,

scanning around himself in a 360-degree arc. The Kiwi vaulted out beside him, quickly followed by Joe and Tiny. Range and Tiny took the right side of the roof, as The Kiwi and Joe moved ahead to clear the left.

Range crept forward, moving on the balls of his feet. He had his eyes glued to the oil drums up ahead of him. There were more of the enemy behind them, he just knew it.

Suddenly, a figure broke cover and made a run for it. Instantly, Range had him in his sights. But it looked to be a young kid, no more than thirteen years old – a kid with an AK-47 clutched in one hand.

'Drop the gun!' Range yelled. But his words were muffled and distorted through the gas mask. 'Drop the fucking gun!'

Within seconds the young kid was cornered on the edge of the roof. Range advanced towards him, keeping him covered. The kid took a fearful step backwards. Range's bulky NBC suit and mask made him look twice as large as normal, and no one had ever called him small. He towered over the kid.

The youngster jerked his head from Range to Tiny and back again. He took another step backwards, his AK dangling in his hand. The edge of the roof was now right at his back, and he had nowhere to retreat to or to run.

'Drop the gun!' Range growled.

As if in answer, a voice rang out in Arabic from beside him. The words were clearly directed at the kid, but there was something about the tone that seemed oddly familiar.

As he swung his weapon around to cover the threat, a tall, rangy figure stepped out of the shadows. He had his hand held out towards the kid, while the other was open at his side, making it clear he had no weapon. He spoke to the kid again, and although the Arabic was lost on Range, he could tell he was trying to talk the boy down.

Then, a few words were fired out of the corner of the figure's mouth, in English. 'Steve Range . . .'. He spoke in an unmistakable drawl. 'Man, did you guys take your freakin' time to get here . . .'

It was Randy.

'The kid's just the house boy,' he continued, as he edged towards him. 'He ain't got nothin' to do with AQIM.' He flicked his eyes across to Range and Tiny. 'Lower your weapons, guys, just for the time it takes me to bring him in.'

For a split second Range wondered if this was a set-up. *TNF: trust no fucker.* Was this some kind of an ambush or a trap? But if it was, Randy was doing a damn good job of acting as if his only concern was for the boy's welfare. Range lowered his weapon. He signalled for Tiny to do the same.

As Randy coaxed the boy down from his fear, he gradually managed to bring him back from the edge of the roof. Range put out a call over the Cougar. He gave the word that they'd got their man. They'd found Randy, alive and well. O'Shea's team had brought the Escape Hoods and spare suits in with them and Range needed them up on the roof right now.

Comms done, he turned back to Randy – who by now had the kid gripped firmly around the shoulders.

'Fucking good to see you, mate,' he announced, knowing as he said it how inadequate it sounded. 'But there ain't no time for swapping war stories, 'cause we got to get the fuck out of here. There's a building below full of nerve gas, plus the dead and dying of AQIM. There's only one way down from the roof, right?'

'Right,' Randy confirmed. 'The same way that you guys came up – the stairwell.'

'That means going back through the gas,' Range told him, 'which means you got to suit up.'

'Sure thing, dude,' Randy drawled. 'But this time, you ain't gonna be leaving me behind now, are ya?'

For a moment Range didn't know how to respond. He felt this unerring sense of unease, like it was all balanced on a knife-edge here. Was Randy really joking? Or did he detect just the faintest hint of bitterness in the tall American's voice.

'No one's leaving you behind,' Range countered, 'not unless you want us to.'

There was a long moment's silence, and then Range felt a figure appear beside him, and a bag full of NBC kit was thrust into his hand.

'NBC gear.' He passed it across to Randy. 'Like I said, suit-up. Quicker you do so, sooner we get you out of here.'

Randy grabbed the bag. He glanced at Range. 'Kid's coming with us, right?'

Range shrugged. 'Can't leave him here. So yeah, he's coming some of the way. We'll work it out as we go.'

In truth, the kid was a problem. The Colonel had been adamant – no witnesses – and the kid was the biggest eye-witness you ever could wish for. Once they'd taken him down through the gas he'd have seen everything. But what were the alternatives? No one was about to kill him, and they couldn't exactly leave him to be found by the Libyan authorities, or whoever was first to investigate. Range figured they'd take him with them and work it out along the way.

'Tiny, help the kid suit-up,' Range prompted.

He turned away from them all and spoke into his radio. 'This is Alpha One: listen up. We're on the roof preparing to come back through the building. We muster by the front gate. Make sure that all – repeat ALL – AQIM are dying or dead. We want no survivors. And remember: find Moussa ag Ajjer. If he's still alive, get him out into the open air.'

That done Range readied himself to exit the roof. He turned to check if Randy and the boy were ready. He noticed the kid's AK-47 lying where Randy had left it, propped against the edge of the roof. As he reached for it, he sensed the American eyeing him through the round eyepiece of the Escape Hood he was now wearing.

Range checked the magazine on the weapon, then handed it to Randy. 'Full mag. Just in case there's any of those fuckers still left alive in there.'

Randy took the assault rifle in one of his huge, bear-like hands. 'Those fuckers who saved my life, you mean?'

Range did a double-take. Had he really heard him say that? Randy didn't have a radio, so his words were muffled and badly distorted via the Escape Hood, which looked like a bulkier, lightweight version of his own mask.

Range saw the American's eyes crinkle into a smile behind the perspex eyepiece. 'Lighten up, buddy, I'm just shittin' you.' He took a step towards Range, and punched him playfully on the shoulder. 'We're good.'

Randy turned towards the stairwell leading down into the building's interior, taking the kid with him. Range went to follow, but as he moved he caught a shadow darting behind the planks of wood to their side. He saw a figure raising his weapon: they'd missed one of the bastards.

Range swivelled his gun and squeezed the trigger, but the noise of his silenced AK-74 was drowned out by the bark of the enemy's assault rifle. There was a flash of muzzle flame as he fired off a wild burst, and Range could see that Randy and the kid were right in the line of fire.

He dived forward, cannoning into the lean American and slamming him onto the deck, and bringing the kid down with them. Luckily, the bulky NBC suits cushioned the fall. Rounds went pounding over their heads, as the enemy unleashed on automatic. A fraction lower, and the bullets would be hammering into his, Randy and the kid's skulls.

Ahead of him Range saw a second figure steal around

the pile of wood. It was The Kiwi. His weapon barked: *pzzzt, pzzzt, pzzzt!*

The enemy fighter was blasted off his feet, his weapon still firing off its last rounds as he fell. The Kiwi followed him down with his gun sights, until he lay on the roof, his bloody torso tangled in the washing. Range could see a spreading pool of blood staining the sheets a deep red.

He untangled himself from Randy and the kid. The former Navy SEAL turned to face him. 'Thanks, buddy. Close thing, huh?'

'Yeah, he pretty nearly fucking nailed us.'

As Range said those words he felt a sharp pain in his jaw. He figured he must have been hit. He lifted his hand to check, but could feel nothing through the heavy over-gloves. He shone his torch beam on the black rubber of his glove. There was a small patch of blood. It couldn't be anything serious. Most likely it was a flesh wound from a stray AK-47 round. He'd deal with it later, once the assault was over – and for sure it had to be nearing its end.

They hurried across to the ladder leading down into the building. Range was the last to leave the roof, figuring that way he'd have to spend the least time inside. He checked the area one last time, then took a step down into the gas-filled interior. As he descended, the Sarin swirled around his knees. It was like a thick fog in there. A second later the gas was up to the eyeholes of his mask and then he was in over his head.

Suddenly, he took a choking, burning gasp. He felt his windpipe clamp shut, as he was hit by a wave of searing pain. *He couldn't breathe!* He clutched at his throat, as he tried to work out what the fuck was happening. Then the nausea swept over him and his muscles seemed to lose all control, and an instant later his body crashed down the metal steps and he landed in a heap on the floor.

With the last of his energy he tried to speak into the radio, but he couldn't manage even the one word. All that came out was a choking, rasping series of gasps. 'Craaaak . . . Craaaak . . . Craaaak . . .'

Up ahead The Kiwi heard the gasping. It sounded ghostly and horrific. He had no idea what was happening. Ahead of him Randy, the kid, Tiny and Joe were all moving quickly toward the stairwell leading down to the floor below. That left only Range. He turned. With a shock he caught sight of a figure slumped on the floor in a twitching mess.

'RANGE IS DOWN!' he yelled. 'RANGE DOWN!'

In one swift move he dived back to the foot of the metal steps. He grabbed Range and rolled him onto his back. His torch beam glinted in a slick of blood and shattered rubber at the big man's jaw, plus a scum of vomit flecking the inside of his gas mask. In a flash The Kiwi realised what had happened.

During the firefight on the roof Range must have been hit, and the round had punctured his mask. He had inhaled some of the gas. The Kiwi began scrabbling in his chest pouch. The thick gloves made it all but impossible to find it, but suddenly he had the syringe of ComboPen in his hand. He raised it above his head and plunged the big needle downwards. It penetrated Range's NBC suit and his combats, and then The Kiwi punched the syringe of drugs into him.

The Kiwi was as tall as Range, yet of a far slighter build. But he was lithe and wiry, and possessed of an incredible stamina and strength. In one swift move he bent down and hauled the big man up onto his shoulders.

'Find fucking Moussa!' he yelled at the others. 'I got to get Range out of here.'

With that The Kiwi turned and ran for the stairs. He clattered down and thundered onwards, vaulting over shadowy figures scattered across the floor in their last death throes. He made the bottom of the second stairwell and charged towards the door of the building, yelling into his throat mic as he went.

'Alpha Two, exiting via front!'

He crashed through the shattered remains of the doorway and out into the cool night air. He dumped Range in the cover of the perimeter wall and reached for his knife. He grabbed it, slipped the blade under the rubber restraining straps of the mask and sliced through them, before ripping it off his face. He used his over-gloves to clear the worst of the vomit away, which was smeared into Range's nose and eyes and into his close-cropped sandy hair.

The Kiwi was the best-qualified and most experienced medic on the B6 team. He understood the effects of a nerve agent like Sarin pretty well. It killed by attacking the nervous system. It did so in such a way that nerve impulses were permanently being fired – on send – hence the twitching and convulsions that Range was exhibiting now.

Death usually resulted from the inability of the muscles involved in breathing to keep functioning properly. In other words, as a result of your own body's muscle malfunctions you suffocated to death.

Sarin was toxic even in minute doses – which is what would have seeped into Range's mask via the bullet graze. The worst kind of exposure was via inhalation, and the treatment required the antidote, injected three times in quick succession. The Atropine would treat the symptoms of the poisoning, but Range would also need the Pralidoxime and Avizafone, to try to get the muscles that controlled his breathing working properly again.

They'd also have to decontaminate Range pretty quickly now, by stripping him out of his NBC suit, which would have been heavily contaminated with Sarin. Nevertheless, The Kiwi was pretty certain he could save him.

He felt around for the syringes he had in his smock pocket, and readied to plunge the next one into Steve Range.

CHAPTER EIGHT

'It was supposed to be bloody you in the hospital bed recovering from the gas,' Range croaked. His voice had yet to recover fully from the effects of the nerve agent.

Randy gave a smile and a shrug. 'Yeah, well, you know how it is . . . A man who's come back from the dead – he don't need no second killin'!'

Range tried a smile. 'Yeah, mate. Fair one.' But it hurt to smile and it hurt to talk. In fact, Range hurt all over.

He'd been here for a good week now, in a private room in an exclusive Harley Street hospital, one that employed the kind of medical staff who would ask few questions about what appeared to be a case of nerve poisoning. He had tubes and needles sticking out of every limb, and he'd been put on a morphine drip that was self-administering. Whenever the pain got too much – or he just felt like a shot of the good stuff – he pressed the nozzle, and sweet release flowed into his veins.

As a result, Range was pretty much on a permanent high, and he'd spent a great deal of time sleeping. But a week was more than enough for a man like him to do either. He was itching to get out of there and back to the business of living. Trouble was, he'd taken a good dose of the Sarin, and his doctor wanted him in there for another week at least – for tests, observations and recovery.

Randy checked his watch. 'Say, dude, I gotta run. The Hogan got my folks flown over, did you hear? Kinda like a Reiner welcome home party. I promised to take 'em to the Tower of London, to see the Crown Jewels. You be good now – all them cute nurses . . .'

'Yeah, like I can do anything trussed up like some kind of pervert,' Range growled. 'Have fun at the Tower. My regards to your family.'

'Got it. Gotta run.'

Randy was at the door when he hesitated. He half-turned to Range. 'Listen, buddy, you took a bullet for me back there on that rooftop. Not to mention some gas. Any debt of life – it's been paid.'

Range waved him away. 'Too bloody right. Way I see it, *you owe me*.'

Randy gave a laugh. He turned and was gone.

In spite of what he'd said, Range sensed there was still a weird, wired tension between the two of them, of the kind that Range had first detected on that Tripoli rooftop. But gradually, Range – the guy who had ordered that Randy should be left behind – and Randy – the guy who had been left for dead – seemed to be coming to terms with each other. Doubtless, Range being here and recovering from a bullet graze, plus a bad case of nerve poisoning was aiding that process.

With Randy gone Range was alone again. O'Shea had been in earlier and dropped off his personal effects – the gear that Range had left at the Wadi Idhan base, prior to the assault going in. In his every spare minute O'Shea seemed to be calling by, and Range appreciated it, for he had a lot of catching up to do.

He'd barely been conscious when they'd pulled out of the assault, and for most of the long journey home he'd been out of his head on the antidote drugs and the morphine. There was a lot of stuff he needed to get sorted, and O'Shea had the patience and the loyalty to sit by his bedside and help him.

He'd promised to be back that afternoon. In the meantime Range had two long hours to kill before the next highlight of the day, which was lunch. He reached across for his bag of kit and rummaged around for the phone. He pulled it out, flipped it on, and waited for a signal. There were several beeps as text messages came in, then the familiar sound of his ring-tone.

Voicemail.

He listened through several messages, well-wishers mostly, and then there was this.

'Mr Range, this is Jean-Pierre de Saint-Sébastien, calling from Geneva. I am afraid I need you to call me, most urgently. It is not good news, I am afraid. Please call me.'

Isabelle's father. His voice had sounded empty and desperate. Range hoped that Isabelle hadn't done anything stupid. He had visions of her lying in a bed in some Geneva hospital, recovering from an overdose. There was no way she'd have killed herself, of that Range was certain; she had far too much vitality and life for that. But a desperate call for help? That was all too possible. Maybe that was why she'd kept texting him: *Please come to Geneva; we need to talk. Please.*

Range checked his text messages. There had been none from Isabelle since the last one he'd received when he'd been at their Wadi Idhan base. He felt guilty now for not having responded, but fuck it, they'd had a mission to execute. She'd known that. Range had told her they were going in to get Randy, so surely she would have understood?

He punched the dial button and called her number. He got through to a recorded message, first in French and then in English: *This number is no longer in service. This number is no longer in service. This number is no longer in service.* What the hell? She must have changed her mobile number, but why hadn't she texted him to alert him to the new one?

With a growing sense of foreboding he dialled her father's number, but it went through to voicemail. He left a message, hoping his rasping croak of a voice would be audible to her father.

'This is Steve Range. I got your message. I've been away on a job, hence the delay replying. I'm on this number, awaiting your call.'

That done, he lay back in the bed to wait. What else was he to do? He glanced at the bag of morphine solution suspended from the metal hook above him. He tweaked the button, and heard the faint whirr as a few drops fed into his system. At least it would kill the boredom and the worry.

Range felt a hand shaking him awake. O'Shea's face swam into focus. 'Hey, buddy, how are ya?'

No matter how often O'Shea visited, he always seemed to show a real interest in Range's recovery and remain upbeat and positive. He'd put up with a lot of moaning from Range. It seemed like water off a duck's back to the tough, wiry American.

'I feel like shit – only worse,' Range grunted.

O'Shea smiled. 'As good as that?'

Range noticed that his lunch lay untouched on the table they'd pulled across his bed. He'd slept through feeding time again. He picked at the cold food, using his free hand to check his mobile. No text messages, no missed calls. What the hell had happened to Isabelle and her father? Why had no one called?

'So, you want to hear about the kid?' O'Shea volunteered. 'That's where we left off last time.'

Range tore his attention away from the phone. 'Yeah. Why not? Hit me with it.'

'So, we left him at the Wadi Idhan base, when we flew you home. They'd got you stabilised at Wadi Idhan, so it was just a case of gettin' you back to a facility like this one. We've since briefed The Colonel on the kid, and on the fact that he's an orphan. The Colonel's getting him a visa to the UK, so he can start getting a proper education. And whilst he's at it, they figure they'll put him through the odd bit of hypnosis, to blank his memory of anything from the assault.'

'You what? They can do that?'

'Yeah. Apparently they can,' O'Shea confirmed. 'And that way, they keep it all quiet. The Libyan papers are blaming the assault on rogue elements of their security services. There's not a hint of any suspicion of foreign involvement. It was the discovery of Gaddafi's Sarin canisters that decided it. So, we can't exactly let the kid go and talk.'

Range grunted an agreement. 'And Moussa ag Ajjer?'

'Put it this way, he's in a far worse state that you are. It's gonna be a while before he'll be saying anything to anyone. But we reaped an intel bonanza anyway – in the form of Randy. Seems the crafty son-of-a-bitch got himself well in there with Moussa, and some of the other AQIM high-ups. Randy's debriefings are ongoing, but it's led to some very juicy intel.'

Trust no fucker. Just how close had Randy grown to the AQIM leadership, Range wondered, and just how had he managed it? Maybe that was the only way he'd had to ensure his survival, but even so it raised some questions in Steve Range's mind.

'So how did he come back to life again?' Range probed. 'After we left him? Anyone worked that one out yet?'

'He's been in to see you, yeah? Didn't you guys talk . . .?'

'Nope,' Range cut in. 'We haven't yet had a heart-to-heart about how we left him to die and how he managed to cheat death. But you're close to him. Closer than anyone. If anyone knows it's you, mate.'

'Well, he's told me about as much as he remembers,' O'Shea conceded. 'Or maybe as much as they told him. You wanna hear it? It was kinda a private conversation.'

'I want to hear.'

'Well, okay. But it's between you and me, okay?'

Range inclined his head slightly. It was about as much as he could move it without suffering real pain. 'It's between me and you.'

'After we hit the Fort of the Mount, AQIM sent some of their people in to investigate. They retrieved their dead, traced our movements. That led them to the cairn of rocks, under which they found Randy. At first they only wanted to fuck with the grave, but then someone noticed the body was still warm. It was forty-eight hours after we'd left Randy for dead. Apparently, he showed none of the usual signs of dying.'

O'Shea threw Range this look. 'The rest gets a bit freakin' weird. Apparently they took him to some female Tuareg doctor. But she ain't no doc like we know it. This is some tribal spiritual doctor shit. Anyhow, when Randy finally came to he was under her kinda . . . care. There were shed-loads of armed guards around, but she was the one who seemed to have . . . well, *healed* him.'

'How exactly?'

'Randy doesn't seem to know. He described to me all kinds of bags of leaves and piles of bark and bones and potions and shit. He told me about her beating him with a *live chicken*, for fuck's sake. Apparently, the chicken took all of the bad and hurt out of Randy and into its own body.'

'The chicken died?' Range prompted.

'The chicken fuckin' died.'

They both started laughing.

'You saying he owes his life to a fucking chicken?'

O'Shea shrugged. 'Fuck knows, buddy. Probably. I just don't do all that fucked up tribal witchcraft shit.'

Range shrugged. 'Maybe you should try it some time. Tribal knowledge. Traditional medicine. There were a lot of guys in the Regiment swore by it. Mostly it's a load of hocus-pocus and bullshit. But other times it can be pretty powerful ju-ju. Tell you what, you don't know if she's free right now, do you? I could do with some of her voodoo chicken-bondage to get me out of this place.'

O'Shea laughed. 'Sure. I'll make some calls.'

'Fruit?' Range inclined his head towards the bowl beside his bed. O'Shea kept filling it up with heaps of grapes and other sickeningly healthy stuff, in an effort to aid his recovery.

O'Shea took an apple and polished it on his shirt, turning it over and doing each side methodically, before finally biting into it. Like everything the guy did, he couldn't even eat an apple without real precision and total dedication to the task.

Range unpeeled the banana that had come with his lunch, and took a bite. His jaw still felt sore whenever he ate, from where the bullet had grazed him. 'So, what're the high-lights of the intel Randy's delivered? Any chance of a job for us lot?'

'Not for you, buddy. There won't be any chance of any of that for a good while now.'

'Fuck off, mate. I'm not dead.'

O'Shea smiled. 'Doc's orders.' His expression switched to serious. 'Randy was about to be deployed. In fact, most of those fuckers we wasted in that compound were. But here's the thing: they were supposed to target a cruise liner somewhere off the coast of Somalia. And Randy's role – he was the vital "foreign element". Being an American, they planned to get Randy – plus a bunch of other foreigners – onto the ship, posing as passengers. They planned to take it in a two-pronged assault: one force from inside the ship, the other from the sea . . .'

'Yeah, but Randy wouldn't have had a passport, remember? We were sanitised for the Gaddafi mission. Completely. So how could he travel anywhere . . . ?'

'If you'll just listen, buddy, I'll freaking explain,' O'Shea cut in. 'The regime in Libya is seriously schizophrenic. There are those that hate AQIM, but also those who can't get enough of their shit. Someone in the Libyan foreign ministry acquired Randy a US passport. It's likely fake, but you'd never know it. That's why his AQIM brothers were watching him so closely. Those who hadn't completely bought into Randy's act feared he was gonna do a runner with the passport, and disappear.'

'So, the attack on the cruise liner?' Range probed. 'It's foiled, I take it?'

'Not necessarily. Randy was to fly to London, to board the ship somewhere in the UK. Trouble was, he was linking up with several other AQIM members, all of whom are either European or US passport holders. The plan was fuckin' genius. They'd board the ship dressed like any other wealthy passengers. It's not like air travel: on a cruise liner your luggage doesn't even get searched. They'd have their guys on the ship as she set sail for the Indian Ocean, all armed.'

'Once into pirate waters, those cruise ships rely on speed mostly to stay out of trouble,' O'Shea continued. 'Often, the pirates' skiffs just ain't fast enough to catch a hundred-thousand-tonne liner cruising at speed. Most have a secure locker full of weapons, which can be issued by the Captain to his crew in case of attack. But only if the Captain's still in control of his ship . . . The six guys on that ship – they were going to take it *from the inside*. Once they'd stormed the bridge, they'd bring the ship to a halt, and call in their pirate buddies by satphone.'

Range discarded the half-eaten banana on his plate. 'But it's been stopped, right?'

'Maybe. Maybe not. Randy didn't know the identity of the ship. The AQIM leadership held all of that kind of stuff back until the very last moment. He knew the code-names of the blokes who were to join him on the ship, but not their real identities. He didn't even know which port they were to sail from. And get this: an advance party has already left to liaise with the Somali pirates. Apparently, AQIM has very strong links to piracy operations, and to Al Shabaab, the Islamists who pretty much run Somalia. It's like a marriage made in hell.'

O'Shea finished off the apple and dropped it in the bin. 'It's also potentially a pirate's freakin' goldmine. You got thousands of mega-wealthy passengers on that cruise ship. They're dripping in diamonds and gold, and then there's the kidnap and ransom potential as a bonus. And as for AQIM – imagine the terror it would spread, and all the media they'd get? They'd choose a handful of passengers for hardcore treatment – maybe the ex-military guys, any Jews on board – you know the kind of shit.

'And get this,' O'Shea continued. 'That advance party headin' out from Tripoli, they were makin' for a port which is Pirate Central as far as Somalia goes, and one of the few places they can handle a ship that size.'

'Do we have a name?'

'Yeah,' O'Shea confirmed. '*Al Mina'a* . . . The Harbour in

English.' He glanced at Range. 'I think it's the same place where that fucker Amir hailed from?'

Range nodded. 'It is. I studied the file on him before we did the Isabelle pick-up. He was based at Al Mina'a all right. That's where they held Isabelle, at least until they started to move her down the chain to make the handover.' Range eyed O'Shea. 'It's a small world, mate.'

O'Shea gave a thin smile. 'Buddy, it sure is.'

The call woke Range with a start. He'd been dozing through the last of the afternoon sunshine that streamed through the window of his private room. Long visits like O'Shea's tended to exhaust him. The effects of the gas – not to mention the antidote drugs, which were also toxic – would take time to work themselves out of his system.

He flailed around for the phone. 'Range,' he croaked.

'Mr Range, this is Jean-Pierre de Saint-Sébastien calling from Geneva.'

Range tried to lever himself up in his bed and shake the drug-addled fog from his mind, but he could barely move with all the tubes and the needles. 'Sir, your call left me worried.'

'Mr Range, I believe my daughter and you were somehow close, although you had spent barely days together. That is why I am calling you. There is no easy way to say this. Isabelle is dead. I am afraid she took her own life, and we can only conclude it was the trauma of the . . . kidnapping, that drove her to it.'

'Sir, I . . .' Range was at a complete lost for words. He felt a mixture of shock, anger and the pain of loss swirling around in his morphine-clouded brain. 'Sir, I'm in a hospital,' he blurted out. 'I got injured on a job. I'm sorry it's taken me days to get back to you . . .'

'I understand. You were not to know.'

'Sir, I am so very, very sorry. When did this happen?'

'Five days ago. We had the funeral this morning, which is why I have only just called. I called you because I thought you would want to come, and I believe Isabelle would have wanted it. I did not know, of course, that you were away, or now hospitalized. I hope your injuries are not serious?'

'No, it's nothing,' said Range, quickly. 'Nothing.'

'Mr Range, I would like to make a suggestion. I would like to invite you to Geneva. Isabelle left something for you. I know she would want you to have it, and I should myself like to see you. Do you think that might be possible?'

'Sir, I'll book myself a flight soon as.'

'No, no. You will not book a flight. I will send the Gulfstream. To London's City Airport? It is the most convenient, I believe. And please, feel free to bring any of your team you may wish to, and who you trust most absolutely. Maybe the American, Mr O'Shea?'

'Sir, consider it done.'

'When will you be well enough to travel? When would you like me to send the Gulfstream?'

'Sir, I can't stand hospitals. I'm going to check myself out this evening.'

CHAPTER NINE

Normally, the approach into Geneva International Airport put Range on a real high. With the historic city clustered around the southern end of Lake Geneva, and surrounded by towering, snow-capped peaks, this had to be one of the most dramatic cityscapes anywhere in the world. The airport itself sat right on the French border, which sliced through the northern end of the city. Half of Geneva was in Switzerland, half was in France, and this was truly a global playground.

But as the Gulfstream lined up for its final approach, powering across the glittering surface of the lake, Range felt only a burning anger and an emptiness eating away at him. *Isabelle was dead.* All he had now were the memories – and precious few they were: a hostage handover at a remote African border; a few hours' laughter and light – not to mention code-breaking – in a Kenyan hotel. That was it. All of the promise, all the thrill of anticipation, all the dreams of what might have been. All of it was gone.

Range felt consumed by a murderous rage at those who had brought this young woman to such a place where she would take her own life. And he felt guilt. Guilt that he hadn't replied to her last message. Guilt that he hadn't jumped on the first flight to go see her. Guilt that he hadn't been there for her, in her hour of need. Sure, directly after Tripoli he hadn't been capable of going anywhere – it had been trouble enough getting the hospital to discharge him even now – but any guilt he had felt over leaving Randy for dead had been eclipsed by the guilt of leaving Isabelle alone in Geneva, to take her own life.

Of course, he knew that in reality she hadn't been alone. But in this glittering city of wealth and privilege, who could have related to what she had been through? Few would understand such dark, brutal suffering, or the trauma that would have followed. But Range would have been able to relate to it. He would have understood. Sure, he'd have been bound to seduce her too, but as she'd said herself: *If you need anything, you only have to knock on my door*. And at least he might have been able to talk her out of the darkness in which Amir and his sort had imprisoned her.

The Gulfstream touched down with an almost imperceptible shudder. Range glanced across at O'Shea. He knew he was proving shitty company right now. The very worst.

Rarely, if ever, had his mood been blacker. But true to his nature, the American had agreed to accompany him, and Range was grateful. He was unsteady on his legs, and all through the flight he'd been fighting the urge to vomit. For the first time in a decade of friendship and brother soldiering, he needed O'Shea to nursemaid him through the next few hours.

O'Shea helped him through immigration, from where a de Saint-Sébastien driver whisked them into central Geneva in one of the family limousines. The father had booked them into the Hotel d'Angleterre, a place of elegant, cultured luxury set right on the waterfront. The hotel was rumoured to have been the watering hole for British spies during the Cold War, and somehow it still retained some of the romantic, cloak and dagger feel.

Not that Range paid much heed to it now. He had found the journey as exhausting as his doctor had warned him it would be. After O'Shea had checked them in, he let the wiry American help him to his room, whereupon he collapsed onto his bed fully clothed. Mr de Saint-Sébastien had suggested they meet at eleven o'clock the following morning, to talk. Range fell asleep as he lay, and his last thoughts were that whilst he had finally made it to Geneva, he'd done so too late for the much longed-for rendezvous with Isabelle.

'To my mind it is simple,' Mr de Saint-Sébastien told them. 'My daughter was killed by her kidnappers. Maybe not at their hands. Maybe not in Somalia. But still, it is they who killed her. They put those pills into her hands and killed her, almost as if they had put a bullet in her brain.'

The old man spoke with venom, and for the first time Range sensed the bitter loss and rage that he had been suppressing. Until now, he'd been a model of decorum – polite, understated, welcoming. But that had been over mid-morning coffee on the hotel's terrace overlooking the water. Now, they'd retired to a private room so they could talk without any danger of being overheard.

'I believe I can speak frankly with you, Mr Range, and you, Mr O'Shea,' he continued. 'A British man, an American . . . and a Swiss. We are the decent, democratic, freedom-loving peoples of the world. Could any one of us hold a young and innocent girl hostage *and treat her such as they did*?' He spat out the last words. 'And all for monetary gain? She went to their country to help. *To help!* And what did they do? Out of sheer greed, spite and hatred, they drove her to her own destruction.'

The old man's fist pounded into the polished wood of the table around which they were gathered. The force of the blow shocked Range. Mr de Saint-Sébastien had seemed so hunched and shrunken in on himself, as if the shock of his loss had withered him to a husk, but within his wizened frame there burned real anger and passion, not to mention considerable strength of will.

'But none of this helps explain why I have brought you

here,' the old man went on. 'Revenge.' He let the word fall into the silence of the room. 'Revenge. I have called you here because I seek revenge. I do not know if you are religious men. For my part, I was born and raised a Christian. But I prefer to adhere to the Old Testament sentiment: an eye for an eye, as opposed to the more contemporary teachings of forgiveness. Forgiveness! How can I forgive? An eye for an eye! And then, maybe I can forgive once I have had my revenge!'

The last words were almost shouted across the room, and each was lent weight by the fist thumping the table. Range worried that in his grief the old man had partially lost his mind, for his earlier composure was completely gone. But who could blame him? If Range had had a daughter and the same had happened to her, would he have kept his grip on sanity? And as for forgiveness – well, fuck that. Rather than being forgiven, those like Amir and his ilk deserved a hole in the head.

'But this is not purely about vengeance alone,' the old man continued. 'Even now, they are plying their evil trade. Ships are being seized. Innocents taken hostage. More ransoms are paid, ransoms that fuel the evil trade. Gentlemen, the circle has to be broken. The serpent has to be decapitated. And so I have brought you here to ask you one thing: are you the men who might be willing to help me do this? I am an old man. You can see that. Were I young like you, I would go. But as I cannot, I can at least ask of you if you are willing?'

Range was surprised to hear O'Shea answering for them. 'Sir, the will is most certainly there. It's just the objective, the means and the timescale that we're lacking. Those things being given,' he threw a momentary glance at Range, 'we will go into harm's way, sir, on a mission of your bidding.'

'I think what my friend's trying to say, sir, is do you have some kind of a plan?' Range added. 'Some kind of a concrete proposition we can consider?'

The old man snapped his fingers. 'Pierre, the file.'

Pierre was his head of security. A Frenchman, he had a distinctly ex-military bearing, though Range doubted he hailed from any particularly elite unit. The very fact that he ran the old man's Geneva security, but that men like Range and O'Shea had been called in to execute the daughter's hostage recovery, betrayed their respective capabilities. Range figured Pierre didn't like him much. He had the demeanour of someone who knew when he was outclassed, and Range figured he resented it.

Pierre produced an attaché case, flipped it open on the table, and pulled out a maroon ring binder. It was embossed in gold with a triple 'S' symbol and beneath it was written in smaller type: 'Saint-Sébastien Shipping.' The old man laid his hand across the file, his fingertips pressing into the triple-S symbol almost lovingly.

'The de Saint-Sébastien family business is shipping,' he announced. 'I am French-Swiss, and most of our ships sail

135

from French harbours. Over the centuries the Triple-S Company made our family a fortune plying the seas. The company has now diversified, and at a conservative estimate it is worth perhaps some three billion dollars. Consequently, when you consider what I am about to propose, you must realise that money is no object in conceiving of our plans.

'Before taking over the family business I served for some years in the French navy,' the old man continued. 'But that was a long time ago and I have no pretensions to being a military man now. I am, for want of a better expression, a "shipping magnate" these days. So my plan, such as it is, falls back upon my knowledge of shipping. This,' he slipped a sheet of paper before O'Shea and Range, 'is a map showing the hotspots of piracy off the Somalian mainland. As you can see, the greatest concentration of ship seizures is here, some 25–150 miles off the Somali coast. Ninety-nine per cent of ships seized here get taken to one port, and one port only: Al Mina'a, or, in English, The Harbour.'

'The Harbour – we know it well,' Range remarked. 'Piracy Central. We studied the place in detail when preparing to do the hostage handover for you . . . for Isabelle . . . Trouble is, it's pretty much impossible to attack. Hit it from the sea, and you run into the pirate fleets. Hit it from the land, and you've got hundreds of miles of hostile Somali territory to cross, to get in or out. Hit it from the air, and in the warren of alleyways and boltholes that is the town itself, you'd likely have another Black Hawk Down – a Mogadishu – on your hands. That's why in part it wasn't possible to launch a rescue attempt for your daughter.'

'Yes, Mr Range, I know.' The old man fixed him with a burning look. 'But perhaps there is another way. You are all familiar with the siege of Troy? The Greeks wanted to defeat the Trojans and sack the Trojan city. The trouble was, Troy was a walled city that proved impregnable. When the Greeks supposedly withdrew, they left a giant, wheeled wooden horse at the city gates. The Trojans rejoiced, believing it to be a gift from an enemy that had departed.

'They drew the horse through the gates and into the heart of the city.' The old man balled his fingers together into a fist. 'And that was their undoing. In the belly of the beast was hidden a force of Greek warriors. At midnight, as the Trojans drank and partied and celebrated, those warriors stole out of the horse and opened the city gates, so letting the Greek army pour in. And the rest is history.

'Now this,' the old man passed another printout across the table, 'is perhaps our Trojan Horse. This is the MV Endeavour, a small Liquid Petroleum Gas tanker, known as an LPG-Carrier. She used to be one of the SSS fleet. I have recently had her re-flagged to a Liberian company – a shell that I set up to be totally untraceable. LPG is one of the most explosive substances known to man. It is also highly volatile – it evaporates into a gas very rapidly – but the gas is heavier than air. Indeed, LPG has to be kept under great pressure, hence the vessel's reinforced steel tanks – to keep it in a liquid and transportable form.

'Imagine the following scenario.' As he spoke, Range could see the excitement burning in the old man's eyes. 'The MV *Endeavour* sails down the coast of Somalia. She strays too close to the active pirate zone. The Somalian pirates pounce. The crew has retreated to the ship's citadel – a specially-hardened safe zone in the bowels of the ship. Most merchant ships plying that route have one these days. The pirates cannot break in, but they don't need to. They seize the vessel and sail her into The Harbour. They know the crew's water and oxygen will last for only so long, and eventually they will be forced to emerge. With the vessel anchored in their port they have the prize: they are happy to play the waiting game.

'For several months at this time of year there is an onshore breeze off the east coast of Africa. It starts blowing just before sunrise, and lasts for a good hour or more. The breeze cools the coast in the early hours. But that same breeze would carry a cloud of LPG from the *Endeavour* into the town, were the tanks to be opened at dawn. The gas is heavier than air, so it would pool around the waterfront and gradually get pushed inland. All it would then require is an igniter charge, and you being military men, I am sure you can suggest how we could improvise that.'

'There are loads of ways you could trigger an explosion,' Range confirmed. 'You can pretty much take your pick.'

'So, your plan is you fry the entire population of the port?' O'Shea queried. 'Of Al Mina'a?'

'It is,' the old man confirmed, grimly. 'Every last one of them. Damn them!'

'Trouble is, sir, there will be women and children in there.'

The old man eyed O'Shea for a long second. 'Mr O'Shea, my daughter is – *was* – a woman. Do you think that brought her any clemency from those who kidnapped her? Quite the reverse: they used her womanhood as a means to further terrify her. I am sure you know what I mean.' The old man's chin quivered, as the rage he was trying to suppress almost overcame him. 'And do you know who were some of her worst tormenters? *The Somali women.*'

'And the children, sir? Are they also guilty? Do they also deserve to die?'

'Goddamn it, man! Every single cursed family in that harbour lives off piracy, kidnapping and ransom! Every single one! As to those children you so worry about, they will grow up to be the future pirates. And let me tell you – you cannot decapitate a snake *partially*.'

O'Shea shook his head. 'Sir, it still troubles me. Where I come from . . .'

'But we are not *where you come from*, are we, Mr O'Shea?' the old man interrupted, fiercely. 'No. This is not Houston or New York. You are sat in a hotel on the Geneva waterfront, talking to an old man whose only daughter – a woman

139

you helped rescue – has been murdered by these people.' He paused, as if in an effort to regain some of his former composure. 'But tell me, am I to take it you see no impediment to the plan itself working?'

'Sir, I'm an ex-Navy SEAL. That's Sea-Air-Land elite forces. We specialise in water-borne operations. Your plan of attack might need a few refinements – I can think of several right away – but frankly, sir, it's a peach. We could use you at Coronado, sir. That's the home of the Navy SEALs, and the heart of US special operations. It's just some of the collateral damage that troubles me . . .'

The Old Man ignored O'Shea's last comment. 'And Mr Range? The plan? How do you see it?'

'Sir, I've got to be honest – killing women and kids doesn't sit easy with me, either,' Range replied. 'I've got no problem with murdering every last pirate bastard I come across. But their families? That's beyond savage.'

'But that is the thing with a gas attack, isn't it, Mr Range? Gas does not distinguish between the victims. And if I were to tell you – well, perhaps she shared this with you already; I know you were close – exactly what those Somali women did to Isabelle . . . Perhaps then you would not be so squeamish about putting them where they belong – which is in their graves!'

For a moment Range reflected upon those words. Why was he fighting scared of wiping out those whose hands were dripping in blood, and whose bank balances were swollen by funds raised from such a vicious and inhuman trade as piracy, kidnap and ransom? Did any of them actually deserve his protection? Or were they, as the old man argued, damned by their collective guilt?

'Your moral objections aside, Mr Range, does the plan of attack as I have outlined it work for you?' the old man continued.

'Yes, sir, it does it for me. Long fuse; slow burn; big bang kind of thing. Only one problem – how do those locked in the ship's citadel get away, before the LPG and the ship blow?'

'Easy,' O'Shea cut in. 'You get a pair of rigid-hulled inflatable boats – RHIBs – lashed to the deck. Money's no object, right? We order a pair of Navy SEAL Invaders – state-of-the-art RHIBs that can outrun anything in those seas. They've got dual diesel-electric motors, so they can run on silent stealth mode for several hours if they need to. Before the ship blows, we bust out of the secure room – the citadel – under cover of darkness and make our getaway in those.'

'Yes, this is something like I had in mind,' the old man remarked. 'And I can have a crew manning my yacht, *The Isabelle* – yes, she is named after my . . . late-lamented daughter – standing by at sea, to collect you.'

'Then there ain't no holes in the plan of attack, not that I can see,' said O'Shea.

The old man fixed him with his piercing, eagle-eyed stare.

'So, you are only running scared of the plan because of any pirate children who may end up as casualties. Am I correct?'

'Sir, no one is running scared,' O'Shea grated. 'A Navy SEAL never runs scared. A Navy SEAL stands and fights, to the last man and the last round if need be. But that doesn't mean he willingly murders . . .'

'Then why won't you take on *this* fight,' the old man cut him off, 'which you know in your heart is the right one?' He was practically spitting the words across the table at O'Shea.

'No one's said they won't,' O'Shea replied, evenly. 'Not yet, anyways.'

'And Mr Range?' the old man challenged. 'Do you have similar qualms about *the ethics* of what I am suggesting? Is Isabelle – and countless thousands of Isabelles – not to be avenged because some pirate children might die in the process? Maybe I have something that may convince you to change your mind . . .'

He turned to a figure at his side and held out a shrivelled palm. 'The item. From Isabelle. If you have it please, Pierre.'

Pierre passed across a small buff envelope. The old man reached out and handed it to Range. 'This Isabelle left for you. I thought you might want to open it later, in the privacy of your own room. But bearing in mind your misgivings about the Al Mina'a mission, I think perhaps you should see it now.'

Range nodded. He felt inside and retrieved a gold chain,

on the end of which dangled a glittering, diamond-encrusted angel. *Isabelle's.*

Her father had given it to her as a child; Range had given it back to her on the Kenya–Somalia border, at the moment she'd taken her first steps into freedom; and she in turn had left it for him, it seemed, just before she took an overdose of sleeping pills and killed herself. As he held it in his hands, Range felt consumed by a burning anger and a coruscating sense of loss. Who was he to deny Isabelle's father – and the woman he had so fallen for – vengeance?

'So, Mr Range, the mission?' the old man prompted. 'Are you willing?'

'Mr de Saint-Sébastien, give me the ship and I'll sail her tomorrow,' Range announced. 'And I'll do so with or without my friend here, Mr O'Shea.'

CHAPTER TEN

'Randy knows,' The Hogan remarked. He was holding his wine glass up to the light, admiring the viscosity of the vintage and the thickness of the rim it left as he tilted the glass. Rumour had it that the thicker the 'legs', as they called it in the trade, the better the wine. Personally, The Hogan thought it all a load of rot, but one thing was for sure – it did look pretty in the light.

The Beaujolais wine bar was packed as usual, but Range and The Hogan were pretty much always guaranteed to get 'their' table, which was tucked away in a corner and largely hidden from prying eyes or flapping ears.

'No reason Randy shouldn't know,' Range replied. 'It's no secret what we're planning.'

The Hogan inhaled deeply of the wine's bouquet. 'Ah, yes, but it's not only that he *knows*.' His eyes met Range's over the top of his glass. 'Randy wants in on the mission.'

Range took a good swig of his wine. Tony had tried teaching him how to sip and savour, tried making him a connoisseur, but as far as Range was concerned, if it was an alcoholic liquid he was happy to neck it.

'Tony, he's only just got away from eighteen months' fun and games with Al-Qaeda in the Islamic Maghreb. He needs time to decompress and to be with his family. He needs to fly home, do a few barbies in the back yard, get it on with his missus and throw a football around with the kids. There's no way Randy should be in on this one.'

'And you?' The Hogan chuckled. 'Mr Indestructible? You've only recently discharged yourself prematurely from hospital after a not inconsiderable dose of nerve gas. The phrase "pot calling the kettle" comes to mind.'

'Yeah. Fair enough,' Range conceded. 'Difference is, I don't have any family to spend any time with. And as to getting it on with the missus . . .' Range's mind drifted momentarily to Isabelle, or at least to the memory of her.

'You know what I think?' The Hogan volunteered. 'I think you're mainly doing this because of a certain relationship you built up with a certain Isabelle de Saint—'

'Not that it was ever bloody consummated,' Range interjected, gruffly.

The Hogan raised one eyebrow. 'I wouldn't know. So, are you?' he pressed. 'Doing it only in memory of her?'

Range took a pull on the wine. There was nothing better than drinking with The Hogan. He never paid less than sixty quid for a bottle, and as a consequence Range never seemed to get a sniff of a hangover after one of their late-night sessions in The Beaujolais.

'Does it matter?' he countered. 'There's a very juicy contract on the table from our man in Geneva. When have we ever been offered those kind of rates for a few weeks' work? If at the end of it all we've knocked out Pirate Central, earned a packet *and avenged Isabelle* – then what's the harm in all that?'

'But unlike most of our contracts, Steve, the risks on this one are somewhat insane.'

Range glanced at The Hogan, searchingly. 'Tony, you're not suggesting you're not going to bloody take the contract? 'Cause if you are I'll do it bloody freelance.'

The Hogan waved a hand, dismissively. 'No, no, of course not. Of course we're taking the contract. After all, Blackstone Six has a certain reputation to maintain. Which brings me back to Randy, if I may. Might you have any other misgivings about our recently rescued ex-Navy SEAL and Blackstone Six operative, ones that you're not telling me? Like . . . the TNF factor, for example?'

For a moment Range massaged the stiffness out of his neck and lower jaw. It was mostly gone now, but long conversations brought the ache back with a vengeance. 'Now that you ask, yeah, there is more than a little TNF in it. The Kiwi's the most untrusting of the lot of us, the cynical fucker, but I've got my own reservations.'

'Such as?'

'Nothing specific. Just a feeling. Plus a few things that were said by the guy when we busted him out of there. Plus how was it Randy managed to get himself so close to the high-ups in AQIM? He must be one bloody good actor, that's all I can say. And if he can act so convincingly with them, . . . well, enough said.'

The Hogan leaned closer across the table. 'Range, there's something else you need to know, and this is absolutely to go no further. He's only revealed it recently and during some of the more intensive debriefings. He was tortured in extreme ways by those who . . . saved him. Indeed, they seemed to have wanted to save him first and foremost only so they *could* torture him. Simply horrific is all I can say. I do not want to go into any detail, and I'm sure you don't want me to. And before you ask, none of this is make-believe: he has the scars to prove it.'

'So who's operating on TNF now?' said Range. 'I don't doubt he does have the scars, but extreme torture can make even the toughest of blokes end up in the strangest of places. You can lose track of who your real enemies are, who your friends are and who you need to be hitting back against.'

The Hogan nodded. 'Agreed. And Randy *is* hankering after revenge. No doubt about it. But it's revenge against those who tortured him and tried to break him – that's what he's after. He wants in on your mission because of that: because it's the best way he can see to strike back against Al-Qaeda in the Islamic Maghreb. A good number of their people have deployed to this place called Al Mina'a – The Harbour. He wants in so he can go help annihilate them.'

'So you're saying we take him?'

'Yes, I am. I think it would be wrong to deny him the chance of . . . closure. Plus there's another factor at play here. You say you want a minimum of six. At present we have Tak, Tiny, Joe and yourself. Oh, and The Kiwi, of course: he'd never miss out on such a thing. The others have all said it's too risky, and they've got families to think of. And then there's O'Shea: he says he's most likely out. Doesn't think the "collateral damage" – the innocent deaths – are worth it. You're short of a crew member, Range. You need every good man you can get.'

A week passed in frenetic preparations. Whilst the contractor, Mr de Saint-Sébastien, seemed more than able to procure just about any piece of kit, weaponry or technology from his base in Geneva, it was up to Range and his crew to draw up the detailed plan of attack and prepare the minutiae: lists of arms and explosives; suppliers; maps, communications and navigation kit; and perhaps most importantly of all at this stage, the escape boats.

The US Navy SEAL rigid-hulled inflatable boat was strictly speaking known as a RHIB, but often abbreviated to 'RIB' for short. The RHIB was eleven metres of fibre-reinforced plastic, which formed the rigid V-shaped hull, topped off with air-filled tubes running around the gunwales. The design made the boat fast but also almost unsinkable. She had a top speed of more than forty-five knots and could operate in very heavy seas. The turn of speed was provided by a pair of 2,470 horsepower, turbo-charged diesel engines, which could also be operated on stealth electronic-motor mode.

Under O'Shea's guidance, Range had asked Mr de Saint-Sébastien to procure a pair of decommissioned RHIBs. O'Shea was arguing that he wasn't 'in' on the mission because he couldn't countenance the non-pirate, civilian deaths the attack would cause. But he was still helping with the planning, and Range could tell there was a part of him that was sorely tempted to join them. O'Shea figured they'd need a pair of RHIBs in case one was damaged in the firefight with the pirates or otherwise proved unserviceable. Long experience in maritime ops had taught him it was always best to have a back-up.

It wasn't overly difficult to procure the RHIBs, especially since there were companies who specialised in selling such ex-military hardware. They would be supplied complete with weapons mounts, but without the normal array of guns they carried. With Range and his crew needing to bust out of Pirate Central, they wanted the craft refitted with the most potent weaponry possible: namely, the tried-and-tested weaponry the RHIBs normally carried. With money being no object, Geneva had assured him that procuring those armaments wasn't going to be an issue.

They'd mount the RHIBs on the ship's deck, in place of the lifeboats. Once sheeted over with the ship's heavy tarpaulins, there should be nothing to alert the pirates to them being anything other than an LPG tanker's standard equipment, especially once they'd padded out the mounted weaponry to hide its distinctive shape. From their mounts the RHIBs could be released direct into the sea, and Range and his men would drop into the water beside them. They'd climb aboard, fire up the engines and within seconds they'd be motoring out of Al Mina'a.

Very few vessels in the world could catch those RHIBS – and certainly nothing operated by Somali pirates. Once they were underway, they would be pretty much home and dry. If they did run into any pirate craft, they had more than enough weaponry to blast them out of the water. Mounted on their state-of-the-art weapons pivots, each of the boats' .50-cal heavy machinegun and 40mm grenade launcher had an accurate range of approaching two thousand metres, even when firing on the move. Nothing was going to get close to those RHIBs to do them any damage.

With a 190 nautical miles of range on standard tanks, the crew would be more than able to make the planned rendezvous with the pick-up craft. The de Saint-Sébastien motor yacht would be unable to carry a RHIB, so they would have to set charges in the boats and blow them up once they were done with them. It would be sad to see fine craft like the RHIBs sent to the bottom of the ocean, but such were the needs of the mission. Just in case they missed the RV for any reason, O'Shea had ordered the RHIBs to be loaded with extra jerry cans of diesel, to provide enough for them to reach Kenyan waters. That was their fallback escape option.

Roles were going to be very tightly delineated on this mission. Whilst Range and his team were tasked with preparing all aspects of the assault, and the escape and evasion that followed, readying the LPG tanker in all its forms was left to Pierre, Mr de Saint-Sébastien's head of security, working with one of the Triple S shipping line's most trusted ship's crews.

Range and his men would fly out to rendezvous with the ship in Sri Lanka. Ironically, this was one of the key staging posts for anti-piracy crews joining ships as they sailed into pirate waters. Teams of armed men – mostly British, US and Allied ex-soldiers – shepherded the ships through pirate-infested water, before disembarking once they had reached safety. By contrast, Range and his crew were joining their vessel with the specific aim of getting captured by the pirates – and they had no illusions as to the risks they were running on this mission.

Soldiers who'd served in recent conflicts and had left the military were finding lucrative work running such anti-piracy missions. Almost a decade earlier Range himself had pioneered the anti-piracy runs, and back then they had been forced to do them unarmed. They'd had to mock up weapons using wooden cutouts, and hope they could bluff the pirates from a distance. Plus they'd 'hardened' the ships – welding shut all access points and stringing razor wire along the decks and the main stairwells.

The golden rule of those early missions had been never to stop or slow the boat. If the captain did, it would give the pirates a chance to board her, and then you were finished. Range had experienced some close calls on those early jobs – several dashes across the Indian Ocean with pirate mother-ships steaming after them, and launching their skiffs crammed full of heavily armed Somali pirates.

In more recent years the mood had changed and nowadays guard forces went onto the ships properly armed. But even having crack teams armed to the teeth onboard hadn't managed to deter the pirates. It didn't help that different countries had different laws about whether ships were allowed to carry armed men through their waters.

The maritime police of some of the nations bordering Somalia had started boarding ships and 'confiscating' weaponry, claiming that it contravened their laws to carry arms through their waters. Invariably, though, not long after the weapons had been removed from the ship, a flotilla would appear on the horizon manned by pirates brandishing assault rifles and rocket-propelled grenades. The pirates were earning so much money from the kidnap and ransom industry that they could afford to bribe the authorities in neighbouring countries, and so the maritime police weren't just disarming the ship's guard force: they were radioing ahead to the pirates to give them the go-ahead to attack defenceless vessels. And on occasion they were even selling the arms they'd confiscated on to the pirates.

Piracy was a dirty – and highly lucrative – business, and with the waters off the Horn of Africa being a major cross-roads in terms of global shipping, the pirates were seeing no end of action. This year alone there had been over two hundred attacks by pirates off Somalia, and twenty-eight successful hijackings of ships. Several dozen vessels were being held in Somalian ports – Al Mina'a being first and foremost amongst them – with 198 crewmembers held hostage.

The hijackings were almost always about the crew and not the ship. Shipping companies were insured for the loss of a ship and its cargo. It was the human victims the companies paid the big ransoms for. A ship's crew might yield ten million dollars or more in payments. In some cases a Somali pirate could earn forty thousand dollars per crew member ransomed, which was a fortune in a country wracked by civil war and where the average wage was six hundred dollars a year. With so much money at stake, the pirates had made it crystal clear what the fate would be of any security teams captured. *They would not be ransomed.*

Yet despite the dangers, most of the twenty-thousand ships sailing through the Gulf of Aden and the Indian Ocean

– the waters off Somalia – weren't getting hit by pirates. That was why Range and his crew needed to sail their ship into the heart of the piracy zone, so as to ensure they were amongst those who were targeted.

If necessary, they'd steam right into The Harbour itself to make sure the pirates got their 'prize'. It would seem odd to see a ship doing this, but with Range and his team locked in the ship's citadel, the pirates wouldn't be able to ask them too many questions. In any case, the pirates were unlikely to look such a gift horse in the mouth. Instead, the dollar signs would be flashing before their eyes.

Somalia was a 'failed state', and the entire south of the country was wracked with civil war. The hard-line Islamist terrorist group Al Shabaab held sway in many areas, and as a result the pirates could operate more or less with impunity. The Somali clan structure, wherein any individual's loyalty was first and foremost to the clan, as opposed to either the country or the rule of law, meant that communities closed ranks to protect their own.

Sri Lanka had been chosen as the start point for their journey for one main reason: it was possible to get all sorts of works done to the tanker ship there without anyone asking too many questions. Mr de Saint-Sébastien had ordered some very specific modifications be made to the LPG carrier, to transform her from a standard tanker to what amounted to a weapon of mass destruction.

The ship's crew would then sail the modified vessel until

they were just off pirate waters, at which point they would transfer into Mr de Saint-Sébastien's luxury yacht. From there it would be left to Range and his skeleton crew to pilot the ship into the danger zone.

Apparently, navigating the vessel from the handover point to where they were most likely to get hit was a simple enough process: the captain would have set her on a course, bearing and speed to take her right into Al Mina'a if need be. All Range and his men had to do was keep a look out for any vessels that might be on a collision course with them, and keep their eyes peeled for the pirates.

When – not if – the pirates struck, Range and his men had to give an impression of putting up something like a fight, before bringing the ship to a dead stop. That's what they would be ordered to do anyway, for the pirates' modus operandi was always to force the ship to a halt with gunfire and rockets, and then board her. The main priority was then to get his men below decks into the hardened sanctuary – the citadel – for they had to avoid getting captured at all costs.

The plan required that they last out until the following morning, at which point they would trigger the LPG and make their getaway. They had to presume that a pirate guard force would be stationed on the ship, to keep watch. So they'd be fighting their way out of the citadel to get to their boats and make their getaway. That was most likely doable under cover of darkness, so they agreed that they'd make a call on when exactly they made their escape depending on when they sailed into Al Mina'a. Because the gas-release mechanism on the ship had an override function, it could be controlled from Geneva, and with the GPS tracking systems available to him, Mr de Saint-Sébastien would know full well when the ship had docked in The Harbour. This meant that if circumstances dictated, the team could make their getaway in the depths of the night and the gas release could be triggered at dawn, remotely from Geneva.

Because of the distinctly nautical nature of this operation, Range really did want O'Shea on this one. Of course he had Dive Shack Joe on the team, who, being ex-Special Boat Service, was well-versed in navigating a ship at sea. He also had Randy, but neither of them had served at the kind of level that O'Shea had, as a Lieutenant-Commander in the Navy SEALs. O'Shea was also the only man in their number who had captained a ship of any considerable size. During his days in the SEALs Range had commanded a Mark V special operations craft – a jet-powered, arrow-shaped, high-speed assault vessel, one capable of long-range insertions at speeds of over fifty knots.

The Mark V drew only five feet of draught, but it was large enough to carry two RHIBs, which could be launched from the sloping deck of her rear hold. That had made her ideal for hunting Abu Sayaf terrorists in the shallow bays and inlets of the Philippines – a nation that remained a close ally of the United States.

O'Shea had led a team of Special Warfare Combatant

Crewmen (SWCCs) on several tours of the Philippines – the SWCC being specially trained for operating such fast assault boats. Though they were little known about, the SWCC were the sister unit to the SEALs, and SEALs often rode on SWCC-operated craft as they went in to hit their targets.

A Mark V was nowhere near the tonnage of the MV *Endeavour*, but even so O'Shea was the natural candidate to captain such a ship. More was the pity then that he had decided he was off the coming mission. If only there was some way to distinguish between males of fighting age and women and children during the coming attack, then O'Shea would have been on it like a flash.

But the thing about gas – whether nerve gas or liquid petroleum gas – was that it made no distinction between its victims. It was an indiscriminate killer like no other. Apart from wind direction there was no way whatsoever to focus the attack, or to steer the gas to hit one victim whilst safeguarding another.

After a hard day's planning and preparations at B6's Mayfair office, Range was sat in his London flat transfixed by the TV news. It was twenty-four hours before their departure for Sri Lanka and the start of the mission. He had a beer grasped in one hand, yet it had been left all but untouched. He was glued to the ticker tape newsflash running across the TV screen, in a loop that kept repeating over and over.

Breaking news. New piracy outrage threatens thousands off Somalia: Golden Achilles *cruise ship seized. Breaking news. New piracy outrage threatens thousands off Somalia:* Golden Achilles *cruise ship seized.*

The details known about the cruise ship hijack seemed to be very sketchy right now, but Range could only presume that Randy's former AQIM brothers had proceeded with their plan, and without Randy being amongst their number. Even if it wasn't Randy's old lot, there was no way that Range could refuse Randy a place on the mission now. This would only serve to quicken his appetite for revenge, and Range didn't have it in him to deny him that indulgence.

In any case, wasn't he doing this mostly for revenge? Range glanced around his flat. Sparsely furnished but well-appointed was how an estate agent might describe it. With three bedrooms, one of which he used as an office and one as a spare, it wasn't lacking in space. And with the flat being in West Knightsbridge, if he had to go out and buy something similar now he shuddered to think what it would cost him. No, he wasn't doing the coming job for the money, that was for sure.

In any case, after the Gaddafi mission of the year before he figured he'd be hitting a monster payday in the not too distant future. When they'd gone in to lift the last surviving free son of Colonel Gaddafi, they'd also managed to get their hands upon a king's ransom in gold. The Gaddafi family wealth – mostly made up of 400-ounce London Good

Delivery Bars – had been co-located with the last Gaddafi family member still at large, or rather with the Tuareg-AQIM forces that were holding him.

It had made every sense to lift the gold at the same time as lifting Sultan Gaddafi. Range and his team were waiting for the dust to settle a little from that mission, before someone – most likely The Hogan – went out and fenced the bullion, at which point they'd all hit pay dirt big time.

No, Range certainly wasn't doing the coming mission for the money.

Range felt around in his pocket and pulled out a crumpled buff envelope. It was the one that the old man had given him in Geneva. He felt inside and retrieved the gold chain, on the end of which dangled the glittering, diamond-encrusted angel. *Isabelle's.*

Range stared at it for a long second, his mind lost in bitter memories. No, he knew for sure why he was doing this mission.

It was just about the most insanely dangerous tasking that he'd ever taken on, but he owed Isabelle, and as far as Range was concerned, that made the risks immaterial. Maybe Amir himself would be there, as the gas drifted silently into the streets and alleyways of Al Mina'a. Certainly some of his murderous crew would be – those who had treated Isabelle worse than an animal and driven her to take her own life.

In a way, Range hoped that Amir survived the attack –

preferably with terrible burns that left him confined to a wheelchair for the rest of his life. That way, he would have to live with what Range had done to him and his people for the rest of his days. That would be pure, sweet revenge.

Range was pulled away from his dark thoughts by a buzzing on the flat's intercom. He had a visitor. He strode across to the door and peered at the tiny video screen to see who was outside. All he could see was an arm holding up a piece of paper to the camera. On it was scrawled in black marker pen:

Count me in . . . O'SHEA.

Range smiled. He buzzed O'Shea into the communal hallway, opened his door and ushered him into the flat. He showed him to one of the stools at the breakfast bar in the kitchen.

'Brew, mate?'

'Yeah. Coffee. None of that British tea shit.'

Range fired up the kettle. 'Instant do you?'

'That ain't coffee. That's pisswater. But if it's all you got . . .'

'Quit complaining.'

'So, you saw the news?' O'Shea remarked, grimly. 'The cruise liner? They reckon it could be as many as five thousand passengers.' A pause. 'So, buddy, I came to ask if you got room for an extra one.'

Range handed him the mug. 'Here you go. One cup of pisswater. One way or the other I was going to have to persuade you to join us. Who else is going to captain that ship, at least when our man in Geneva's crew do the handover? I guess the news did the persuading for me.'

'You figure it's this AQIM crew Randy warned us about?' O'Shea asked.

'No way of knowing. No details on how they took the ship yet. But if it was an inside job as much as it was the pirates, I reckon it'll be AQIM.' Range threw O'Shea a look. 'Mate, I am well glad you're coming with us on this one. I mean it. What I said in Geneva, I'm going with or without you? That was bullshit.'

O'Shea smiled. 'Aw, buddy, you're all heart.'

CHAPTER ELEVEN

Range paced backwards and forwards across the breadth of the ship's deck. He was always like this in the hours prior to the mission going in: pumped up with a tense, nervous energy and a burning desire for the action proper to begin. The worst of all times were these – the final hours of preparation and of waiting before battle was joined.

The MV *Endeavour*'s forward deck was hardly the best of places for what he was about to do, but he'd delivered final mission's briefings in worse places. The fierce sun beat down from an azure sky and was thrown back by the ocean's surface in a thousand dazzling shards of light. The voyage up to this point had been largely uneventful, and they were now approaching the crew handover. Range and his team were wound up as tight as springs by the combination of the boredom and the crushing weight of anticipation.

There was only so much sunbathing and card-playing a bunch of blokes could do during a three-week journey on the high seas. The Indian Ocean had proven baking hot and millpond calm, and with its dodgy air-con the ship's accommodation had proved only borderline endurable. About the sole relief from the discomfort and the tedium was the daily internet feed, which was available for just one hour every evening.

That was how Range and his men had learned the fate of the *Golden Achilles*, the cruise liner hijacked just prior to their departure. Under her pirate crew the *Golden Achilles* had been steaming fast for the coast of Somalia, at which stage she would have been well beyond any hope of rescue. A NATO warship had been shadowing the vessel, but with dozens of nationalities being held hostage onboard, no one had been able to break the international logjam and order a hostage rescue assault.

As the hours went by and the Somali coast drew ever nearer, the *Golden Achilles'* crew and passengers had grown frustrated and angry as hell at seeing a friendly warship on hand, yet apparently unable to intervene – and so they had taken matters into their own hands. They had armed themselves with whatever makeshift weapons they could find – ship's shovels and axes mostly – and overpowered a handful of the hijackers.

But then the leaders of the Somali pirates had woken up to what was happening, and the danger that they were about to lose their prize of all prizes. In the bloodbath that had followed, hundreds of passengers and crew had been killed and injured, but by force of numbers alone the hijackers had eventually been defeated. They'd run out of bullets, at which point vengeful passengers driven wild with grief had started to tear them to pieces with their bare hands.

The pictures broadcast around the world were horrific and deeply shocking. Many had been filmed on passengers' mobile phones and the very worst images hadn't even made it onto the mainstream news. But traumatised and grieving passengers had posted their videos and photos onto internet sites anyway, and if you searched hard enough you could find them.

If ever any of Range's team needed a reason to believe that their present mission was the right one, the *Golden Achilles* hijacking was it. The pirates had spared no one: grandmothers, mothers, the few children on board – all had been slaughtered as the battle raged for control of the vessel. Children had been thrown live over the ship's railings, and left to drown in the sea below. After learning of the horrors that had befallen the cruise ship, Range had noticed a reinvigorated yet grim determination in all of his men, O'Shea foremost amongst them.

Apart from viewing those terrible and bloody images, Range had killed the time with fishing. The MV *Endeavour* cruised too fast for most open ocean fish to catch her, but not the tuna. On many a previous voyage Range had learned that tuna would go for just about any kind of bait. All you needed to do was cut up an old Coke can, fashion a spoon-shaped plate out of it, attach that to a rod and line with a hook and toss it over the side of the ship.

He'd caught a couple of real whoppers on this trip, and the ship's Burmese chef had become expert at flipping the fillets on a scalding hot barbecue bolted to the ship's deck, so they were lightly browned on both sides. The entire ship's crew was Burmese – apart from the captain – and they sure knew how to work their butts off, and how to look after Range and his men.

As far as the Burmese crew was concerned, this was all just another job they were doing for Triple-S Shipping, and Range and his men were the gunmen who would keep them safe from the pirates. And that meant that they held Range and his team in suitably high esteem – for they were the blokes who just might be called upon to save their lives, or at least their liberty.

At the rendezvous point with the yacht, the Burmese deckhands would be given some cock and bull story about an unexpected 'crew change'. They'd be sent below decks on the yacht, as O'Shea turned the MV *Endeavour* westwards and sailed her into the heart of hell. They'd be left none the wiser as to the MV *Endeavour*'s real mission, but they'd be paid handsomely for their time and given a 'cancellation bonus', which should serve to keep them happy.

By contrast to the Burmese crew, the ship's captain – a bearded Ukrainian with skin like parched leather – looked as if he had more than a sneaking idea what Range and his men were up to. Range figured Captain Kolokov had to be well into his sixties, especially as he'd let slip that he'd once served in the Soviet Union's armed forces. He still had the military bearing, although he looked as if he'd run just about every scam you could possibly imagine since he'd gone civvie.

In spite of the Captain's age there was a hard, fierce, wolf-ishness about his gaze, and Range felt certain Captain Kolokov missed just about nothing that went on in his ship. The Captain must have been given some explanation as to why he was headed to a deep-ocean rendezvous, at which stage he was to hand over his ship to a bunch of foreign mercenaries. But money was always a powerful persuader, and Range figured he was being paid enough to stay schtum on this one.

Either way, Captain Kolokov struck Range as being a useful kind of a bloke to have in command of your ship when the Somali pirates came after you. In fact, Range had to keep reminding himself that their present objective was to *get themselves captured* and not to ram the pirates and send them to the ocean depths, or blow them out of the water – which was why they didn't exactly want a Captain Kolokov manning the ship's bridge.

Range had got his men drilling and drilling for the actions they'd take once the pirates hit the ship. They'd drilled in the cool of the morning and the full heat of midday, for there was no knowing exactly when they would strike. It was all about getting his men familiar with their routes of evacuation to the security of the citadel, so they could do it with their eyes closed. And it was all about doing so in the quickest possible time. The pirates, Range knew, were fast: he'd once had them try to board a ship he was manning, and they'd been shinning up the ropes by the time Range and his fellow gunmen had managed to blast them back into the sea. But it had been a close run thing.

The pirates swarmed ships. They did so entirely with the aim of stopping the crew – those who yielded the most valuable ransoms – from making it to any hardened secure area. Range and his men had to be faster. They'd drilled it so often they'd got it down to 180 seconds – from the moment O'Shea confirmed he was stopping the ship, to having all six of them in the citadel. Range figured 180 seconds was fast enough. He'd vowed to himself to be the last man into the citadel, and to count all the others in.

To achieve that kind of speed and slickness of operation they'd carried out maybe a dozen dry runs, and all of that time Captain Kolokov in particular had been watching. Range figured the Captain knew full well what Range and his men were going into once he handed over the ship, and he reckoned there was more than a small part of the old Soviet sea dog that wanted to go with them.

Whatever story Captain Kolokov may have been told by Geneva, he'd seemed happy enough to keep O'Shea beside him as he went about his business, and to teach him the ropes. He had recognised in O'Shea a fellow soldier of the sea, and the two had bonded well. Many an evening they'd been up on the ship's bridge swapping war stories over a chilled beer or two – Kolokov from his time with the Soviet Navy, hunting for British and US warships; O'Shea from his time with the US Navy SEALs, hunting for terrorists.

Randy being a fellow SEAL, he was the natural running mate for O'Shea, and Captain Kolokov. It made sense for the two of them to man the bridge once Kolokov was gone and Range's team took over. As for the rest of Range's men, they'd learned well their tasks and their stations.

Tak had bonded well with the Burmese crew down in the bowels of the vessel. More than anything, he just couldn't get enough of their rich, spicy cooking. He and Tiny would be taking over in the ship's engine room, once the Burmese crew was gone.

'So, one last time,' Range began the briefing, pacing back and forth in front of his fellow operators as he spoke. 'We've gone over this a dozen times, but you know the old saying: *fail to plan, plan to fail.* O'Shea, Randy: your station is the ship's bridge. It'll be some five hours' sailing from the handover point to the heart of the piracy zone, no more than seven to make Al Mina'a port itself. Your role is to deliver us as smoothly as possible into the hands of the pirates.'

Out here on the open deck the sun beat down relentlessly, the hot steel of the ship's hatches throwing the heat back at them like a giant oven. Like the rest of his men, Range was dressed only in shorts and T-shirt, yet he could feel the sweat oozing out of his pores and soaking into his clothing. There was precious little breeze at this time of day, and the air felt still and brooding – the calm before the storm.

From below them the steady beat of the ship's engines rumbled and vibrated through the men's feet, punching out a now-familiar rhythm. Over the days spent at sea they'd grown accustomed to the throbbing of those engines, but now the reality of what they were about to do was hitting home, and it had taken on an eerie, menacing feel. Every turn of the ship's screw was taking them closer to the showdown.

'Once the pirates attack, we're to put up token resistance only,' Range continued. 'On my call, O'Shea, you're to bring the ship to a dead stop. But remember: as soon as we see them preparing to board, make for the citadel. Do not delay. Those fuckers use grappling irons and assault ladders to board, and they can swarm a ship in seconds. You have to get to the citadel before they get to you. And remember: the likelihood of our being able to rescue any man captured is just about zero.

'You've each got a Cougar, but we know they're unlikely to work for comms between the citadel and the exterior of the ship,' Range added. Their mission rehearsals had proved the radio signal wouldn't make it through several layers of steel compartment and ship's hull. 'So, there will be no radioing for help by any man trying to resist capture.

'Rest assured, if anyone is captured they'll likely get beaten and tortured in a similar fashion to those poor fuckers on the *Golden Achilles*. They'll torture you in an effort to make the rest of us give ourselves up – to open up the citadel. That cannot happen, and for obvious reasons, which you all understand. So, the simple message is this: *avoid capture at all costs*. Got it?'

There were a series of affirmatives from the men.

'Anyone got any doubts about the inadvisability of getting captured, speak to Randy there,' Range added. 'We all know how closely allied AQIM and the Somali pirates are: at its simplest they're one and the same thing.'

'Dudes, trust me, it ain't a good idea.' Randy spoke in his trademark laid-back drawl. Word had got around by now how he had been treated by his captors. It was an open secret amongst the men. 'Anyone wanna see them, I'll show you my scars.' His teeth flashed white in the sunlight. 'That's why I'm here – *payback time*.'

'Too bloody right,' Range remarked, 'it's payback time for all of us. Tak and Tiny: just as soon as you get O'Shea's orders to bring the engines to a stop, that's your signal to head for the citadel. O'Shea and Randy: my order to you to stop the ship is your green light to get off the bloody bridge and into the citadel. That leaves Joe, The Kiwi and myself standing security. We'll position ourselves depending on the pirate's line of attack. Put warning shots into the water around the pirates' skiffs, but not too many so as to drive them off completely.

'Again, on my call we cease any form of resistance. Or at

least, that's the way the pirates will see it. I want you very visibly downing your weapons, shaking like a leaf and running for the citadel. But we are to be the last below decks. Randy and O'Shea: you confirm you're heading down to the citadel before we break position and head for it ourselves. Is everyone clear?'

'Got it.'

'Kiwi, you figure you can handle that – shaking like a dog taking a piss on a thistle?' Range queried. 'I know it goes against everything you Kiwi mountain men are bred for, but believe me, on this one the secret is to give up the fight, get below decks and start preparing for the real battle – when we fry them all.'

The Kiwi cracked a thin smile. 'It's not in my nature to run. But run to fight another day, I can do that.'

'None of us will question your manhood because of it,' Range quipped. 'Now, you all have memorised the six-figure code, the one that gives access to the citadel. No one – I repeat *no one* – writes it down. Not even you, Tiny, and we all know you're two sandwiches short of a picnic.'

There was a ripple of laughter from the men. Even Tiny smiled. The best jokes were sometimes the old ones. It was good to throw in the odd wisecrack, Range figured, even when facing a mission such as this. Humour was essential in keeping the guys positive and to build their *esprit de corps*. If the laughs ever stopped completely, Range would know that things had gone terminally wrong.

'No one writes the code down for obvious reasons,' Range continued. 'If you get captured and they find the code, they've got one less barrier to get through to break into the citadel.' He paused. 'We've drilled and drilled for this. We're as good as we're going to get. It's a case of train hard, fight easy. That's what we're going to do over the next twenty-four hours, and we're going to take out a lot of evil piratical fuckers in the process.'

Range surveyed his men. He could see the strength in their expressions – steely-eyed bringers of death each and every one of them – and he knew that they were ready. O'Shea, Randy, The Kiwi, Dive Shack Joe, Tak, Tiny – he couldn't have chosen a better half-dozen fighters to be going into action with here, Randy included. Any nagging doubts he may have had about the man's true loyalties had long since dissipated.

'Right. Questions?'

'What happens if they take the ship, but don't take us directly into Al Mina'a?' O'Shea queried. 'They anchor a lot of their captured vessels a mile or so out to sea. So what if they opt to do the same with us, and we're too far out for the LPG to have any effect? A mile out it'd spread over the ocean and fry a load of fish is all.'

'Only the largest vessels get anchored a way offshore,' Range replied. 'That cruise liner – the *Golden Achilles* – if they'd got her all the way to the coast they'd have anchored her a mile out. But a small freighter like this, they're bound to sail her right into port, and especially with us locked in the citadel, for that means they've got to keep a very close watch. And if for some reason they don't, we break out of the citadel during the hours of darkness and sail her into Al Mina'a ourselves, ready for the mother of all fry-ups at dawn.'

'What if they discover the RHIBs?' asked Joe. 'Clock the fact they ain't any normal lifeboats? Disable them or remove them? What's the plan then?'

'Putting it bluntly, we can't let that happen,' Range replied. 'From the citadel there are live links to video cameras covering all parts of the ship. If we see anything like that happening, we bust out and put a stop to them. But frankly I think there's about as much chance of that happening as hell freezing over. The way we've disguised them, there's nothing about the RHIBs suggests they're anything other than the ship's lifeboats. Anything else?'

'What happens if there's a problem with the LPG release system?' The Kiwi asked. 'The whole reason we're doing this is to have the mother of all fry-ups, as you put it. The LPG trigger system is the one thing we know next to nothing about. What happens if we trigger it, and it malfunctions? It'd be a hell of pity to leave the job half done, and especially after the *Golden Achilles*.'

'Geneva's rigged the ship with a back-up system, a fail-safe,' Range replied. 'If necessary, the LPG release can be operated remotely from there. If we experience problems, they'll troubleshoot it from Geneva. Our priority is to get ourselves gone in good time before the ship blows. We need to put a good few miles between us and the coming blast, 'cause it's going to be a fucking monster.'

'Like a mini nuke going up,' The Kiwi remarked, evilly. 'All the more reason to be doubly sure we get to trigger the gas and burn them all to hell.'

'You got it.' Range eyed his men. 'Right, if that's it, get to your stations. The handover's scheduled for thirty minutes from now, at which time we need to be ready to take command and control of this ship.'

'On that note, dude, just who is in command of her?' Randy queried. 'I mean, for the short time we'll be sailing her into pirate waters?'

'O'Shea is captain of the ship,' Range replied. 'I'm overall team leader. Whatever O'Shea says in terms of the running of the ship – that goes. That's how we'll do it.'

'Just one more thing,' O'Shea added. Somewhere deep inside himself he still harboured misgivings about the savagery of the attack they were poised to launch. 'What happens *after* the explosion? You know, if someone goes to investigate? Any danger our fingerprints are gonna be all over this thing?'

Range frowned. 'Investigate? Who's going to investigate? A ship blows up in a Somali pirates' harbour. Who the hell's ever going to investigate? What – they're going to send in a team from the UN and get them kidnapped and ransomed? Come on, mate. You know what the world will think: good riddance to bad news.'

'Yeah,' muttered The Kiwi, 'what goes around comes around.'

Range felt strangely relaxed now that the final stage of the mission was underway. He perched on a bollard on the forward part of the MV *Endeavour*'s deck, his AK-74 cradled in his arms, eyes scanning the distant horizon. The die was cast. The handover with the *Endeavour*'s crew had taken place some three hours back, and it had gone like clockwork. He'd just had a call from O'Shea on the bridge, confirming that they'd entered into the heart of the piracy 'hot zone'.

With all the captured ships at their disposal – not to mention their growing financial clout – the pirates had been able to equip themselves with some state-of-the-art ship-tracking equipment: radar, IDF transponders (an electronic gizmo that supposedly identified ships as 'Friend' or 'Foe'), pin-point accurate GPS navigation systems, plus satphones to effect communications over long range and to call in reinforcements.

Range didn't doubt that they were on the pirates' radar already, and that the first wave of boats had been launched to intercept them. No doubt the pirates would be feeling like today was their lucky day, with a juicy little ship sailing directly into their clutches. Indeed, Range had been expecting the bad guys to have shown themselves for some time now.

They'd been steaming through pirate waters for a good two hours, and hadn't had a sniff of a pirate skiff. It was weird. But maybe they'd caught the pirates napping. It was mid-afternoon – the hottest part of the day – so maybe the pirates were having a nice little siesta. Either way, sooner or later the bad guys were going to steam their way over the horizon.

Range spoke into his Cougar: 'Range, bridge. What d'you see?'

'I see jack,' O'Shea replied. 'Nothing that might be a pirate boat in any direction.'

'What about the radar?'

'Nothing. There ain't another vessel sailin' this part of the ocean in any direction.'

'I guess they keep clear for good reason.'

'Yeah, I guess so,' O'Shea confirmed. 'We're three hours out from Al Mina'a. Standby.'

The MV *Endeavour* droned onwards through the heat of the afternoon. The dull red bluntness of her prow ploughed through the azure water, a school of dolphins jumping and playing in the spray thrown up by her progress. Normally Range would have been watching the dolphins riding the ship's bow wave.

But right now any thoughts of wildlife-watching, or of fishing for that matter, couldn't be further from his mind.

Chapter Twelve

'Got 'em!' O'Shea's cry over the Cougar brought Range to an instant focus. 'Bearing 0300 degrees, fast craft approaching off the starboard bow. She'll be with us in under four minutes.'

Range whipped up his binoculars and scanned the sea to the west of them. It was barely visible, but he could just make out a white flash of water on the shimmering horizon. The bow wave was of the classic shape thrown up by a V-hulled craft, one cutting through the water at high speed – in other words, a typical pirate vessel.

About bloody time, Range told himself.

'I see them,' he confirmed. 'How many boats?'

O'Shea would be tracking them on the ship's radar, which would mean he'd know exactly what kind of force they were dealing with here.

'Visual with one only,' O'Shea replied.

'Say again?' Range queried. 'Confirm one craft only.'

'Standby.' O'Shea would be double-checking boat numbers visually, and doing a sweep of the ocean with the ship's powerful binoculars, plus via the radar.

It didn't make any sense for the pirates to have sent just one skiff. Normally, they'd swarm a target with several fast-attack boats, hitting it from all directions to frustrate the ship's defenders. A force of six couldn't cover all points of a vessel like the MV *Endeavour*, and many ships targeted were far larger. Pirates gambled on one of their boats penetrating the ship's defences unseen, enabling them to pull alongside and get grappling hooks and ladders onto her gunwales – at which point they'd be onto her.

'Confirmed – one fast boat only,' O'Shea radioed. 'ETA 180 seconds.'

This was well weird. They had a pirate vessel bearing down on them fast and alone. If Range and his team *had* been intending to defend the MV *Endeavour*, they'd have no trouble repulsing such a lone attack. Maybe the rest of the pirates were working a half-day, he told himself, wryly. Or maybe the bloodbath that had resulted from the *Golden Achilles* hijacking had tempered their desire to get in amongst a ship such as theirs, one boasting armed defenders.

'Craft is displaying as "Friend" on the IDF scanner,' O'Shea radioed.

'Yeah, what pirates don't these days,' Range replied. 'The

crafty fuckers – they'll have lifted the IDF gizmo from one of the ships they've hijacked.'

'More 'n' likely,' O'Shea confirmed. 'ETA ninety. Coming up on the starboard bow.'

'Joe; Kiwi – remember; hold your fire,' Range grated over the Cougar. 'Let them get close enough to have a good look at the prize. Return fire only if they open up. Do not – repeat do not – do anything to frighten the fuckers away.'

'Got it.'

Range studied the boat more closely as it sped towards them. The two vessels were approaching each other pretty much head-on, and their combined speed had to be approaching 30 knots. It was a typical pirate skiff – a long, slender, wooden-hulled vessel, more normally used for inshore fishing. The hull was painted a dirty off-white, and the guys manning the craft squatted on the skiff's wooden-slatted floor, using whatever they could find to help cushion the ride.

Powered by a single outboard motor, she was nowhere near as fast as your average civilian RHIB, and totally out-classed by the ex-SEAL RHIBs they had lashed under the MV *Endeavour*'s tarpaulins. But in terms of what the pirates needed, she was perfect for an assault on a ship like the *Endeavour*. She could easily outpace an LPG carrier, and she would even give a cruise liner a good run for her money.

Range scanned the pirates' armaments. He counted a dozen figures squatted in the oncoming boat – each a typical, tall, rangy Somalian. Slung around the shoulders of each was an AK-47 – the older, but equally reliable and punchy model upon which the AK-74s that Range and his men were packing was based. But even with a dozen pirates ranged against them, in normal circumstances Range would have had no qualms taking this lot on.

Range and his men had a big, rock-steady fire platform to unleash from – the MV *Endeavour* – whereas the pirates were being thrown about like beans in a can. It was impossible to fire accurately from a small craft moving at speed, not unless you had some seriously well-engineered weapons mounts attached to the vessel – such as their RHIBs had.

A hand-held AK-47 fired from a speeding skiff was about as much use as an ashtray on a motorbike. Five hundred yards. Four hundred. The skiff was closing fast. Range felt the itch to open up on the speeding vessel and nail the bastards, but he forced himself to resist the urge to fire: there was a much bigger prize that they were playing for here.

Range was about to drop the binoculars he'd been using to scrutinise the craft, when he did a double-take. In the prow of the vessel he could have sworn he'd spotted a female – and not your bog-standard Somalian woman draped from head to toe in black. This one looked to be bareheaded, and with her hair tied back in a ponytail. Range could see it billowing out behind her in the wind. What the hell? Since when did Somalian pirates recruit women for their operations?

Range knew enough about the country to appreciate the status women had in that society. In terms of hierarchies, first came the men, then the boys, then the camels – with the women coming somewhere just above the dogs. Girls rarely, if ever, got educated; women had few, if any rights; and in the shariah courts run by Al Shabaab a man's word was worth four of any female. Wasn't it always thus in those hard-line Islamic fundamentalist regimes?

It was that kind of messed-up attitude – plus their hatred of the so-called 'infidel' – that had 'enabled' those who had so abused Isabelle and the hundreds like her, to do as they had done and to believe they had somehow committed no wrong. For an instant Range remembered Amir's sickening words at the hostage handover: *After what we have done to her, do you really think any of us would want to keep her?*

Range lifted his weapon and braced it against the ship's rail. He fixed the skiff in the assault rifle's stark iron sights and swept the boat from end to end, his mind imagining the bullets he longed to unleash tearing into the vessel's occupants. That was the thing with these kind of encounters: the pirates had to get to within spitting distance to be able to put down any accurate kind of fire. By contrast, the ship's defenders could rake a pirate vessel with deadly accurate fire from a good three hundred yards away.

At the sight of Range, plus The Kiwi and Joe with their weapons brought to bear, the pirate skiff slowed and vied away from the MV *Endeavour*'s flank. Range watched it do an about turn some three hundred yards distant, whereupon it seemed as if it had settled into a cruising speed to keep pace with the bigger ship, almost as if they were shadowing her progress. Maybe this was an advance party doing a recce? Now that they'd got a sense of the MV *Endeavour*'s defenders, perhaps they'd call in half a dozen further skiffs packed full of pirates?

Range watched through his iron gun-sights as the distinctive figure in the skiff's bow rose on one knee, and started waving something about in her hands. *What the hell were they up to now?* At this kind of distance Range couldn't tell exactly, but this wasn't like any kind of pirate tactics he had ever experienced before.

Where were the wild warning shots unleashed across the bows? The screams over the loud hailer demanding the ship be brought to a stop? Where was the tallest of the guys brandishing a grappling iron, as he prepared to swing it onto the MV *Endeavour*'s rails? Or the wiriest of pirates with his AK slung over his back, preparing to shin up the rope and vault over the side?

'Range. Bridge: what the fuck is happening?' he growled.

'Signal flags. She's signalling to us,' O'Shea replied. 'I'm decoding what they're saying.'

'Well don't trust a fucking word . . .'

'Trust me, buddy, I won't.'

Seconds dragged by during which O'Shea had to be reading the pirate's message, but since when had Somali pirates started using *signal flags*? It didn't make any sense.

In normal circumstances signal flags were used to communicate between vessels that had no other means of doing so – such as if there were language or technological barriers. Each flag corresponded to one letter of the alphabet, so whilst it was a painfully slow means of communication, it was simple and effective – at least between those who were still taught to read the archaic flag code. O'Shea, being a SEAL commander, had been.

His voice came up on the net. 'Signal reads: FRIENDLY. MOVE TO LINE ASTERN FOR ESCORT. What the hell d'you make of that?'

Range let out a snort of laughter. 'Since when did we ask for a *pirate escort*? What is this – like these guys are the good cops, and the bad guys are lurking over the horizon?'

'Fuck knows, buddy. Fuck knows. So whadda we do?'

'Search me.' Range shrugged. 'Move into line astern for escort, I guess.' He paused, as he tried to make sense of what was happening. 'Ask them where they're taking us.'

O'Shea signalled the pirate ship from the bridge: ESCORT TO WHERE?

The reply that came back was: AL MINA'A.

O'Shea relayed the message to Range. 'So whadda we do?' he asked again.

Range considered their options. There didn't appear to be any, other than to do as signalled. 'I guess we fall into line astern and let them lead us in.'

O'Shea signalled his confirmation of the pirates'

instructions, and the skiff pulled ahead. And it was in that formation that the two vessels began the last stage of their journey into whatever hell awaited them in The Harbour.

There seemed little point in Range remaining crouched over the ship's rail with weapon at the ready, for the pirates were doing nothing much to menace them. Leaving Joe and The Kiwi on guard with strict instructions not to open fire, lest they scare the pirates off, Range made his way across the deck and up the ship's ladders that gave access to the superstructure. At least the bridge had decent air-conditioning. It would be an oasis of shaded cool after the exposed, sun-blasted deck.

It would be somewhere to think, at least.

Range stepped inside. O'Shea gave him a look. 'What the hell is going on, buddy? Since when did Somali pirates—'

'Yeah, I know,' Range cut him off. 'Since when did Somali pirates use signal flags, and offer an escort into their harbour?'

'And who the hell is *the woman*?' O'Shea added. 'Sadie the freakin' Goat?'

'Sadie the what?'

'The Goat. Nineteenth-century pirate. Operated in the waters off New York. Famous for head-butting her victims – hence the name. We studied her in Navy SEAL class . . .'

Range threw up a hand to silence him. 'Whatever. The point is, mate, this is about the most benign form of piracy

184

I have ever encountered. So someone please tell me – what the fuck is happening?'

O'Shea shook his head in bewilderment. 'Buddy, I have absolutely no freakin' idea.'

'Randy?' Range prompted.

'Does it matter?' Randy replied, his voice cool and gravelly calm. 'They're takin' us where we need to go. No matter how we freakin' get there, every turn of the ship's screw gets us one bit closer to payback time.'

'Yeah, but doesn't it strike you as being just the slightest bit messed up?' Range grated. 'I mean, not exactly what we were expecting, is it?'

Randy's eyes met Range. 'Maybe, but remember, I spent a good deal of time with these kind of people. They rarely do what's expected of them. It's in their freakin' nature to act in ways we will never understand. Sometimes, you just gotta roll with the punches.'

'Any other ships in the vicinity?' Range asked O'Shea.

O'Shea ran his eye over the radar screen. 'Nothing. It's us, the vessel ahead of us and hundreds of miles of empty ocean. Go figure.'

Range spoke into his Cougar. 'Range, all stations. We've got one supposedly pirate skiff leading us – escorting us, so they claim – into Al Mina'a. At this kind of speed we'll be there in under an hour. Presumably this has to be some kind of a trap – some new kind of pirate strategy we've not heard of yet. Or maybe it's some kind of response to the

185

Golden Achilles bloodbath: Pirate Central has ordered all crew to tone down the bloodshed as much as possible.'

Range paused, mopping his brow. The air-con had cooled his sweat, making it stick to his exposed skin like a cold and clammy blanket.

'Whatever the truth, keep your eyes absolutely bloody peeled. We do not want to get tricked into a situation where we are vulnerable – where we can be rushed, or taken by surprise, and we can't make the citadel. So keep on high alert and with your weapons at the ready. If they do try to rush us, use all necessary force to buy every man the time to reach the citadel. Understood?'

There were a series of affirmatives.

That done, Range settled down with a pair of ship's binoculars to study the skiff that was racing through the seas some five hundred yards ahead of them. Through the more powerful lenses he could make it out in finer detail. The more he studied the pirate craft, the more he got the sense that the mysterious woman in the prow was somehow commanding the ship. You could tell it from her gestures, her stance and the cut of the figure she made.

It just didn't add up. Since when would a bunch of fundamentalist Somali pirate-terrorists let a women command their number?

Perhaps there was an infamous female Somali pirate no one from the outside world had heard of yet? Perhaps they were the first to make her acquaintance? Perhaps this was

Somalia's version of Sadie the Goat – only Imam the Cobra specialised in kicking her victims hard in the bollocks as her trademark means of attack? Something like that, anyway.

The two vessels ate up the miles. After forty minutes the low, slumbering outline of the coast hove into view. A pencil-thin brown line, it grew in substance until Range could make out the individual squat baobab trees that dotted the cliff-tops, and the rows of slender palm trees that marched down the white sand to the glittering shallows.

Paradise. From a distance it looked like any kind of tropical paradise. Only here in Somalia, this was the coast of hell. This was the skeleton coast of the Horn of Africa. This was where ships, and their passengers, came to die.

At first Range had been at a loss to see where exactly the pirate skiff was making for. But as the vessel drew in closer to the shoreline, he could make out the narrow break in the cliffs, one that hid what he guessed had to be a perfect natural harbour. And as they came in closer under the rocky crags, he could appreciate how these cliffs weren't quite as low-lying as he'd first imagined.

It was hard to judge distance at sea, and especially when all perspective seemed lost in a shimmering heat haze. The afternoon was drawing to a close, the golden orb of the sun sinking fast and red behind the cliffs to the west. On countless previous jobs across Africa, Range had noticed how the sun set in a headlong rush towards the horizon, one that seemed to last barely minutes.

Yet during his last visit to this benighted part of the world, he'd not even had the time to share one sunset with Isabelle, their time together had been so short. Range had nurtured plans to take her back to Africa, on a wildlife safari, most likely to Tanzania, a country that had been at peace ever since independence. In Ngorongoro Crater, Amboseli Game Reserve and Mount Kilimanjaro, that country possessed some of the most spectacular scenery and stunning wildlife that Range had ever seen.

He'd wanted to show her how Africa wasn't all bad, and how maybe her initial instincts to volunteer to help the people of this continent hadn't been entirely misguided. He'd wanted to help her lay her ghosts to rest. He'd figured that would have formed an essential part of the healing process, and it was the one area in which he was particularly well placed to help her.

But now, the only opportunity to slay the demons lay in revenge – and the ultimate revenge mission was just about to come to fruition. Revenge: it wasn't necessarily a noble motive, but it sure as hell felt like a good one right now.

Range glanced up at the cliff-tops that stood sentinel-like on either side of the entrance to the bay. This was more like it: this was what he'd been expecting at Piracy Central. He could see fortified gun-emplacements set atop the cliffs. He recognised the distinctive silhouette of 12.7mm

DshkA heavy machineguns, mounted on tripods and surrounded by sandbagged walls – their barrels poking out like hungry dinosaur necks as they menaced the sea below.

He pointed them out to O'Shea. 'When it's time to get the hell out of here, we'll need to make sure to avoid those.'

'Yeah. Sure thing. Dunno how, though. They got a superb vantage point, and pretty much 360-degree vision from up there. And the DshkA's got over a two-thousand-yard range.'

Range smiled, grimly. 'No one said it was going to be easy. We'll find a way.'

As the pirate skiff nosed through the harbour entrance, it slowed to a dead crawl. From the vantage point of the *Endeavour*'s bridge Range could see why. Before and beyond them opened out a natural amphitheatre, with only the narrowest of entranceways leading out to sea. It was maybe two thousand yards across, and the entire surface of the inlet was peppered with assorted craft and vessels.

Range noticed a raft of skiffs tied up together in a long line like dominoes, and stretching out from the harbour's edge into deeper water. In several of those craft he could see crews working away, seemingly stowing the vessel's kit after a day out on operations – and just about every one of those figures appeared to be armed.

As the *Endeavour* nosed further into the harbour, the gunmen manning those craft stopped what they were doing and stood to stare. The deception engineered by the lead skiff – if that's what it was – suddenly became much clearer:

Range and his fellow fighters would stand little chance against the forces occupying Al Mina'a.

'All stations – standby to make for the citadel,' Range spoke into his Cougar. 'If they attack, break fire immediately and head below. We can't hope to fight the numbers gathered here.'

There was a series of muttered affirmatives.

The six men aboard the MV *Endeavour* were starting to realise just what they'd got themselves into here. Even under the cover of the coming darkness, sneaking out of this place was going to be some challenge. As Range ran his eye across the steep cliffs that surrounded them, he picked out further gun emplacements that dotted the hillside. The place was a veritable Fort Knox, and breaking out of here was sure going to prove more challenging than cruising in had done.

To left and right were larger craft anchored in the deeper waters of the bay, but none appeared to be a particularly rich prize. There were several dhows – large, wooden-hulled cargo ships that regularly plied these seas. The dhow owners were mostly small-scale Arab traders, and they couldn't afford to hire dedicated security teams. As a result, they were forever falling prey to the pirates. Ransoms paid for dhow crew were pitifully small, and often they were simply left to rot – at least until the pirates got tired of them, and fed them to the sharks.

Then there were a couple of rusty tramp steamers – the

kind of vessels used by local shipping lines for transporting produce from the Horn of Africa to the Arab coast a short distance away, and back again. Once again, those constituted a less than lucrative ransom offering. The more he studied the harbour, the more Range realised that their vessel – the MV *Endeavour* – was the jewel in the crown for the pirates based here at Al Mina'a.

Though it was going to have one massive sting in its tail.

CHAPTER THIRTEEN

The skiff that had led their vessel in circled back towards them, its prow cutting a silver slash through the calm waters of the darkening bay. Range had rejoined The Kiwi and Joe down on the ship's rails. He wanted to give the impression of a private security team readying to defend their ship, but just as quickly realising what deep shit they'd sailed into here, and so heading below to safety.

The three men menaced the skiff with their AK-74s, but still it seemed to hang back as it circled the vessel, keeping just to the limit of the range of their weapons.

Then the woman in the prow did a repeat performance with the signal flags. O'Shea relayed the message: ANCHOR. WILL RETURN MORNING.

Range glanced at the other pirate crews. They had pretty much finished stowing their skiffs by now. Men were shouldering their weapons plus cargo, and making their way into the streets of the town that clustered around the bay. 'Town' was a somewhat grandiose name for the settlement that made up Al Mina'a: Rows of tightly packed mud-walled buildings formed narrow, winding streets little wider than alleyways, ones that twisted and turned in a chaotic rabbit warren of human habitation running up the hillside.

Everywhere he looked Range could imagine Isabelle incarcerated in one of those mud-walled hovels – this being the location where she was held for months, as her captors tortured, abused and insulted her. Again, he felt the rage burning through his veins and the almost irresistible urge to unleash his weapon on those responsible. But his AK-74 could do little damage compared to a hundred thousand cubic metres of LPG going up in a massive, searing fireball.

The skiff that had led them here motored off to dock with the row of similar vessels. As it did, Range reflected upon the nature of this new message: 'Anchor. Will return morning.' Again, it was hardly what he had expected. 'Surrender your ship or we will sink her'; 'Throw down your weapons or we kill you': those kind of sentiments would have been more fitting.

What was the point of their maintaining any nice-cop routine, now that the *Endeavour* had sailed into the heart of Al Mina'a, and was under the pirates' very guns? Not for the first time in the past few hours Range found himself wrestling with the odd, unsettling feeling that all wasn't quite right here.

He didn't see how any alternative scenarios could make even the slightest sense – but for sure there was a different way to read all that had happened. What if the 'pirate skiff' wasn't carrying any pirates at all: what if it was simply a group of Somali men led by a mystery woman, guiding them into some kind of safe harbour?

That scenario – as unlikely as it might seem – would fit the events of the last few hours as nicely as the alternative – that they had been 'tricked' into sailing into the pirates' clutches. Range couldn't for the life of him imagine why any Somalis would seek to guide them into some kind of a sanctuary, or even that such a safe-harbour existed in this part of the world. Yet still he felt dogged by uncertainty, and the suspicion that all might not be as it seemed.

The Kiwi joined him at the ship's rail. He nodded in the direction of the skiff, as it dwindled into the shadows. 'Odd. Weird beyond measure. You'd almost think they were tucking us up for the night in a place of peace and safety.'

Range eyed him. 'Why d'you say that?'

'Think about it. No one has fired a single shot at us. No one has so much as attempted to board our ship. No one has even so much as threatened us. All they keep doing is signalling: FRIENDLY. And what d'you make of the woman captaining the skiff? Since when did Somali pirates ever let a woman lead them?'

Range shrugged. 'So where the hell else are we, if we're not in Piracy Central?'

The Kiwi eyed the town high above them. 'You see that? That mosque-like building. Looks like a cross between a mosque and an ancient castle, right? I reckon it's been built over the remains of an early church. I read up on Al Mina'a before we set sail. There was no mention of a historic structure like that, and look at it – it dominates the town. Surely there would have been . . . ? And another thing; Al Mina'a was described as an enclosed inlet some five kilometres across. This one is no more than two klicks from shore to shore, if that.'

'So what're you saying?' Range pressed.

'I'm saying it doesn't add up. I'm saying I want to get those pirate fuckers as much as you do, mate, but I got a horrible feeling we've somehow ended up in a place that ain't . . . right. And if this isn't Pirate Central, no way should we unleash the LPG . . .'

'Tell that to the survivors of the *Golden* fucking *Achilles*,' Range cut in.

He didn't know quite where the anger was coming from. Maybe it was all the accumulated tension and stress of the last few weeks boiling over. Maybe it was in part the hangover from the Sarin attack. He'd sweated out a lot of the nerve toxins during the days spent on the ship, but he knew he wasn't quite fully recovered yet.

The Kiwi's cat-green eyes met those of Range. There was something of a cobra menacing its prey about them. Of all the men in his team Range often thought he'd least like to go up against The Kiwi. The Kiwi was a loner and a hard man to befriend. He was also lightning fast at unarmed combat and he feared no man. Range himself had never been known to back down from a fight, but he'd rather have The Kiwi on his side, for he'd make a fearsome adversary.

'Range, I got to say it,' The Kiwi remarked, quietly. 'You let this Isabelle shit get to you too much, it'll cloud your judgment, and you can't afford to let that happen, not at a time like this. I reckon all may not be as it seems here: the others will be sharing the same concerns. There's not a man on your team who's stupid, Range, not even Tiny, and everyone likes to give him shit.'

Range ran his hands across his face, exhaustedly. 'Yeah, maybe you're right. Maybe I am letting this revenge thing get to me. But what d'you suggest? Time's ticking: zero hour for the LPG to get triggered is 0800 tomorrow morning.'

'Call Geneva,' said The Kiwi. 'I've never met Mr de Saint-Sébastien, but by all accounts – from what O'Shea says – he plays it straight. Sure, he's angry as hell at losing his daughter. Who wouldn't be? But would he want to hit the wrong place and fry a load of innocents? Call him, and get him to double-check the GPS coordinates. O'Shea sailed this ship into a pre-planned destination. Get that destination checked. I can't believe Geneva would have keyed in the wrong grid, but get it checked, just so we're all in the clear on this one.'

'Okay. Keep a close watch. I'll be up on the bridge on the satphone.'

Range strode across the deck, the dusk light shading the steel hatches into dark purples and greys. Come 0800 those hatches would slide open and the LPG would start to pour forth, in preparation for the mother of all explosions. *Surely, they had to be at the target?* He climbed the ladder, his footfalls on the iron rungs ringing in his ears. Range didn't for one moment believe they were anywhere other than at Al Mina'a, but just presuming for one instant they weren't, then where in God's name were they?

'I've got to use the satphone,' he announced, as he entered the bridge. 'The Kiwi figures something's not right about this place: no gunshots, no pirates boarding the ship, us lot left free to occupy her. He figures we need to double check with Geneva that we're in the right place.'

'Ever since taking control of the ship we've been on auto-pilot,' O'Shea remarked, 'and following a GPS bearing for Al Mina'a. You can check yourself, buddy. We're bang on the location where the GPS was taking us.'

Range shrugged. 'I know. I know that. But doesn't something strike you as not quite right here?'

'Sure it does. It's well weird. But a GPS never lies. And like Randy says, he's lived with these kind of people, and the one thing you should always expect is for them to do the unexpected.'

'Where is Randy, anyway?' Range asked.

O'Shea jerked a thumb over his shoulder. 'He went to use the satphone. He's over there in the office room. Said he wanted to talk in private.'

'You dropped anchor?' Range queried, as he made his way across the bridge.

'I'm on it,' O'Shea confirmed.

At the rear of the bridge was a small office. Range reached to open the door, but something stopped him. From inside he could hear the low rumble of Randy's voice – but he was speaking in the distinctive, guttural tones of Arabic. Range froze. He'd simply presumed that Randy had to be speaking to his loved ones – his family back in the States. Who the fuck was he talking to from the MV *Endeavour*'s bridge *in Arabic*?

For a few seconds Range listened to the ebb and flow of the conversation. Then he thumped open the door and barged in. Randy glanced up, his eyes wide with surprise. Range heard him utter a few last words, before he cut the line.

A tense and heavy silence fell between them. The two men stared at each other, as each tried to predict what would be the other's first move.

'Tell me this isn't what I think it is,' Range grated. His voice was low and it resonated with menace.

'What d'you think it is, dude?' Randy's words were suffused with a strange calm, and it infuriated Range.

'Don't fucking dude me!' he exploded. 'Who the fuck is

Joe Frank Reiner, ex-US Navy SEAL and presently Blackstone Six operative, talking to in Arabic on the ship's fucking satphone?'

Randy raised one eyebrow, coolly. 'You figure I'm consorting with the enemy, is that it?'

'Convince me otherwise,' Range snarled.

'Okay, you gonna hear me out, or you just gonna keep fucking with my shit?'

'Try me. But best be quick, before whoever you were calling shins up the fucking anchor chain and slits our throats.'

Randy shook his head, his anger starting to show now. 'Just like they do in the movies, eh? Buddy, you been watching too much James Bond . . .'

Range took three quick strides towards the big, rangy American. Randy dropped into a classic Krav Maga stance, his balance light on his feet, his arms up and ready to defend or to strike. Range thrust out his hand: 'Give. Me. The. Satphone. It's got last number redial. You good for me to make the call?'

'Sure. No worries. But first, you fucker, you hear me out!' The last words were practically spat into Range's face. 'It's long overdue we talked . . . You ordered me left behind in Libya. You left me for dead. I survived. I came through all that, and here I am with my brothers taking the fight back to those fuckers who tried to break me. And how do you deal with that – you and your fucking sidekick, The Kiwi?

You've never once trusted me from the day you broke me free.'

'And you fucking blame us! I just caught you on the sat-phone speaking in Arabic . . .'

'Yeah, and you want to know who to? To the fucking woman who saved my life, that's who! And you know why? Because she fuckin' bore me a kid, that's why! Man, she nursed me back to health over eight fuckin' months. And at the end of that she wasn't just my *doctor*. She was my "wife" out there. Every AQIM operator had one. I ain't making no excuses. I didn't do it only for the cover. But you wanna know who was I fuckin' speaking to just now? Answer: I was speakin' to my other wife and my one-year-old fuckin' kid. My son.'

Randy took a step closer. He rammed the satphone into Range's stomach. 'There you go, *dude*. Do your last number redial. Call her up, asshole. Give her shit in that big fuckin' macho way of yours. Be my guest, if it makes you happy.'

Range sensed a figure appear in the doorway. It was O'Shea. 'Guys, I heard the most of that . . .'

Randy stormed past the two of them, cutting O'Shea short. He thundered down the ship's ladder and out onto open deck. He needed to have some time alone, to see the stars and to get some air.

Range went to follow, but O'Shea stopped him. 'Randy's already told me about his Libyan wife and kid. I didn't know that's who he was calling, but it's the truth. You gotta cut the guy some slack.'

Range stared in silence at O'Shea for several seconds, then took the satphone and headed out onto one of the open wings of the bridge. He needed some fucking space too.

A part of him was feeling guilty about what had just happened, but he didn't see why the hell he should be. Sure, there was a part of Range that did still suspect Randy, but he'd be a fool not to. Range wasn't like O'Shea. He didn't automatically believe in someone, just because they were a member of the Special Forces brotherhood. He trusted someone when they'd proven they could be trusted.

More than likely Randy *had* been speaking to this mystery Libyan doctor, and now wife and mother of his kid. But it was appalling operational security to have made such a call. They were supposed to be on strict comms silence, unless absolutely necessary. And what had necessitated Randy's call to his 'other wife' right now, at this moment, Range couldn't bloody imagine.

The satphone was a completely insecure means of comms. Who knew what equipment the pirates might be using to monitor such calls? They had seized a shedload of kit off pirated vessels, plus they had the money to buy the best. They could be deploying sophisticated signal intercept equipment for all he knew. It was best – it was crucial – to keep comms to an absolute minimum in such circumstances. Range told himself he had no reason to feel the slightest bit guilty. Randy was out of line. Period.

He shrugged it off and proceeded to dial the Geneva number. He had more important shit to be dealing with right now. On the second ring a voice answered. It was Pierre, and Range asked to be put through directly to Isabelle's father.

'Mr Range, I trust all is well?' Mr de Saint-Sébastien's voice rang out clear and strong over the echoing connection.

'Pretty much, sir, yes.' As he spoke he was aware that someone might be listening, and of the need to be circumspect. 'We're at the intended destination. Or at least we think we are. But aspects of it are a little . . . untypical, sir, if you get my drift. Can you double-check on your systems that we're here – here when we need to be, I mean.'

'Of course. One minute.' Range could hear some muttered conferring in the background, presumably as Pierre and the old man double-checked. 'Yes. I can confirm we have you visual on several of our systems. You are exactly where you are supposed to be – in Al Mina'a.'

'You sure of that, sir?' Range queried.

'Absolutely. I am as certain of this as I ever have been about anything, Mr Range.'

Range didn't know what else there was to say. 'In that case, sir, we'll proceed with the time and actions as planned.'

'Excellent, Mr Range. And remember, if there are any problems operating from your end, call me. We can switch to the master system of control that will enable things from here.'

'Understood, sir. Best to keep this short.'

Range cut the line. For a long moment he stared at the handset, his mind lost in thought. What was the phrase Isabelle's father had used: *as certain as I ever have been about anything*. It was an odd choice of phrase. Almost deliberately overstated. Still, English wasn't the old man's first language, so maybe that accounted for the peculiar choice of words.

He wandered back into the bridge. 'The old man's just confirmed it, we're here all right. You've double-checked the ship's nav-systems?'

O'Shea nodded. 'I have. We're here. This is Al Mina'a.'

Range checked his watch. It was eight hours until zero hour – when they'd trigger the LPG to start pumping. The natural walls of the harbour would corral the gas, and the early morning breeze blowing off the sea would sweep it into the town. When the detonation charge triggered, the entire place should go up like one giant volcano. And by that time, Range and his men had to be a long way away from there.

Range figured they could each afford to catch a few hours' sleep. They'd set a rolling watch, three-on and three-off, until 0600 hours. They'd need a good amount of time to get the RHIBs loaded and ready for dropping into the sea, plus he still needed to work out how they were going to bug out of there and not get hit by the pirates' gun emplacements.

Maybe they could sneak past with the engines on silent

electronic mode. Maybe they should race past at pushing fifty knots, weaving the RHIBs from side to side to make themselves a difficult target. It would take an excellent gunner to hit a small vessel moving at the equivalent of nearly seventy mph, and zigzagging across the sea. He'd speak to O'Shea about it.

Their ex-SEAL commander would be sure to know the best option for such an escape.

CHAPTER FOURTEEN

The night hours passed quickly enough. Al Mina'a proved
quiet, the waters of the harbour largely devoid of life. Those
on watch had little to look out for, and those asleep had
little to disturb their dreams. By 0700 the men were gathered on the deck, with their preparations well in hand.

Range gave a short, terse briefing, in which he explained
the plan of attack and of escape. Once the gas-release was
triggered, they'd drop the RHIBs from their cradles and load
up three men to each. With O'Shea driving one and Randy
the other, they'd power out of there at full speed. By the time
those manning the gun emplacements had woken up to the
fact of their escape, they'd be motoring through the seas at
over fifty knots, offering a very hard target.

It wasn't a perfect plan of escape, but the men had rarely
come across one that was. Risk came with the territory.

There was little to do now but watch and wait. Sunrise was at around 0700 in this part of the world, there being little, if any, change with the seasons this close to the Equator. The towering cliffs would keep the harbour in shadow for a good hour or more. Range had brought the LPG trigger time forwards to 0745, sooner if a steady on shore wind blew up earlier. He wanted them out of there as soon as possible, so they could make maximum use of the darkness to mask their escape.

It was 0715 when he felt the first stirring of a breeze. As the sky to the east above the cliff tops lightened with the first rays of dawn, just the faintest breath of wind drifted in through the neck of the harbour. It carried with it the smell of the sea, and a vague suggestion of hot, burning sands and exotic spices. Range sniffed the air. Some two hundred kilometres to the east was the Arab mainland, and the wind blowing off the ocean carried some of the essence of those lands with it.

Range felt the tension building inside him as the breeze started to stiffen. He saw the faintest ruffle flitter across the calm surface of the bay, as a more powerful gust swept in off the open sea. It was almost time. Up above him, O'Shea was at the ship's wheel – the captain remaining on station until the last minute of his doomed ship. When the LPG went up the MV *Endeavour* would be torn asunder, and little would ever be found of the vessel – not that anyone was likely to go looking.

Below him in the citadel lurked the trigger device. Range figured it was only right that he had taken responsibility for operating the mechanism via which the ship's hatches would be set to slide open, and the valves of the LPG tanks set to fully open. They would remain like that for a full thirty minutes, before a massive charge of PE4 – a powerful plastic explosive – would detonate in the bowels of the ship, which would by then be awash with the gas, as would the entire bay.

And at that moment: *kaboom*.

Range knew that in some peoples' eyes what he was about to do was of questionable morality. He'd heard O'Shea's original protestations about the women and children here in Al Mina'a. There was a small part of him that felt over-burdened with the enormity of what was coming. What was the population of Al Mina'a, he wondered? One thousand? Five thousand? Maybe more? The way they packed families into the buildings here – they were heaped up on each other row upon row – it was impossible to tell.

Range had spent a good deal of his time as a private warrior on jobs all across the African continent. Over time he'd warmed to the lawless, freewheeling familiarity he'd experienced with many of the people here. More than anything he liked the way the locals so often got the British sense of humour. He'd gone fishing with a rebel leader on the Sudanese Nile and they'd laughed their rocks off when a local had paddled over in a canoe and offered them a hippo's leg for sale – *for dinner*. He'd trained the Presidential bodyguard of a West African nation, and one of the guys had forever been texting on his mobile phone. To teach him a lesson Range had confiscated the phone, and put it at the target end of the range. Everyone had been falling about with laughter, as they shot seven bales of shit out of that cell phone.

No doubt about it he'd had some good times in Africa, and murdering several thousand villagers didn't exactly sit easy with him. But the people of Al Mina'a had chosen their role in life: they were pirates, ransom negotiators, or those who lived off the ill-gotten gains of the brutal business of piracy, kidnap and ransom. They preyed on their innocent victims – most recently, the men, women and children on the *Golden Achilles* – and that made them fair game in Range's view. And that meant he wasn't overly disturbed about embracing his chosen role in life right now – *that of the avenger*.

He was torn away from his thoughts by a squelch of static in his Cougar earpiece: 'Skiff approaching. Port bow. Same crew as before.'

Fuck. Range glanced at his watch: 0720. What the hell were they doing out on the water at this time? He strode down the length of the ship, joining The Kiwi on its bow. There before them was the pirate skiff, motoring across the calm bay towards the *Endeavour*. Range eyed it warily for a long second: he counted a full crew in the boat, plus Somalia's only bloody female pirate standing at the bow.

This changed everything.

'Joe, Tiny, Tak, Kiwi – keep the fuckers well away,' Range snarled into his Cougar. 'O'Shea – remain on the bridge. Randy, get down into the citadel and prepare to trigger the LPG. It's your baby now. I got to stay here now we got a pirate craft in bound. O'Shea, I'll radio through the trigger order when we're good to go. Relay it to Randy via the ship's phone, in case he's got no radio signal down there.'

'Got it.'

For a split second Range wondered why he'd given Randy the role of triggering the gas. He'd done so instinctively. He had to remain on deck now, from where he could properly command his men – and especially if the bullets were about to fly. *But why had he chosen Randy?* He figured when the shit hit the fan, maybe he did trust the bloke after all. He wouldn't have done this otherwise. And maybe in his heart he figured Randy deserve to be the trigger guy, after all that AQIM had done to him.

The skiff kept coming. She was powering across the water. It was somehow ominous, as if the boat's occupants were on some seriously time-critical business. For an instant Range's mind flipped back to the bridge of the previous evening, and to Randy's Arabic satphone call. But there was no way that he could countenance that Randy might have somehow double-crossed them by calling through a warning. *No way.*

The skiff was 250 yards out when Range unleashed the

first shot. As soon as he'd seen the boat coming, he'd grabbed his silencer and screwed it onto the weapon, signalling for the others to do likewise. The last thing he wanted was gunshots ringing out across the bay and alerting the rest of the pirates to what was happening. The single shot was all but noiseless – *pzzzt* – but the plume of water it kicked up at the skiff's bow still had the desired effect.

The boat slowed dramatically and pulled around until it was barely drifting in the water. The figure at the prow reached down for something. Range cursed: not another bloody session with the signal flags. *We do not have time for this.* If she tried that he'd put a burst of bullets into the water beside the craft, to get them to back the hell away.

She straightened up and a voice rang out across the harbour. 'Cease your goddamn fire! And put away your goddamn guns!'

Range and The Kiwi stared at each other in utter bewilderment. The woman was using a loud hailer, her amplified voice carrying clearly to them across the still water. But it wasn't that which had shocked them. She was speaking in a thick American accent, such as a New Yorker would use. She sounded pissed as hell, and all in all it was the last thing either of them had ever been expecting.

'And while you're at it, throw down a goddamn ladder so I can come aboard!' the woman yelled.

'Who. The fuck. Is that?' Range grated.

The Kiwi shook his head. 'Mate, I have no fucking idea.'

'You gonna answer me or what?' the voice rang out across the stillness. 'You speak goddamn English?'

'Who. The hell. Are you?' Range bawled back at her, trying to regain some of the initiative.

'Either you throw down a goddamn ladder,' she yelled, 'or I'll get Yassir here to throw a rope up to you, and I'll goddamn board ya anyway. Hell, what does a woman have to do around here?'

'Turn your boat around and back the hell off,' Range countered. 'We're—'

'Now just a goddamn minute,' the loud hailer cut in. 'I am comin' aboard whether you like it or not, so you either throw down a ladder, or you step aside as Yassir here throws a line on to your bows.'

Range saw the woman issue a few curt orders to the crew at her back, and the boat started up again. It accelerated forward, each turn of the screw bringing it closer still. Either Range fired again, in an effort to stop them, or they were going to have that mystery woman trying to clamber around their ship. Range felt his finger tighten around the trigger, but something stopped him from opening fire.

The last thing they needed right now was a full-on firefight with this lot. But more than anything it was the pure burning curiosity of what the hell was going on here that had made him hold his fire.

'You listen here, big man,' the figure yelled, 'you get your weapon down! I got some vital intelligence I gotta pass across to ya. And trust me, when you hear it you'll thank me ten times over.'

Range cursed under his breath. 'Joe, drop the stupid cow a ladder. But she's got five minutes, no more. After that, we throw her to the sharks.'

There was a faint, hollow thunk as the wooden prow of the skiff made contact with the steel flank of the MV *Endeavour*. A few seconds later the mystery woman appeared, clambering over the ship's rail. She jumped onto the deck, brushed herself down and stood to face the four men who were there to receive her. The first impression Range got was of Imam, the supermodel, but without the wrinkles. But there was a real sharp intensity and anger burning in her wide, smoky eyes.

'What the hell you lot starin' at?' she demanded, fiercely. 'Never seen a woman before? Gawd, how long you guys been at sea?!'

The four of them stared at her in silence. She swung her eyes onto Range. 'You the big guy, huh? You gonna apologise for almost blowing my ass out of the water? Well, are ya?'

'The seas around here are dangerous,' Range grated. 'Sometimes, you got to shoot first and ask questions later.'

The woman snorted. 'They sure are dangerous with the likes of you around! Yeah, and the way you kept threatenin' us yesterday, we figured you took us for a goddamn bunch of Somali pirates.'

Range fixed her with a look. 'You were – *are* – a bunch of goddamn Somali pirates.'

The woman threw back her head and laughed. 'Do I sound like a freakin' Somali? Do I look like a goddamn pirate?'

Range didn't so much as smile. 'You don't. Funnily enough, you sound like some brass-neck New Yorker. So, mind telling me what the fuck is going on here?'

'Well, first off, Mr Big Man, *this ain't Somalia*,' the woman cut in. 'Second off, we don't do piracy. We're more of the guide-you-into-a-safe-port-and-save-your-sorry-asses sort of people. But whoa, hey, who're we to expect any thanks.'

Range stared at her in silence for several long seconds. *Just what the hell was going on here?*

'You sound like a goddamn Brit,' the woman added. 'Where is your oh-so-famous English hospitality. Cup of tea, ma'am? Served in Her Majesty's finest china, ma'am?'

'The refreshments come later,' Range rasped. 'There's a bit of confusion we've got to clear up first . . . So, if this isn't Somalia, where the fuck are we?'

The woman arched one eyebrow. 'How cool is that – a bunch of sailors don't know where they're sailing to . . . It's like this. Yesterday you steamed onto our radar screen, moving fast and making right for this place, by the looks of things – for Al Mina'a. We sailed out to warn you that the waters around here can be a shitty kind of a place to be, and to guide you in—'

'So we *are* in Al Mina'a?' Range cut in.

'Your Arabic's goddamn atrocious . . . But yeah, you are in Al Mina'a – a port in southern Puntland.'

She glanced around at the expressions on the faces of Range and his men. 'You never heard of Puntland? Okay, here goes . . . Puntland is an autonomous region that covers the north-east of Somalia, closely allied to the semi-independent and neighbouring region of Somaliland. For those of you who don't do big words, we're a sovereign nation in everything but name. We got our own government, own parliament, own flag, own army, own navy, own police force. And we try to have as little to do with our anarchic and bloodthirsty Southern neighbour, *Somalia*, as is humanly possible.'

She glanced around at Range and his men. 'You got it? And just so there's no confusion here, the people of Puntland do not do goddamn piracy.'

Range jabbed a thumb in the direction of the gun emplacements atop the cliffs. 'What about those?'

'Defences. With neighbours like the Somalians, you'd want 'em. Sometimes they try to come this far north, to raid us. We learned to meet fire with fire.'

'We were making for Al Mina'a, *in Somalia*,' Range grated.

'Right name, wrong country,' she fired back at him. 'There is an Al Mina'a in Somalia, you got that much right. But you really don't wanna go there. Oh no, those guys would eat you alive – 'cause that place is goddamn pirate central.'

214

'So where exactly is the Somalian Al Mina'a compared to here?'

She jerked a thumb south. ''Bout a hundred miles that way, as the crow flies. But like I said, you *really* do not want to be goin' there.'

Range cursed under his breath. He glanced at The Kiwi. 'Hold her here a minute. I got to make a call.'

'No one holds me anywhere,' the woman countered, her eyes flashing angrily.

Range snapped his AK-74 into the aim, its barrel pointed at her head. 'Listen, we are not fucking around here. You will do exactly what you're told, unless you want a bullet in the head.'

He turned on his heel and was gone. For a second she went to try to follow, but The Kiwi blocked her way. She was about to protest, but one glance into his cold gaze was enough to stop her. 'Ma'am, you'd best do as the boss man says.'

Range took the iron rungs of the ship's ladder in leaps and bounds. He had absolutely no idea what was going on any more. As he raced towards the bridge, he could feel the confusion and the anger boiling in his guts and cooking up a storm. He sensed the cool wind blowing steadily off the sea now. These were the ideal conditions in which to release the LPG, yet he had never felt less certain about doing so.

He reached the bridge and made a grab for the satphone. 'Don't even ask,' he snapped at O'Shea.

He dialled the number for Geneva. A voice answered on

the second ring. Once again, Pierre passed Range across to the old man, and then his distinctive voice came on the line.

'Mr Range, I trust all is going to plan? You are very near the time we set as zero hour.'

'Yes, sir. But not exactly, sir, no. You see, we appear to be in bloody Puntland, not Somalia, and whilst the harbour here is called Al Mina'a, it isn't the pirate stronghold—'

'And how exactly do you know this, Mr Range?' the old man cut in.

'There's this woman. She sounds like an American, looks like . . . Well, bugger what she looks like – she claims that there are two Al Mina'as – or ports called The Harbour. There's the one in Somalia, which is what we're after, and then there's the one here, which if what she's telling me is right is clearly not our target. Sir, I can't see us triggering anything at our present location. But we got a major round trip if we're going to relocate to the right location . . . Sir?'

Range realised the satphone had gone silent. He figured the connection must have been lost. It did happen sometimes over long distances, and under certain atmospheric conditions. He redialled the number. It rang and rang, but there was no answer. He checked the number and dialled it for a third time. But again, it rang out without being answered.

He was burning up with frustration. Right now he had no idea just how much of what he'd been saying the old man had heard, before the communications went down.

He turned to O'Shea. 'Lost the connection. Can't seem to get it up again.'

'Buddy, that is one weird coincidence,' O'Shea replied, 'cause by the looks of things I have just lost control of my ship.'

Range strode across to where O'Shea was hunched over the ship's control panel. 'Like how?'

O'Shea pointed to the computer-like screen on which all the ship's vital functions were displayed. Range read the words that had appeared there.

PRIVILEGED ACCESS.
CONSOLE CONTROL MODE – REMOTE.
ENTER CODE TO RESUME CONTROL FROM SHIP'S BRIDGE.

Range flicked his eyes across to O'Shea. 'Code? What bloody code?'

O'Shea shook his head. 'That's just it – there isn't one. Not one that I've been given, anyway.'

'Kolokov didn't say anything . . .'

'Not a fuckin' word.'

At that moment an alarm started to sound on the bridge, and Range could see a red icon flashing on the console. A sentence flashed onto the screen.

SHIP'S HATCHES OPENING.

Range leaned forward, so he could see down onto the ship's deck. The seal on the nearest of the hatches that closed off the ship's hold cracked open a fraction. As the alarm continued to bleep, the massive steel door began to roll backwards, gradually revealing the shadowed bowls of the vessel and the fat cylinders of gas that sat within, plus the massive charge of C4 plastic explosives that was primed to blow the LPG sky high.

Range turned to O'Shea. 'He's taken control from Geneva! He's going to get the LPG to blow! We've got to launch the fucking RHIBs!'

O'Shea shook his head again. 'The lifeboats're triggered via the ship's console, and the RHIBs are rigged up to the same system. We're locked out!'

Range let out a string of curses. 'What about a manual override? It's a lifeboat release, right? There's got to be a manual override.'

O'Shea stared at him for an instant, then spun around and was gone. As he thundered down the steps the American was yelling into his Cougar, getting Joe to go check on the RHIB on the starboard bow, whilst he did that on the port. There had to be a person-operated mechanical system that acted as a back-up release. *There had to be.*

Range spoke into his Cougar, his voiced laced with urgency: 'All stations – Geneva has taken control of the ship. The gas is gonna start pumping any second now . . .

Get everyone into the RHIBs. Tak – head for the citadel and get Randy. Every second counts, so get moving, but do not – repeat do not – leave without your grab bags. And Kiwi – take the woman with us. I have no idea what the fuck is going on here, but I have a feeling she may just prove to be our witness and our alibi.'

As he finished speaking there was a hollow thwack and a geyser of water spurted up on the port side of the bridge. Result! O'Shea must have located the emergency release, and the first boat was in the water. Seconds later a fountain of spray erupted on the starboard side, as boat two hit the sea.

'Boats in,' O'Shea announced.

Grabbing a pair of the ship's binoculars and the satphone, Range thundered down the ladders. He had a plan forming in his head now. But it was one born out of sheer bloody desperation . . .

Plus the growing sense that somehow, he and his men had just suffered the mother of all betrayals.

CHAPTER FIFTEEN

Range used both hands to flick the seawater out of his eyes and hair. His clothes were dripping wet and the RHIB was awash with several inches of water from where it had dropped from the ship. Not that it was any threat to the craft – they were pretty much unsinkable. Range had been the last to jump, and he'd been the last man they'd hauled aboard the boat.

As O'Shea worked to get her engines started, The Kiwi was busy un-sheeting the weapons, and slamming a round into the breech of the .50-cal, plus a stubby grenade into the 40mm launcher. *It was always good to be ready.*

Range was painfully aware how he was making this up as he went along now. He was more than winging it. If the plan that was forming in his head worked, they might just live to fight another day. If not, at least one boatload of B6 operators would end up very, very dead.

He glanced across at the woman. She was staring at him, a look like bloody murder in her eyes. True to his nature, The Kiwi hadn't messed around. He'd bound her wrists and ankles with plasticuffs, just as soon as he'd got her into the RHIB.

'So, who're the goddamn pirates now . . . ?' she spat.

'Shut it,' Range snapped. 'You listen to me and you listen good. Your beloved Al Mina'a is about to get bathed in fire and blood – that's unless you do exactly as I say.' He jerked a thumb at the ship. 'See that. It's a Liquid Petroleum Gas tanker. And you smell that?' He sniffed the air. 'Smells like rotten eggs. That's the gas gushing out of her tanks. Luckily, we're upwind. But your crew at the bow – they're not. They stay where they are, they'll die of suffocation.'

Being heavier than air, LPG displaces oxygen as it spreads – hence the death by suffocation that comes with the cloud of gas, at least prior to its being ignited. Range figured it'd take twenty minutes for the gas to be blown across the bay and into Al Mina'a town itself. They had to do what he was planning in less than half that time, or a lot of people – his men included – would die.

'Tell your crew to head for shore,' Range told the woman. 'Get them to spread the word. Keep everyone – *everyone* – back from the water. Get the townspeople up onto the high ground – the higher the better. And get everyone into cover. They do that they may just live. Anyone does otherwise, they're dead.'

'And why should I listen to a goddamn . . .' She cursed. 'You just triggered . . .'

Range's look was enough to silence her. 'You don't have to *like* us to believe what I'm saying. *Smell the gas*. If you don't do what I'm telling you to do everyone will die. It's your call.' He gestured to the loud hailer that was slung on the belt at her waist. 'If that thing still works, I suggest you use it.'

He turned to O'Shea, at the boat's wheel. 'Ready?'

O'Shea gave a grim thumbs up. 'Good to go. But—'

'Yeah, I'm working on a fucking Plan B,' Range snapped. 'Take us out as far as we need to be safe from the blast. Full speed. I'll brief you when we get there.' He jabbed a finger at the woman's loud hailer. 'Use it, 'cause we're about to get underway.'

Her lips tight with anger the woman raised the megaphone. She called out a few sentences in Arabic. There was a yell of reply from the direction of the skiff, and then Range heard the engine fire up. He caught the driver blipping the throttle, as he powered the craft away from the MV *Endeavour*.

Range spoke into his Cougar. 'I've sent the skiff to shore. You see them trying to mess with us in any way, you blow them out of the water. We got bigger fish to fry here. Boat Two – on us.'

He could hear the twin diesel inboards throbbing throatily, ripples of raw power vibrating through the boat's hull beneath him. He flicked his eyes across to the woman. 'Best you hold on.' He nodded at O'Shea. 'Let's go.'

O'Shea rammed forward the RHIB's twin throttles. The roar of the engines rose to a screaming howl, like a flight of jet aircraft were tearing overhead, and the boat seemed to take off. One moment she was flat on the water, the next the bow had risen, the stern plummeted as the propellers dug in, and the craft was flying across the surface of The Harbour, throwing out a wall of white spray behind her.

The sheer brute power of the thing had taken even Range by surprise. One moment they'd been bobbing on the still surface of the harbour: the next, they were tearing across it like a rocket, O'Shea ramping the RHIB into a tight turn as he made for the entranceway to the bay. They tore through the narrow neck of water, the howl of the inboards reverberating from the rocky walls to either side – and then the open ocean beckoned.

Range crabbed his way across to the woman. It was next to impossible to move about on the speeding RHIB. He crouched down so he was eye-to-eye with her. 'I'm Steve Range. And you are . . . ?'

'Sarah,' she muttered.

'It's not a very . . .'

'Duh! It's Sarah Aisha Imam Greenfield if you gotta know. White father. American. Black mother. From around here.'

'Okay. Sarah, I don't have time to explain anything much. All I got time for is this: *right now we are the good guys*. Right now, we're about all Al Mina'a has got. We're going to try to save this one. All I want you to do is to watch carefully, okay?'

Sarah Aisha Imam Greenfield nodded, sullenly. She gestured at the ties holding her hands. 'Do I got an alternative?'

Range felt around in the pouch at his waist and pulled out a Gerber multi-tool. He flicked it open and levered out the short blade. As he reached forward he saw her eyes widening with fear.

'Hold 'em out. The ties.'

He slipped the blade under the plastic and sliced through, freeing her hands, then reached down and did the same with her feet. Just as he'd finished he heard a yell from O'Shea.

'We're here!'

O'Shea throttled off, and the boat decelerated as if it had hit something like a brick wall. Within seconds they were drifting through the swell, the comparative silence of the open ocean all around them. It had been impossible to use the Cougars as they powered through the sea. The roaring of the slipstream alone would have drowned out any radio comms. Range needed to do an urgent brief of his men.

Boat Two pulled in alongside them. Dive Shack Joe reached out and grabbed hold of the rope slung along the side of Range's vessel, The Kiwi doing likewise with theirs. Together, they pulled the RHIBs closer, until they were in easy speaking distance of each other.

'We just switched to Plan B,' Range announced. 'Boat Two remains here. You should be a safe distance from any blast. Boat One – that's us lot – heads in to trigger it. The sooner we do so, the less harm will be caused to Al Mina'a. If we get hit by the explosion, come in and try to salvage what you can. Got it?'

'Got it.'

Range turned to Sarah. 'Swap boats. No point you risking what's coming.'

'No friggin' way,' she retorted. 'I'm goin' where you're goin'.'

Range shrugged. 'It's your funeral.' He strode across to the 40mm grenade launcher. 'O'Shea, let's go. Kiwi, we get within range, we hit her with all we got . . .'

His last words were lost in the roar of the engines, as their RHIB powered up to speed. O'Shea did a stomach churning u-turn, bringing the prow around until the craft was arrowing back towards The Harbour.

Range braced his legs against the smack of the hull as it skimmed over the swell. He had his hands grasping the spade-handle-like grips of the grenade launcher, and his eyes down the thick, stubby barrel of the weapon. In terms of accurate range, The Kiwi had the edge with the .50-cal. But in terms of sheer destructive firepower, the 40mm grenade launcher was king. In any case, range wasn't really the issue here.

Range took a peep at his watch. It had taken them barely five minutes to power out of The Harbour, and to get the briefing done and the boat turned around. It would be no more than ten minutes since the gas was first triggered by the time they lobbed in the rounds. With a wind speed of around five knots, the cloud of gas would have spread across the bay until it was lying just offshore.

Every second was precious now: they had to blow the fucker before the gas was blown onshore and seeped into the streets and houses of Al Mina'a town.

Range didn't kid himself that there wouldn't be casualties. People would die. But it would be nothing in comparison to the apocalypse they had been planning. And if the skiff's crew had done as they'd been ordered, keeping people back from the water and in cover, the deaths might be even less than Range feared.

The challenge now was to get their RHIB into a position where they could lob rounds through the narrow entrance to The Harbour, so as to hit the ship, and without getting caught in the blast. But that was O'Shea's baby. Range hunched over the weapon, eyes glued to the large flip-up leaf sight, and poised to open fire.

In theory, the grenade launcher had a maximum range of fifteen hundred yards. But when used from a speeding RHIB – and even with the weapon slung on its pivot mounting – that was massively reduced. The Kiwi's .50-cal was accurate up to beyond two thousand yards, but it would likewise be hampered by the way the RHIB was hammering through the choppy swell.

O'Shea brought the craft around in a sharp, carving turn, the V-shaped prow of the RHIB like a spear aimed at the entrance to the harbour. As the boat sped across the water, the sun was breaking above the horizon behind them and lighting up the cliffs ahead a golden orange. They rounded the nearest headland, the still waters of the harbour sweeping into view. LPG being a colourless gas, there was nothing from this distance to betray the fact that anything was amiss in Al Mina'a.

They swung in from the north-east, the first sign of the MV *Endeavour* being a fierce flash of sunlight as the glass of the superstructure threw back the dawn rays in a blinding burst of light. As the ship hove into view, O'Shea spun the boat through 180 degrees, so the bow was pointing out to sea again.

Firing over the stern of the RHIB, The Kiwi unleashed with the .50-cal an instant before Range was able to open fire. The Mark 19 grenade launcher was capable of letting rip with sixty 40mm grenades per minute, the .50-cal able to maintain a far higher rate of fire. The first rounds from the heavy machine gun tore into the ship, the long burst unleashed by The Kiwi going high right and raking across the exposed side of the bridge.

Range felt his weapon kick, as the fat muzzle of the grenade launcher spat fire. *Kerchunk! Kerchunk! Kerchunk!* The belt-fed magazine punched through the grenade rounds, as he kept his thumbs pressed tight on the butterfly trigger.

The first grenades erupted in a shower of spray, as they tore into the calm surface of the harbour just a few yards short of the ship.

The concentration of the gas would be heaviest in the vessel's hold – the point of release. The pressure of the gas pumping out would force it over the sides of the ship, whereupon it would sink down to lie as a layer above the surface of the water. As it was blown inland, the gas would be mixed with air, the concentration of LPG growing less and less the further away from the ship.

The hold, where the gas would be thickest, was where Range was instinctively aiming for. But he figured the LPG would only ignite in the presence of oxygen, which meant they'd have to hit the target in exactly the right place to trigger the blast.

Range leaned his weight on the weapon, raised the barrel a fraction and fired again. This time he saw a series of white-hot flashes bloom along the side of the ship, as the 40mm ripped through the steel hull. The grenades were capable of piercing five centimetres of armour, and the lethal blast range was anything up to fifteen metres, but the ship's hold must have been completely purged of oxygen, for the grenade rounds still didn't blow her.

He leaned his weight on the weapon and swung the muzzle up and back towards the rear of the ship. The onshore wind was blowing in from the sea, fresh air mixing with the gas where it met it gushing out of the ship's tanks and the open hatches. That was where he now aimed for – the meeting point of gas and air.

He fired again.

The rounds struck the ship at the rear of the deck. The instant the 40mm grenade exploded, the LPG caught in a fiery blast. For the barest instant the MV *Endeavour* was silhouetted in a ghostly flare of light, and then the entire vessel was transformed into a white-hot seething fireball.

The explosion flashed outwards from the epicentre of the blast, the firestorm flaring and snorting as it sucked in oxygen like a dragon hunting its prey. Range felt O'Shea gun the engines and the RHIB leapt forwards, but the exploding cloud of LPG was faster. Already the fearsome blast wave was flashing out across the ocean towards them.

The crushing wave of pressure tore across the surface of the sea, as a vast mushroom cloud of smoke punched skywards above the harbour. For a moment it looked as if the amphitheatre of rock had been transformed into an erupting volcano. The thick smoke was lit an eerie white as explosions flashed across it like lightning bolts, fire ripping through the pockets of gas that had spread like fingers throughout the harbour.

But it was too late for the occupants of the speeding craft to see much of those deadly pyrotechnics. The blast wave caught the prow of the RHIB, driving it down into the waves, and flipping the boat over like a giant's hand had tossed it out to sea.

The blast wave flashed outwards, punching into Boat Two like a mini-tornado. The second RHIB was spun around like a leaf in a whirlpool, but by now the force of the explosion was weakened to such a degree that it was unable to tear the second craft out of the water.

Moments later the blast wave collapsed in on itself, and there was an eerie in-rush of air as the vacuum formed by the firestorm sucked oxygen back in on itself. The moment passed. Silence settled upon the ocean. Randy, the operator commanding Boat Two, scanned across the sea, searching for their sister craft.

And then he saw it – the upturned hull glinting in the early morning light, its silhouette stark against the bright blue of the sea.

Chapter Sixteen

As they rocketed across the swell, Randy could make out figures clinging to the hull of the RHIB, although at this distance he had no idea who it was exactly. He counted two. *Where were the others?*

They neared the stricken vessel, slowed, and then he spotted something atop a wave crest. He swung the RHIB around and made for that location. Those clinging to the hull could hold on for a while longer, but whoever it was in the water was clearly struggling.

Randy brought his boat to a dead slow. He saw Range lift one arm from the water, holding it above his head in a crook shape. The other was looped around the neck of the figure whose head he was desperately trying to keep above the waves. Range was kicking fiercely, trying to tread enough water to keep two waterlogged human beings from sinking below the surface of the sea.

Randy aimed the RHIB so its starboard passed a yard or so to one side of Range's raised arm. As the boat slid by, Joe and Tak reached out and hooked their arms around Range's, and went to drag him out of the water and into the boat's interior. But the weight of two bodies proved too much for such a lift – an emergency extraction procedure used by maritime Special Forces – and the two figures dropped backwards, momentarily disappearing beneath the waves.

Randy ramped the RHIB around in a screaming turn, and they came in for a second pass. At the moment the boat was almost upon him, Range raised his arms above his head, forming an inverted U-shape, each hand grasping the other's wrist, whilst below the water he linked his legs around the unconscious figure and held tight.

As Range started to sink below the surface of the sea, Joe and Tak got their arms through his and hauled. For a second or two Range was dragged through the water by the boat's momentum. Then as Tiny joined them on the heave, with a superhuman effort the three men hauled the figures inside.

Range lay in the bottom of the boat, where they'd dropped him. 'Why. The fuck. Didn't. She tell me. She couldn't. Swim?' he gasped.

Beside him, Joe was already at work pumping the chest of Sarah Aisha Greenfield. Within seconds she started to vomit up seawater. She spluttered and coughed for a good few seconds, before her eyes opened, and she glanced all around herself, confusedly. Her gaze came to rest on Range.

The glazed look dissipated, and as the pupils pulled into focus the memory of what had happened flooded back in.

She flicked her eyes downwards, almost as if she was embarrassed to have betrayed such a weakness. As for Range, all he could think right now was this: *Sarah Aisha Greenfield – you'd do more than all right in a wet T-shirt competition*. It was weird the way the mind worked when you'd come that close to drowning.

He lay back exhaustedly, trying to catch his breath and get his pulse under control again. He told himself it was over. Or at least this stage of whatever fucked-up mission they were on now was done with. Plan B had worked, or at least it had partially. Range knew they had injured – on the upturned hull of the RHIB they had one of their number in rag order right now.

Range had seen it happen. As the blast wave tore towards them, he'd felt time run down to an agonising slow-mo loop. He'd seen the billowing blast front smash into them, lift the RHIB up and spin it through the air, the boat's occupants being thrown clear. But The Kiwi had been flung against one of the RHIB's screaming propellers, and it had gouged into him as he fell.

Range had no idea how badly wounded the man was. If he was still clinging to the upturned RHIB then at least he was alive. But from what Range had seen of it, it looked as if the guy had taken a horrific pounding.

*

233

A good hour passed, during which time Randy had got The Kiwi and O'Shea off the upturned hull and safely into the one usable RHIB. Once there, The Kiwi had pretty much seen to his own treatment. An expert Special Forces medic, he had no illusions as to the seriousness of his present injury. The boat's screw had torn across his chest, ripping his shirt to shreds and gouging out great hunks of flesh.

He figured he'd broken all of the ribs on his left side – the side where the propeller had churned across him – and he was only able to breathe with real difficulty. Each rasping intake of breath was accompanied by a sharp, agonising stab of pain, which likely meant he had a broken rib pressing onto a lung. He'd bathed the wound in seawater – it being about as sterile and healing a solution as it was possible to find around here.

Back at mission start O'Shea had made sure that each RHIB was fitted out with a medical kit. The Kiwi was able to pack out the wound with absorbent gauze. That done, he'd got two of the blokes to wrap a bandage around and around his torso, as tight as they could get it, in an effort to hold the broken ribs in place.

There was nothing much you could do to treat them anyway – except to lie up and take it easy. With rest, the ribs would heal in their own time. He'd lost a lot of blood, but he figured he would live. As to lying up and taking it easy, The Kiwi figured there was fat chance of that happening for a good while now.

O'Shea had got a rope lashed to the upturned RHIB, to stop it drifting away. Plus they'd retrieved the extra jerry cans of fuel that the boat had been carrying, most of which had been thrown free as the boat flipped over. Range figured they had a long journey ahead of them, and they were going to need all the diesel they could get their hands on.

To the west a towering plume of dark smoke drifted over Al Mina'a. It obscured from view the bay itself, which was thick with fumes and with the eerie flash of secondary explosions and burning. But what was done there was done. The deaths; the damage – there was no turning back the hands of time. What they needed now were answers, before which no cogent plan of action was possible.

Range shared his ideas with his battle-worn men, plus the lone female who somehow seemed to have become one of their number. It was 1000 hours. If all had gone according to the plans drawn up in Geneva, they would have turned the boats east and headed into the open sea. That night they had a supposed rendezvous with Old Man Geneva's yacht, at which they were to be picked up and sailed away to safety.

But Range doubted all of that very much now. Maybe all this had been a mistake. A misunderstanding. Words lost in translation over a broken satphone link. But it didn't seem very likely. Yet at the same time he had no idea what, if anything, was true any more. It was all smoke and mirrors now.

Had the old man lost the satphone link, and set the gas to release without hearing Range's words of warning – *if what she's telling me is right, this place clearly isn't our target?* Range didn't think so. But the alternative made no sense at all. If he *had* heard and he *did* know, why had the old man taken control of the mission and blown apart a peaceful Puntland fishing village?

'I figure the only way we can start to get some answers is to head for tonight's RV as planned,' Range told his men. 'Or at least a variation on it.' The fatigue in his voice was clear for all to hear. 'We have a set of GPS coordinates to head for. We leave the one boat,' he jerked his head at the upturned vessel, 'on that grid. Then we stand off a good few kilometres and we watch and we wait.'

'What you expecting to see?' Tiny asked.

'One of two things,' Range replied. 'One: maybe, just maybe, the yacht comes in to pick us up, and someone explains to us just how the old man can have got this so very, very wrong. I figure there's about zero chance of that happening. Two: what I think we'll see is some kind of a clean-up operation. Kolokov is aboard that yacht, and he's a hard, wily bastard. I figure they'll look to blow us out of the water, to sink any witnesses to what took place here today.'

'What's the danger of them spotting us?' O'Shea asked.

Range shrugged. 'They may do. They've got radar. But so have we. We can keep a watch on them just as much as they can on us. Plus they won't be expecting it. And if it comes to it we can easily outrun them, and I figure we'll outgun them too. Either way, like this we flush out their real intentions.'

'And if they do what you expect 'em to, what then?' Randy asked. 'Do we blast 'em out of the water?'

Range shook his head. 'Nope. We stay silent and hidden and we watch. The old man is not on that yacht, that I am sure of. He wouldn't have risked it. He's in Geneva with his security people, at the heart of things. If we can leave them thinking they've got us, we gain the element of surprise.'

'Surprise for what?' Randy asked.

'Surprise for whatever's coming.' Range shrugged. 'Guys, I am making this up as I go. But whatever we discover tonight, I am pretty certain there's going to be a stage two of this mission, and it's going to be played out in and around Geneva.'

'How do we move the upturned boat?' The voice was that of The Kiwi. He sounded totally drained with the pain of his injury.

'O'Shea figures he can flip it back over,' Range answered. 'We either drive it there or tow it there, depending on how badly damaged it is.'

'And me?' a quiet voice faltered. 'Where do I fit in with all your . . . plans?'

Range turned to face Sarah. She was propped against the side of the boat, looking very much the worse for wear. The fierce sun was drying all of their clothes, which were steaming visibly in the heat, but it would take more than that – much more – to dispel the darkness that had crept into Sarah Greenfield's heart.

'So, how're you feeling?' he asked. 'You know, it's a good idea when you're on a ship to warn your crewmates you can't swim – that's if you can't.'

She smiled weakly. 'I didn't think a bunch of pirates would care much. But you rescued me, so I guess on one level I got you all wrong.'

Range cracked a smile. 'Look at us.' He gestured at his men: unshaven, bandaged, bloodied and seriously battle-worn. 'Looks like a bunch of pirates to me.'

Sarah gave a half-smile. 'I don't know.'

'As to what you do now, it's your call,' Range told her. 'We can drop you on the coast, within walking distance of Al Mina'a. There's got to be a lot of people in real need there right now, and you may be able to help. You got any medical training?'

'A little.'

'Then there's people there could use your skills.' Range paused. 'We did our best to minimise the damage. We did all we could. I hope you can see that?'

Sarah shrugged. 'Kind of. You and your men risked your lives . . . for something. But there's so much that I don't understand. Like what in God's name were you coming here for in the first place? We just thought you were a tanker ship that had lost its way.'

'It's a long story,' Range told her. 'And if you want to hear it, you're staying with us, 'cause we have got to get moving.' He jerked his head in the direction of the massive pall of smoke spreading across the bay. 'Sooner or later someone's going to come and investigate all this. I mean, Puntland must have some kind of maritime security force, right?'

She nodded. 'It does. The mainstay of the economy is fishing. Korean and Chinese trawlers were raping the fisheries around here. The Puntland Government set up a unit to stop them. It was even your British Government who helped fund and train them. In fact, that's who I work for.' She indicated the discreet logo displayed on the breast pocket of her damp overalls. *GPMSTF: Government of Puntland Marine Security Task Force.* 'I'm the Al Mina'a GPMSTF tourist liaison. It's 'cause I speak good English, that's why they gave me the job. Not that we get many tourists around here . . .'

'It's a nice logo.' It wasn't quite what Range was thinking. His mind was more on what lay beneath it. 'Right, so if your Task Force people are on their way we got to get moving. Wherever we're going, we're seeking answers. You're welcome to stick with us for as long as you feel able. I figure we owe you that much, for without you we'd have fried the entire population of Al Mina'a.'

She stared at him, eyes wide with shock. 'So that's what you were sent here for . . . But in God's name, why?'

'I don't know.' Range shook his head. 'I got no answers

for you. I don't know myself. None of us do. At least not yet.'

'My grandmother lives in that village,' Sarah remarked, quietly. 'She is eighty-seven years old, and every morning she gets up before six to milk her one cow. I came out here from America because of her. And every morning since I arrived she's set a glass of warm milk by my bedside, to awaken me. It's what she did this morning, before I roused my crew and we sailed out to speak to you. What harm had she – or the thousands like her in Al Mina'a – done to you?'

'No harm. Nothing.' Range paused. 'I got a lot of questions I need to ask of the man who set this whole thing up. We all have. That's why we have to get moving. So you need to make the call: you sticking with us, or d'you want putting ashore?'

She levelled her eyes at Range. 'I will come with you until we get some answers. And then, God willing, we – the people of Al Mina'a – may also get our revenge.'

Darkness had swept across the ocean quickly, like a thick cloak had been thrown across the sky. With it the air temperature had dropped, until it was cool enough to lie back and relax in the one serviceable RHIB. The sea lapped softly against the tough hull, as the seven occupants watched and waited.

Before setting off, O'Shea had pulled some slick SEAL manoeuvre to get the upturned craft righted. He'd rigged it with ropes in such a way that when he accelerated under full power in the lead craft, the upturned boat had been flipped out of the water and had righted itself.

It was still largely unusable. The force of the impact with the water had stove in much of the boat's superstructure, flattening the raised radar housing and breaking the steering. But at least the craft was on an even keel again, and the lead RHIB had been able to tow it at a gentle pace east across the ocean to their scheduled rendezvous. Now all there was to do was wait.

Some five thousand yards to the north of them, the damaged craft had been left at the grid for the RV. O'Shea had anchored it there by its thrusters – small propellers set into recesses in the hull, more normally used for executing tight manoeuvres when docking. Because the thrusters produced a sideways motion in either direction, he'd been able to programme the GPS-navigation system to keep the RHIB stationary on the grid.

Using empty jerry cans drained of their diesel, together with the seat-covers, tarpaulin and their clothing, they'd rigged up hunched shapes roped to the RHIB's seats. At a distance, and in the darkness, it should give the impression that the boat was occupied. It wouldn't stand a closer examination, but as decoys went, and with the material they had to hand, it was about as good as it got.

They'd arrived at the RV a good two hours early, but the scheduled rendezvous was barely minutes away now. O'Shea was bent over the radar scanner, searching for signs of the yacht. Randy was stood beside him, keeping O'Shea company. To the rear of the craft, The Kiwi was trying to rest. He'd even gone as far as taking a phial of morphine.

Range had never known the man take any form of painkiller when injured on ops. He was a fanatic for keeping his mind alert and functioning, at least whilst he and his fellow operators were still under threat from a hostile force. The fact that he'd gone as far as injecting himself with a phial of morphine reflected just how bad the injury and the pain had to be.

To either side of the RHIB, Tak, Joe and Tiny had cleaned and oiled the heavy machinegun and grenade launcher, just in case it all went noisy again. That done, they'd reloaded the weapons and taken up their battle stations. And funnily enough, Sarah Aisha Greenfield had taken up her favourite position in the prow of the boat, though right now she recognised she was very much not in command of this craft.

Beside her sat Range, cleaning and reloading his AK-74 in what he hoped was companionable silence. As he worked the gun's mechanism, he ran through the last few hours in his mind. The worse part of it all – the one part he did not want to face up to – was this: *how far did the betrayal go, if betrayal it was?*

No matter which way he looked at it, he could only think that the old man had set them up to annihilate that fishing port. The question was, why? Why on earth did he want it destroyed? And if it was a set-up from the start, just how far back did it all go? To Kenya? To a hostage handover on the remote Somalia–Kenya border? *To Isabelle?* To the old man's own daughter? To a so-called romantic liaison between his daughter and Steve Range, a liaison which maybe wasn't anything like it had seemed?

The more Range tried to fathom what had happened, the more he felt his head start to spin. Scenarios crashed into his mind seemingly from out of nowhere, the conspiracies and deceptions getting darker and darker still. At the end of it all, only one thing remained clear: instead of wreaking revenge on those who were deserving of it, they had killed a lot of innocent people today.

Sure, it was also possible to argue it the other way around: if they hadn't done as they had done, and risked their lives and taken injuries, a whole lot more of the residents of Al Mina'a would now be lying dead and injured. Most likely all of them. So, you could say they'd saved countless lives today.

But from where Range was sitting, it didn't exactly feel that way right now.

CHAPTER SEVENTEEN

Range checked his watch for the umpteenth time. There were barely minutes left until the scheduled RV. By rights, the old man's yacht should have been visible on the radar screen for a good hour or more now.

'Anything?' he prompted.

'Still no sign of the vessel,' O'Shea confirmed.

The seconds ticked by. Maybe the old man knew that Range and his team were onto him, or at least that they were full of unanswered questions and suspicions. But if that was the case why not make the RV and try to finish it, here and now? It was far easier to sink a RHIB full of deniable operators here in the Indian Ocean, than if Range and his men survived and took this argument to the shores of Europe.

'I got something,' O'Shea snapped. 'Moving fast on an

intercept bearing. Too fast for a surface ship. We got a helo inbound – ETA at the RV approximately five minutes.'

So the old man has sent someone after all.

'Just the one?' Range queried. 'No vessels?'

'One helo. No surface craft,' O'Shea confirmed.

'Right, so he's sending in a reception party by air.' Range's mind was racing now. 'What're the chances the helo's tasked to pick us up? Lifting six guys from a RHIB in the open ocean, that's a job for a Special Forces aircrew, not a civvie operator, and we have to presume this is some kind of private contractor. Let's say it's unlikely they're coming with the best of intentions. What's their flight profile?'

'Sticking low to the water,' said O'Shea. His face was lit an eerie blue by the glow from the radar screen. 'They're almost lost in the chatter of the waves – that's why the radar didn't see them until now. They're twenty miles out and closing fast.'

'Okay, fire up the engines and move off on a southerly bearing,' said Range. 'Move at the kind of speed a civvie craft – say a skiff – might go. We have to presume they'll pick us up on their radar, and we want them to see us as just another boat on the open ocean . . . Maybe a bunch of pirates returning home from a bit of late-night murder and mayhem.'

Those last words broke the tension a little, but not by much. If this was what everyone suspected it to be – an attack helicopter – it would carry weapons with a far greater range and lethality than those on the RHIB. And this being the Horn of Africa, no one doubted Geneva's ability to rustle up the odd gunship or two – not with the kind of financial muscle the old man had to hand.

'We have to presume they'll come to check us out,' Range continued. 'If they do, this is the plan. They'll need to get a good look at us before they can attack, 'cause most likely we are just a civvie craft. I figure they'll use the helo's searchlight. They'll need to get within a few hundred yards of us to do so and get eyes-on. The moment they switch on the searchlight they'll be visible and we use that to target them. Fire into the light, and use the .50-cal to try to get a drop on 'em.'

'Not only the .50-cal,' a voice rasped. It was The Kiwi. Range had thought him completely gone on the morphine, but obviously he was somehow keeping with them. 'They get that close, we can unleash with everything – the Mark 19, plus the AKs. Get down, brace it on the gunwale – an AK-74 is accurate up to four hundred yards or more.'

'Even better,' Range agreed. 'Most likely, they'll be coming at us from due north. Tak: take the .50-cal. Joe: man the 40mm. Everyone else on the AKs, apart from O'Shea. O'Shea: take evasive action only if they fire on us. Otherwise, keep her steady on this bearing. That's what any civvie craft would do, and it'll make her a more stable fire platform.'

Range took up position kneeling against the rear of the craft, weapon braced against the gunwale. Tiny and Randy took up positions to either side of him. Then The Kiwi appeared, weapon grasped in hand.

'State I'm in, I'll more likely to miss,' he muttered, as he took up his firing position. 'But who knows, I might just get lucky.'

Range turned and searched for Sarah. He could see the fear in her eyes. There was nothing worse than facing such an attack with no role and no way to fight back.

He gestured at his weapon. 'You know how to use one of these?'

She nodded. 'They taught me a little.'

'O'Shea, pass her your AK. You won't be needing it at the wheel.'

O'Shea unslung his assault rifle and handed it across to her. She took it, cocked the weapon, slammed a round home and flicked off the safety. Having done that, she joined the line of figures kneeling at the RHIB's rear, weapon at the ready.

Range glanced at her. 'So who's the pirate now?'

The throb of the diesel inboards drowned out any noise of the helicopter, but still they knew it was coming. O'Shea was giving a running commentary, counting down the miles to the RV. The helo was three miles out from the empty RHIB when there was a stark flash of light on the horizon. An instant later a thin line of flame shot across the sky, like a shooting star falling through the heavens, and then the surface of the ocean was lit in a momentary, ghostly flare.

'There's your answer,' Range growled. 'A clean-up operation.'

Seconds later the thump of the distant blast washed over them. They were now some ten miles south of the RV point, but even at this distance they could see that the helo had gained altitude to launch the attack. A second missile flared out from the aircraft, presumably to send whatever wreckage remained of the RHIB to the bottom of the sea.

A few seconds later a beam of light stabbed the distant horizon, as the helo circled the RV point, its searchlight playing across the ocean below. The aircrew seemed happy with their handiwork, for the searchlight flicked off again and the helo went dark.

'Turning south,' O'Shea reported. 'On an interception bearing, ETA two minutes.'

'Fire on, Tak,' Range ordered. 'When Tak fires, open up with everything.'

It made sense to let the .50-cal, their most accurate and potent piece of weaponry against an aircraft, lead this.

O'Shea kept a running commentary going as he gazed into the radar screen. 'Eight miles out . . . Seven . . . Six . . . ETA one minute. Four miles out . . . Three . . . Two . . . One . . .'

By now those in the boat could hear the juddering beat of the rotor blades slicing through the night air. The fact that the helo was showing no lights only served to reinforce the sinister and deadly nature of its mission.

'She's climbing to altitude,' O'Shea remarked. 'Eight hundred yards and closing.'

All of a sudden there was a momentary glint of moonlight on metal high in the sky to the north of them. In that instant, the silhouette of the helo became visible, soaring through the dark heavens as if in preparation to pounce. Tak didn't miss a beat. The .50-cal spurted a long tongue of fire, and a stream of heavy-calibre armour-piercing rounds went punching out towards the distant aircraft.

The 40mm grenade launcher began pumping out its high-explosive rounds, and four AK-74s opened up, pouring fire into the distant target. It was a stroke of luck they'd got sight of the helo before she'd got close enough to use the searchlight. But they wouldn't keep the element of surprise for long – and all the men in that craft knew exactly what it was they were up against now.

That flash of moonlight had revealed they had a Mi-24 HIND inbound – a Russian-built helicopter gunship that boasted thick armoured plating and a fearsome array of weaponry. Developed in the 1970s, the HIND had been built to find and kill NATO main battle tanks. It was designed to lurk below the horizon, blip up and unleash a fire-and-forget missile – radio or laser-guided – and slip out of sight again before the tank could return fire.

Although the HIND was a 1970s concept, the Mi-24 Super-

Hind – the much updated and improved version – remained in service with the Russian military. It was a cutting-edge and potent killer. The Russians had exported scores of HINDs around the world, and not a small number of them had gone to Africa. Basically, if anyone had the dollars and the need, the Russians would flog them one. Corrupt governments, warlords, genocidal regimes, Moscow hadn't been picky. And right now one of those fearsome gunships was bearing down on them.

The wall of fire thrown out by the gunners on the RHIB hammered into the target. Range could see rounds sparking and flaring along the HIND's flanks. But it needed a direct hit with a .50-cal round, or a 40mm grenade, to penetrate the HIND's armoured skin and to hit the aircraft somewhere terminal. The Russians had nicknamed the HIND the 'flying tank', and for good reason. Small arms would have negligible effect, unless they scored a very lucky strike.

Range saw the pilot jink the aircraft to left and right, executing a series of rapid turns to evade their fire, and then the helo let rip. Flame bloomed beneath the HIND's stub-wing, and a missile streaked towards the patch of ocean where Range and his team were mounting their desperate defence.

The incoming missile was a 9K114 Schturm (Storm) – radio-guided and pinpoint accurate. The only drawback with the Schturm was that the gunner had to keep the crosshairs of his sight on the target, to steer the missile in.

That meant the HIND had to remain visible with the target to do so, which meant Range and his team could keep pounding in the fire.

As the missile tore towards them O'Shea blipped the throttle and threw the RHIB into a stomach-churning turn, dropping it down the face of a wave and into a trough between the swell. The missile tried to follow, but it clipped the wave top in a plume of spray, flipped over and tore into the sea to their rear. The explosion punched outwards, the blast wave ripping across the RHIB, but Tak and Joe remained on their feet and on their weapons, pouring in the fire.

Range felt his AK-74 click empty. He went to slot on a fresh magazine. The RHIB was corralled between two wave crests now, and the HIND was closing in for the kill. O'Shea opened the throttle to the max, and the RHIB tore along the trough, but there was no way they could outrun the gunship.

The HIND climbed into view above the wave-tops, and then it unleashed a second Schturm. For a split second the missile was tearing down their throats, before Range saw a fierce explosion tear apart the HIND's cockpit. One of Tak's 40mm grenades must have found its mark. Belching black and oily smoke and spitting gouts of orange flame, the HIND tore itself apart in mid-air – rotor blades disintegrating, and chunks of armour plating blasting off in all directions.

The big, ugly gunship plummeted towards the waves.

Deprived of its gunner and its guide, the Schturm tore through the air above the heads of those on the RHIB, and an instant later it was gone. It would keep flying blind until the rocket motor burned out, whereupon it would drop into the ocean at the limit of its five-kilometre range.

The HIND had disappeared almost without trace. The heavily-armoured beast was gone, sucked into the ocean depths. If any of the crew had survived the explosions, they wouldn't have survived the crash. The heavy turbines would have flipped the helo over, pulling it downwards into the ocean depths. Even if one of the aircrew had been conscious when the HIND hit the waves, it would have acted like an armoured coffin, dragging them down to a deep-sea burial.

But Range didn't kid himself that the old man wouldn't know. The pilot was bound to have radioed in that they were hunting a second RHIB. And even if he hadn't done, the very fact that the HIND and its crew were never going to return from the present mission would alert Geneva that some at least of Range's crew had very likely survived.

No doubt about it, the element of surprise was blown now. Wherever the hunt for answers might take Range and his team, they had to assume that Geneva would be watching.

They pulled a good few kilometres south of the attack zone, just in case of any follow up. O'Shea had brought the RHIB to a stop. As the boat drifted gently on the swell, the six men and one woman talked. A quick glance at the map showed the very limited options open to them. East across the ocean lay Yemen and Saudi Arabia, neither of which countries were the kind of places Range and his team felt like visiting right now.

North, the options were even less enticing: Eritrea – known as the 'North Korea of Africa' – and Sudan, ruled by a brutal Islamic extremist regime. Due south was Somalia, which was perhaps the biggest no-no of all, but beyond that, further south, there was a possible option. If they could run the one-thousand kilometres of the Somali coastline, they'd reach Kenya, the nearest friendly nation where they could feasibly make landfall.

In the extreme north of Kenya at the remote Manda Bay, the US Navy SEALs had a very private and very secret base. It was located within a larger Kenyan military compound, and it was there to provide eyes and ears – and a hunter force – to keep a watch on Somali piracy, and the terrorists who operated alongside the pirates.

O'Shea had once commanded a Mark V special operations patrol craft based out of Manda Bay, and some of the fellow SEALs and SWCCs that he'd served with might still be stationed there. O'Shea had also become good drinking buddies with the Kenyan base commander, a Colonel Julius Mwelu. He figured Manda Bay was their best bet, in terms of a semi-official point at which to put in to land.

The journey to reach Manda Bay would be some thirteen hundred kilometres. With the spare jerry cans of diesel from both boats, they should just have enough juice to make it. They'd travel at night only, cruising at the RHIB's most economical speed of around twenty knots an hour. It would take them a good five nights to make it, and they'd have to find lying-up points on remote stretches of coastline along the way.

They'd have precious little to eat, bar the few ration packs they had stowed in the RHIB, but the main problem was drinking water. The boat had been equipped with a twenty-four-hour supply, for that was all they figured they would need. Food they could live without for five days, but not water. The only option was to scavenge food, and more importantly water, along the way. If they could pull into remote rivers at night, they could replenish supplies that way, and they had enough water purification tabs in the medical kits to make it potable.

It wasn't the best of plans. It was far from perfect. Once again, they'd be sailing through the heart of pirate territory, but at least now they knew for sure they could outrun any hostile craft they might come across – that's if they weren't running out of diesel by then. On balance, it was the least worst of all the options. And so, the plan agreed, O'Shea turned the prow of the RHIB towards the south-east and they commenced their epic journey.

They were thirty-six hours into the journey south, and Somalia during the day had proved to be as hot as a furnace. The RHIB had been dragged as far as possible into the heart of a mangrove swamp, so they could lay up in hiding during the hours of daylight. The thick, impenetrable coastal forest made for a perfect place of concealment, for no sane individual would be coming through this way any time soon. But at the same time hiding out in such terrain was about as close to a living nightmare as you could possibly get.

The thick, tangled mangroves grew out of the coastal mud of the Somali shoreline, being half-submerged at high tide. The interwoven branches cast a dense pool of shade over the RHIB, but it made only a marginal difference to the discomfort, for the dense swampy terrain was abuzz with every kind of flying, biting insect that east Africa had to offer. All the occupants of the boat could do was lie low bundled up under a blanket, in an effort to keep the worst of the bloodsucking critters at bay.

Like that, sleep was almost impossible, and it wasn't an option anyway for those standing watch. At first they'd rotated the watch between the six B6 operators, but then The Kiwi's wounds had started to get the better of him, and Range had relieved him from watch duty completely. The hard-as-nails ex-SAS operator would never have shirked on his duty, not even if it had killed him, and Range had had to order the man to stand down.

The previous day had been spent laid-up in similar horrendous conditions, the night zipping through the coastal waters at a steady twenty knots. But as the hours had dragged by, Range had grown increasingly concerned for their wounded man's survival. Sarah was using her limited medical training to try to help him, but what The Kiwi needed was proper treatment in a proper hospital.

The Kiwi's injuries weren't life-threatening, or at least they wouldn't have been had they not been on the run. It was the continued exposure to the heat and the dirt that was going to kill him. He was running a horrendous temperature, in spite of all the drugs he was taking. At times he appeared to be half-delirious. That meant infection, and if the infection was getting into his lungs or his bloodstream as Range feared, out here in these conditions it could quickly kill him.

Range felt a cold, icy fury grip him when he thought about losing one of his team. Of all of his fellow B6 operators, he'd soldiered longest with The Kiwi. They'd been together on several tough operations, when the Kiwi had served with the British SAS. They'd fast-roped into the Sierra Leone jungles and torn apart a rebel base, rescuing a dozen-odd British soldiers held hostage there. They'd taken out a hijacked airliner at Britain's Stansted Airport, and they'd headed into the badlands of Afghanistan to raid an Al-Qaeda/Taliban heroin-processing plant.

They'd survived all of that and more. If Range lost The Kiwi now, to this mission – to a tasking defined by subterfuge, mass-murder and betrayal – he would not let himself rest until his fellow operator and friend had been avenged. More to the point, he was determined not to let The Kiwi die, and that was why Range had made the decision to complete the last leg of the voyage – which they'd originally planned as three overnight relays – as one sustained burst.

They would set out that evening at last light, with a voyage across 720 kilometres of open sea ahead of them. They'd blast the entire distance at close to fifty knots an hour, which meant it should take them just over eleven hours to make landfall at Manda Bay. In theory, it was all doable in the hours of darkness. The main risk was their dwindling fuel supply, but O'Shea figured they'd make it, just. They'd be sipping on air by the time they got there, but hopefully their tanks wouldn't run dry.

O'Shea had decided to hold back their last two jerry cans of diesel, so they would know exactly when they were down to their final forty litres. If they hit that point, they'd have to head inland to the nearest port or settlement, and steal some diesel fuel at gunpoint.

It was a plan born of desperation, but better that than have one of their number die a slow death on the burning Somali shoreline.

Chapter Eighteen

The RHIB cut across the inky darkness, the twin propellers powering through the pre-dawn seas. The hours of thumping over the waves had left Range feeling numb and shaken, and it was like every nerve-ending in his body was on fire right now. *Surely, they had to be getting to their destination sometime soon?*

Thankfully, the Somali coastline was pretty much a dead straight run. It had made the mad dash across the ocean that much easier. O'Shea had simply pointed the prow south-south-west and set the throttles to the max. For sure, there would be those along the sparsely populated Somali coastline who had heard their passing, as the diesel inboards howled and the hull smashed through the swell. But few would have seen them, and fewer still would have been tempted to follow. In fact, apart from the long hours of discomfort, the run had been pretty much drama free.

Behind him, Range felt O'Shea ease off on the throttle, as he checked his GPS navigation unit one more time. Gradually, he brought the boat down from its maximum cruising speed, and soon she was puttering along at a sedate five knots an hour.

The thickly vegetated coastline was just a few hundred yards off the starboard bow. O'Shea had cut the speed to this kind of a crawl, for they were crossing over into Kenyan waters, and that meant comparative safety.

'Okay, Manda Bay should be coming up any minute now,' O'Shea announced. 'The base has a jetty, and last time I was here you could pick it out by the abandoned caterpillar dump truck that sits beside it. Keep your eyes peeled, 'cause when you see it we're pretty much home 'n' dry.'

That dump truck had once been the property of a US military contractor, O'Shea explained. The driver had noticed a SEAL team coming in from an operation, and the SEALs had waved in a friendly kind of a way. The truck driver had misread the signs, left the road and headed down the beach to somehow 'help'. The SEALs had tried to wave him back, but he'd just come on even stronger thinking they were in some real kind of trouble.

The big truck had sunk up to its axles in the mud. Because it was a contractor vehicle, the US military hadn't been able to work out who actually owned it. And because of that, they hadn't been able to get clearance to pull it out.

The Kenyan military had offered to do so, but the US commander couldn't get clearance to let them act either . And so it had been left where it was until it was a rusted hulk of a thing. It had now become the landmark for the SEAL base at Manda Bay.

O'Shea used the silhouette of the truck's massive bulk as the marker to steer their RHIB into shore. He let the craft drift to the jetty-side, whereupon Joe and Randy jumped ashore and lashed her fore and aft to the wooden posts set there for that purpose.

That done, O'Shea killed the engines. A quiet descended upon them, one that was punctuated by the steady beat of a myriad night-time insects. It struck Range as being the first time he'd not had the inboards throbbing beneath him, the wind roaring in his ears, or the boat slamming the base of his spine into the hard seat below for a good eleven hours.

The silence was beautiful.

To the east, the first hint of dawn was lightening the sky, and it was a fantastic feeling to have made it to a friendly country, and a potential slice of sanctuary – somewhere where they could heal their injured and lick their wounds.

O'Shea took Randy with him, as he went to make the first foray onto the base. Security would be tight here, for they were less than thirty kilometres south of the border with Somalia. Pirates had penetrated this far into Kenyan waters, hunting for soft targets along the coastline. To the south lay the island of Lamu, a Mecca for tourists seeking sun, a laid-back, easy time of it and an Indian Ocean island-paradise getaway. But that was before the pirates had struck, and now more and more of the tourists were keeping away.

O'Shea and Randy were gone a good twenty minutes, but they returned with positive news. Whilst the SEAL commander couldn't let Range and his crew stay in their part of the base – US military camps were horrendously rule-bound – the Kenyan commander was more than happy to give them a disused hut to doss down in. In return, O'Shea had agreed to gift him the RHIB, an arrangement with which the commander had seemed well happy.

As a bonus, the SEAL commander had agreed to get food, medicines and whatever else they needed shipped into their makeshift quarters – it was just their staying on a US base that he couldn't stretch to. More importantly, he'd agreed to get The Kiwi into their sickbay, because he could argue his was a humanitarian emergency and so one for which he didn't have time to seek any clearances.

In short, it was all-good. They helped The Kiwi hobble his way into the SEAL side of the base, which was enclosed in a ring of tall security fencing, after which they headed for the Kenyan side of the camp. The disused Kenyan Army hut proved to have a semi-functioning air-conditioning unit, and after getting some US Army cots slung around the place, Range and his team spent the day sleeping the sleep of the dead.

They woke that evening to discover the SEAL commander had dumped a stack of US Army ration packs outside their door. And so it was that Range and his team had got a fire going, so they could heat up some boil-in-the bag meals. Beef Teriyaki, Meatloaf with Gravy, Chilli with Beans – the way Range was feeling he reckoned he could scoff the lot.

The food eaten, they settled around the cooking fire. Somehow, Tak had befriended one of the Kenyan gate guards and had sent him into the local village with a fist full of dollars to buy beer. By the time the guard had cycled back with the bottles and delivered them to Tak, the beer was barely chilled. But after what they had been through in recent days, no one was complaining.

As he lay back beside the fire, Range felt himself beginning to relax a little, for the first time in what felt like an age. He took a pull on the Tusker beer and thought for the umpteenth time about all that had happened. He knew that whilst they were relatively safe here, the challenges and the dangers were far from over. In fact, there was a part of him that felt they were only just beginning.

'So, I hate to talk shop,' Range remarked to his fireside companions, 'but anyone got any sense of what the fuck Geneva's motive may have been for all that's happened?'

No one – O'Shea included – had any bright ideas.

'Okay, so I figure there's only one way we're going to find out,' Range mused. 'We're going to have to make our way to Geneva and ask the old man. He'll know we've escaped

– or at least some of us have. He'll know about the gunship going down. He'll have doubled his security and he'll be looking for us. Head for Geneva, and he's likely to pick us up as soon as we step foot out of the airport. So, we're going to need some serious lateral thinking to crack this one, and some bright 'n' shiny ideas.'

Range glanced around the circle of faces lit by the flickering firelight: Tak, Joe, Tiny, O'Shea, Randy and Sarah – the newest member of their crew. There were shrugs and raised eyebrows all around: *don't look to us for any answers* . . . He laughed. He had the beer bottle balanced on his belly, and it bounced up and down as he chuckled.

'That looks like a lot of don't-ask-me's,' he remarked. 'Which makes six of us, 'cause I don't have a clue either. Maybe The Kiwi will have cracked it, with all the time he's had to think in the sickbay.'

Range changed tack. 'Let's think logistics. Who has their passport? I lost mine when the RHIB turned over, and it threw the grab bags into the sea. I presume The Kiwi's lost his too. O'Shea?'

'Gone, buddy, gone.'

'I never had mine,' a voice piped up. It was Sarah. 'You never told me to bring it, did you?'

'So, Sarah-the-Pirate, how long are you intending to stick with our motley crew, anyway?' Range asked. 'You can see how dangerous it can be now, not to mention hot, flyblown, boring, dirty and uncomfortable . . .'

She laughed. 'Like I said, until we get some answers. And maybe a little payback too.' She paused. 'By the way, you still got that satphone? I've been meanin' to call Al Mina'a, to see just how bad it is there.'

'Not on the satphone, you won't,' Range told her. 'It's at the bottom of the sea somewhere off Al Mina'a. And even if it wasn't, it's about the most insecure means of comms ever now. That was the old man's satphone, and he's sure to be monitoring every means of communication he's ever had with us, to see when and where we come up on comms.'

'I've heard so much about this old man in Geneva,' Sarah muttered, 'the bastard who seems to be behind all of this. Fancy fillin' me in, now we're taking it easy on a beach in Kenya, suppin' our beers and with all the time in the world?'

Range shrugged. 'Sure. Now's as good a time as any.'

He proceeded to relate to Sarah the basics of the job they'd been sent out from Geneva to do. He saw the occasional flash of anger in her eyes, but after the events of the past few days she was pretty much beyond being shocked any more.

'Then it's from him – from this bitter and murderous old bastard – that we've got to get our answers,' she declared. '*Bastard*. We've just got to.'

Range raised his beer bottle. 'I'll drink to that.' He had to admit, he liked the way she said *bastard*, with real passion in her voice, not to mention venom that could kill.

'You say he's surrounded by a heavy screen of security,'

she continued. 'And with wealth like that, he can afford . . . well, anything. But every man has his weakness. You know what the hierarchy of loyalties is in Somalia?'

Range shook his head. 'Nope.'

'It's this.' Sarah began to recite an old Somali saying:

Me and my country against the world.
Me and my clan against my country.
Me and my family against my clan.
Me and my brother against my family.
Me against my brother.

'Other than to ourselves, our first loyalty is always to our nearest and dearest – our family,' Sarah added. 'That's pretty much what it means. So maybe this twisted old man has a family, and if he does, maybe we can use them to get to him.'

Range thought about Isabelle for a moment. Did the old man even have a family? He really didn't know any more. Was Isabelle even his daughter? Had she been a genuine kidnap victim? Or was she part of some wider scam, one that was somehow designed to drag him and his men into . . . Well, into what? What would have justified putting together such a wide-ranging conspiracy, and all to blow up a peaceful African fishing village?

There was a piece of this jigsaw they all had to be missing, but Range was buggered if he could think what it was.

Maybe Sarah was onto something here. For sure, it would be a challenge getting through to the old man direct. Maybe he did have a family. And if he did, maybe they could use his wife or his children to get to him. . .

As The Kiwi would say: *use a lesser evil to fight a greater one.*

Range glanced at O'Shea. 'The Kenyan base commander has a landline, right?'

'Sure does. There's several in his office – least there was last time I was here.'

'Right, take Sarah and use whatever powers of persuasion you need to get her a few minutes' use of the phone.' He turned to Sarah. 'That way, you can call up Al Mina'a and find out . . . Well, whatever you find out. Using a landline from here is perfectly secure, or at least it is in terms of Geneva listening in.'

With O'Shea and Sarah gone, Range settled down to enjoy another beer and few minutes' space in which to think. They'd need to get replacement passports, but that would be simple enough. In Nairobi there was a US and New Zealand consulate, plus a British Embassy, and they were more than used to having to replace travellers' lost passports.

They'd need flights out, but Range wasn't exactly sure yet where they should be flying to. If Geneva was watching, it would be their old haunts in Lo don they'd be scrutinising most closely. The B6 office was a complete no-no, The Beaujolais wine bar probably too . . . Their homes were also out of bounds. Their phones were obviously hot – or at least any of their numbers that Geneva had access to or could have traced.

Range wondered whether he could afford to make contact with The Hogan in any way. The B6 boss would have expected to have heard from him and his team several days ago, if only in a satphone call from the old man's yacht giving a brief heads-up on the mission. There was a secure email drop-box that Range could use, to leave The Hogan a short message. He figured he'd do it that way. All he would tell him was that they were out, but still on the job.

Range didn't want anyone else getting mixed up in this who didn't have to be. For some reason his mind flipped to thoughts of Randy's 'other wife' in Libya. Randy had phoned her on the old man's satphone, and as he was the bill-payer he'd have access to all the numbers called on that device. If he had her number then in theory he could trace her, which meant she was potentially in danger, as was Randy's young son.

'Who used the satphone to make any calls, other than to Geneva or B6?' Range asked. 'Randy, I know you made the one to your wife.' Range left it unsaid which wife he was referring to. He didn't know who around that fire was aware of Randy's recently acquired second family. 'But did anyone make any other personal friend or family calls?'

There were a series of negatives from the men.

'Right, one of you blokes head over to check on The Kiwi.' Range nodded at Tak, Tiny and Joe. 'Better still, why don't you all go? See if you can't sneak him in a beer. Plus, double-check he's not put any calls through that were personal. And whilst you're at it, see if you can't blag some more – *cold* – beer from any friendly SEALs.'

The three men wandered off to do Range's bidding.

Range turned to Randy. 'Mate, Geneva has the phone number of your . . . wife in Libya. That means your son too. You need to get onto them and get them a warning. Head over to the Kenyan base commander's office and see if he won't let you use the phone too.'

Range was expecting Randy to jump to it, but he remained seated by the fire. He took a swig of his beer and glanced at Range. 'Buddy, I appreciate the concern . . .' He paused. 'There ain't no easy way to say this. I'm not proud of what I'm about to tell ya, but it wasn't my Libyan wife I was speaking to.'

Range shook his head, confusedly. 'What the . . .?'

Randy held up a hand to silence him. 'She has a son from a former marriage. That son joined AQIM. He was part of the crew deployed to Al Mina'a – the real Al Mina'a – the Somalian Al Mina'a. I was speaking to him. I was giving him a warning to get the hell out of the town, before . . . Well, before we killed them all.'

Range shook his head in disbelief. 'Fuck me, mate, you could have blown the entire mission . . . That's if we had been in Somalia, which of course we bloody weren't.'

Randy stared into the fire. 'I know,' he muttered. 'I ain't proud of it, dude. Divided loyalties, and all that.'

'Anything else you haven't told me?' Range asked. 'Randy, you can't afford divided loyalties when working in a team like ours. You'll fuck up. You'll fuck yourself up. And probably a whole lot of your brother operators too.'

'Nope. I got nothing else to add. No more divided loyalties. I'm done.'

'But her son's still with AQIM, right?'

Randy shook his head. 'Not any more. He was killed during the *Golden Achilles* hijacking. That's what the person I was speaking to told me.'

'You reckon he was telling the truth?'

'No reason not to. He was speaking to me like I was still a part of AQIM. The leaders – they keep information compartmentalised. They don't share anything unless they have to. The only people who would know about the raid on Tripoli are the top leadership. The rest they treat like mushrooms: they keep 'em in the dark and they feed 'em on shit.'

Range stared at Randy across the glow of the embers. 'Look, mate, I keep trying to believe in you. I keep trying to bury the TNF rule. You know TNF, right?'

'Sure. Trust no fucker.'

'It's a rule we lived by in the SAS. But every time I reckon you're all-good, you spring another one on me. You can't keep doing this, mate. Otherwise, you'll always be TNF to me and the rest of the guys, and that makes it unworkable.'

'I know. Like I said, I'm all done, dude. That's the last

TNF moment just gone. I didn't need to tell you. I did so to wipe the slate clean. I'm all done.'

Range settled down beside the fire again. He let his mind drift and it ended up somehow in Geneva, with a girl who was supposed to be dead at her own hand. It had never even occurred to him before, but was Isabelle – or whatever her name was – really dead? Had she really necked that bottle of sleeping pills? All he had was the old man's word for it, and he knew now how little that was worth. He'd never even thought about it, but was Isabelle maybe still alive, and her supposed death all part of the bigger scam?

He heard voices. Two Americans, talking softly as they moved back through the dark beneath the trees. O'Shea and Sarah took up their places again by the fireside.

Range threw her an inquiring look. 'What news?'

'Well, I guess it could be worse,' she announced, quietly. She stared into the flames. 'Around two hundred dead. Mostly, fishermen who were trying to save their boats. My crew tried to stop them, but those boats were their only means of livelihood, and of course the LPG – well, it was invisible. It didn't seem like a real and tangible threat.'

'There's maybe triple that number injured.' She glanced at Range. 'But most of the townspeople – they survived. Al Mina'a – the town itself – has been saved. The greatest damage was to the fishing fleet. It's pretty much gone.'

'Holy shit, two hundred. That's bad,' Randy muttered, giving voice to what they were all feeling right now.

'I'm sorry for all the victims,' Range remarked, gruffly. 'One innocent death is too many, especially when it's at our hand.'

'Thanks,' Sarah remarked, 'but you know something? The strategy – your strategy – in a way *it worked*. There could have been thousands of deaths. There would have been, had that bastard in Geneva had his way.' A smile momentarily lightened her eyes. 'And my grandma – she's fine. And so is her goddamn cow.'

Range did his best to return the smile, but he felt burdened by the dead and injured they'd left behind them. 'Glad the cow made it. That's something, at least.'

'You know something else? If the attack had gone ahead as planned, you know what that would have done to the country? The castle-like building on the hill, you noticed it, right? It's a mosque built upon a church, built upon even older foundations. They're from an ancient African religion, one that existed before foreigners brought their beliefs here. And you know what? At Al Mina'a those with the ancient beliefs – the animists – and the Christians, and the Muslims, they all gather at that place and worship side by side.'

'Puntland is a place of amazing tolerance and peaceful co-existence. It's a place of democracy, justice and the rule of law. But had that place of worship been blown apart and the entire population of Al Mina'a burned, I shudder to think what would have happened. It would have been obvious this was the work of outsiders, and of those with advanced

271

technologies. No one from Puntland could have – would have – launched such an attack. So who knows, maybe the whole nation would have risen up against the foreigners . . . ?'

'Like a second Somalia,' Range interjected.

'Exactly.' She paused. 'As it is, two hundred innocent fishermen have died, and the fishing fleet is lost. It's a disaster for Al Mina'a, but not for the entire nation. The people are up in arms and a lot of questions are being asked, but right now they seem to have the lid on it. Had the attack caused the mass-murder and mayhem intended, well, who knows where it would have ended up. Yeah, maybe it would have been like the next Somalia. Who knows?'

'But what would Geneva have to gain out of all that?' Range asked. 'Puntland doesn't have an economy large enough to register . . . It still doesn't add up.'

'It doesn't.' Sarah levelled her dark eyes at him and they glittered in the firelight. 'There is more to this, something of significance that we don't know or understand. Which leaves only one option: we got to go to Geneva to find out.' A beat. 'So, Mr Range, do you have a plan as to how we're gonna go nail that bastard?'

He smiled. He just loved the way she said that word – *bastard*.

O'Shea and Range had stayed up late around the dying embers of the fire. They were trying to come to terms with all the death and destruction they had unwittingly caused, and to come up with some form of a plan to nail the Geneva connection. But every which way they looked at it, there was no easy way to get to the old man. He would be forewarned, and they had to presume he would be actively hunting them.

'One thing I don't get,' Range remarked. 'How come the ship's GPS and our own both said we were in Al Mina'a Somalia, not Al Mina'a in Puntland?'

'Been bugging me too,' O'Shea replied. 'It's gotta be 'cause Puntland's an independent country in everything but international recognition. So on maps and GPS systems it'll still show as part of Somalia. Until it gets proper recognition as the world's newest country, I guess it'll stay that way.

'Plus we wanted to believe it,' he added. 'After Isabelle and the *Golden Achilles* hijacking, we all did. We wanted to believe it was Pirate Central, and so we convinced ourselves. If I'd checked the charts properly, I'd have noticed there were two Al Mina'as. But I didn't.' O'Shea shrugged. 'Too late for any of that now.'

Range found the glow of the fire mesmerising. He shifted about on the sand, trying to get comfortable. He figured it was maybe time to hit the sack. They'd look at their options again with fresh minds in the morning. As he moved about he felt something in his pocket digging into him. He reached in and pulled it out.

It hung on the end of its chain, spinning around and glittering in the last flickering shades of the firelight. A few days back that golden angel had been a precious keepsake from a woman he had . . . Well, he didn't want to think about that now.

'What you got there?' O'Shea asked.

'Dunno exactly,' Range replied. 'But I got my suspicions.'

He placed the angel on one of the rocks that they'd pushed together to form the hearth. He picked up a smaller one, and before O'Shea could stop him he smashed it down hard on the golden figure. Gems sprung free, the metal split and twisted, and the angel was left in pieces on the flat of the stone.

Range reached forward and pulled out the tiny silver disk that was lying in the centre of the debris. He held it up to the firelight – half to study it, half to show it to O'Shea. It was about the size of a small button, and completely smooth on all sides. There wasn't a mark on it from where the rock had smashed into the angel pendant, and it looked pretty much indestructible.

He handed it across to O'Shea. 'Any idea what that is?'

O'Shea was B6's resident expert on all things kit- and hardware-related. He studied it for a moment. 'Yeah. It's a transponder. Gotta be. And to get it down to that size, it's gotta be a state-of-the-art piece of kit.'

Range eyed him. 'We're being tracked?'

O'Shea nodded. 'Sure looks like it. You got this from . . . ?'

'Geneva.'

'So, the old man's been tracking us all the way to Manda Bay. Lucky we're in a Kenyan Army base, or most likely he'd have had another go at hittin' us.'

'Why didn't he when we were coming south from Al Mina'a?' Range asked. 'When we were out on the open sea?'

'Moving at the speed we were, at night, plus sticking close to the Somali coast . . .' O'Shea mused. 'I'd like to have seen him try. Plus he'd have had to rustle up a crew to intercept and hit us. That ain't so easy, buddy, and it takes time.'

'Why not contract another HIND?'

O'Shea smiled, evilly. 'One down, remember? Word gets around. That freelance gunship community, it's small and tight. Gotta be. Who else would want to come get some from a bunch of ex-SAS and SEALs driving a RHIB, and all gunned up for war?'

Range held out his hand for the transponder. O'Shea leaned across with the tiny device. Range took it, placed it back on the flat stone and went to smash the smaller rock down for a second time, this time breaking the tracking device apart. But O'Shea was quicker. His hand shot out and stayed Range's arm.

'Whoa . . . Hold on a minute, buddy.' O'Shea reached for the device. 'Think about it first. There's a better way . . . Watch.'

He moved across to the nearby hut. He searched around for a few seconds, then slipped the device into a tiny gap between the roof and the wall. He jammed a couple of loose rocks in behind it, so it was doubly secure and completely hidden from view.

He turned back to Range. His eyes glittered. 'Far as Geneva is concerned, we're stayin' here for a good long while.'

CHAPTER NINETEEN

For the eighth morning in a row it was the call of the
muezzin that had woken Range. He'd settled into a rhythm
now – as much as ever you could when staying as the guest
of an absent host in a strange city in a Muslim nation that
lies at the southern border of Europe. Every morning he
would drag himself out of bed, shower in the beautiful
bathroom that adjoined his suite and head out for a run.

Istanbul. The divided city on the banks of the Bosporus.
One foot in Europe, the other in Asia – a Muslim city with
a thoroughly European feel. Being billeted in Bebek, one
of Istanbul's most exclusive areas, had the odd drawback,
though; Range had experienced a few problems finding an
inexpensive pair of running shoes, but other than that it
was good to be here.

As he pounded the promenade that ran along the riverfront, he drove himself murderously hard. He beasted himself until the sweat was pouring off him, even despite the early morning chill. The promenade was all but deserted at this hour. It was why he chose to rise at five a.m. with the Muslim call to prayer, and to run and run.

He knew he was driving so hard in part to punish himself. He knew how comprehensively Old Man Geneva had suckered him in, although he didn't yet know the reasons why. He realised now how a fake 'relationship' with a fake 'daughter' had blinded him to all the warning signs. He knew how the girl's 'death' and the Old Man's false pledges of revenge had combined to make him all the more driven, and to carry his men with him.

But the last chapter of this dark mission had been opened now, and hopefully there was a plan in place that would put an end to it once and for all. One way or the other, the next forty-eight hours would be decisive. The risks were still legion – to Range perhaps more than any other member of his team – but even so there were risks enough there for all.

The plan they had come up with was a good one, and Range knew he couldn't have done it without the Turkish connection. As he ran, he cast his mind back to the mission on which he'd made that connection – when he had rescued Turkish shipping magnate Emin Sabanci from all but certain death.

Range had been stationed in Basra, where he was running a private security contract. Sabanci, a Turkish billionaire businessman, had been exploring business opportunities in the southern ports of newly liberated Iraq. When Sabanci was seized, no one knew if it was terrorists or a kidnap gang that had got him. Often, they worked hand-in-hand in what was then the lawless power vacuum of post-war Iraq.

If it was Al-Qaeda, no amount of money would persuade them to show any clemency. They'd behead Sabanci, and they'd do so in live, close-up detail – putting the pictures on the internet. When the first ransom demand had been phoned through to Sabanci's wife, she had collapsed in tears of relief. Maybe, just maybe she would get him back again alive.

Fast-track ninety days from there, and a bearded and wild-eyed Sabanci had been kicked out onto a chaotic street in downtown Basra. His ransom had been paid. The kidnappers had released him. Just no one had thought to join up the dots and get a reception party deployed to bring him in. With Sabanci being a Turkish national, no one seemed to have the authority to launch a pick-up operation: not the Brits who supposedly patrolled Basra, nor their US or other allies.

Then Range had heard about it. He'd got a call from a pal of his who was flying down to Basra. The bloke was ex-SAS, part of the brotherhood. He'd asked Range to find a local car and weapons, and to be waiting for him at Basra's main military airport. He'd flown in and they'd loaded up the car – a big, beaten-up Dodge 4x4, with a load of white garden furniture strapped to the rear. It was the wagon Range and his crew used to cut about in, dressed as locals and posing as furniture delivery men.

The garden furniture was so incongruous it seemed to provide the perfect cover. Range and a fellow operator had once driven through the heart of an insurgent gathering, and without being rumbled. So the two of them had mounted up the Dodge and headed into Basra to track Sabanci down. Find him they did – wandering the streets dazed and confused, and terrified that another gang was going to grab him, and this time of the internet-video-beheading kind.

When Range had pulled the Dodge to a halt and opened the doors to drag Sabanci in, at first he had tried to run. It was only when he'd heard the British voices, and seen the blue of Range's eyes, that he'd realised Range and his fellow operator weren't the bad guys. They'd bundled Sabanci into the vehicle, and all the way back to the British base he'd wept with relief and thankfulness.

They'd got him through the base gates, and the British commander had quickly taken over, but not before Sabanci had got to use Range's satphone, so he could call his wife and tell her the good news. And Sabanci had done one other thing before being parted from his saviours – he'd revealed to Range that he was one of Turkey's wealthiest busi-nessmen, and that he owned one of the nation's largest shipyards. As if to prove it, he'd shown Range a photo of his private yacht, which was up there in the superstar league. And he'd promised Range that if he ever needed anything – *anything* – he only had to ask.

When Range and his team left Manda Bay, Range had figured they'd best avoid Nairobi. Sure, they'd left the tracking device secreted in the wall of the hut, but if Range had been Old Man Geneva he'd still have had his people watching Nairobi's airport. It was the main hub for flights into and out of East Africa, and the obvious route via which Range and his team would make their way back to Europe.

Instead, they'd headed east and made for Uganda. Uganda was a very close and loyal ally to Britain and the US, and had been for many years. It had proved easy enough to get replacement passports issued for all at the relevant consulates and embassies, and from Uganda's Entebbe airport Turkish Airlines very conveniently ran three flights a week, direct to Istanbul.

Back at Manda Bay Range had put a call through to Sabanci, from the Kenyan commander's landline. He hadn't needed to explain very much at all. Sabanci had booked the flights they needed and put one of his 'spare' guest villas at their disposal, and he'd had a driver waiting to collect them on arrival at Istanbul airport.

Sabanci hadn't asked Range much of what it was all about. His only interest was in how he could help. He owed Range a debt of life. It was a debt he could never fully repay, no matter what. But right now, in Istanbul, he could sure make a start. Range had explained the information he needed: it concerned one Jean-Pierre de Saint-Sébastien, who supposedly ran the Triple-S shipping line out of Geneva.

Sabanci being a fellow shipping magnate, it hadn't taken him long to find out what Range needed. Jean-Pierre de Saint-Sébastien had been born Arnault Kurtz. He was of Austrian-Swiss heritage, and his first language was German. Of course, being a Swiss national and the country being bilingual French-German, Kurtz also spoke near-perfect French.

Kurtz had married into the de Saint-Sébastien family, the patriarch of whom at that time ran the Triple-S shipping line. As the family business had had no natural heir – there being no son born to the parents – Kurtz had become the favoured successor. But the old man was only willing to hand over the reins if Kurtz changed his name to that of the family line. Hence Arnault Kurtz had become Jean-Pierre de Saint-Sébastien.

At the time that Kurtz had taken over the Triple-S shipping line it was a multi-billion-dollar business. But more recently there were reports of mounting debts, and of shady deals being carried out behind the scenes. Subsidiary companies were rumoured to be involved in a variety of illegal business ventures – all of which were apparently aimed at propping up the core business, the Triple-S line.

Over the space of twenty-four hours Sabanci had pulled

together a detailed dossier on Arnault Kurtz's – or rather Jean-Pierre de Saint-Sébastien's – business interests and the location of his private residences, of which he had several in and around Geneva. It was amazing what an insider like Sabanci – one blessed with financial clout and connections – had managed to find out. And on the basis of that dossier, Range's first team had already set out on the long drive to Geneva, to set in motion stage one of the coming operation.

Range had chosen The Kiwi to lead them. A few days in the SEAL medical centre at Manda Bay had worked wonders on him. He was far from back to full physical strength, but this stage of the mission required a sharp mind and guile more than it did fighting ability, and in that department The Kiwi had few equals. He had with him Dive Shack Joe, Tiny and Tak. They'd hired a car and driven north, Range figuring an overland arrival from southern Europe would be the route of ingress into Geneva that de Saint-Sébastien would least expect.

Randy and O'Shea had set out forty-eight hours later, taking the same route into Geneva. They'd carried with them some very specific equipment, of the kind that Sabanci had had no problems acquiring. None of it was illegal; none of it was lethal; but if everything went to plan, that kit would nail de Saint-Sébastien just as comprehensively as if they'd put a bullet in his brain.

Range was to carry out the third stage of the three-pronged operation, together with Sarah. Or rather, he'd do so with her watching from a distance as he walked into the trap, so she could give ample warning to the others. Sarah was the only 'clean skin' amongst them. The old man could have no way of knowing of her presence on their team, and that was why she had been assigned the role of the watcher.

Range pounded along the cobbled street that led back to the villa, breathing hard as he gave it one last push. The residences here were places of understated, tasteful opulence, hidden behind tall palm trees and high walls. Sabanci's villa had been the perfect private base from which to plan and to strategise, and from where to send out his teams.

For the last forty-eight hours it had been just Sarah and him billeted there. Sabanci had been called away on business, so they'd been left very much to their own devices, just the two of them. *And of course it had crossed Range's mind* . . . Now she was out of Africa and had discarded her Government of Puntland Marine Security Task Force overalls, she'd taken on an altogether more alluring air. Sabanci had equipped the villa with a wardrobe of clothes for Range and his team – one more suited to life in the finest part of Istanbul – and right now she was wearing a flame-red, body-hugging dress by some exclusive designer.

Think a younger, sassier version of Naomie Harris from *Skyfall*, with bags of New York attitude, plus a rack you could hang your hat on. Range for sure was tempted. Of course, she was far harder to read than Isabelle had been in that Nairobi hotel – *or had seemed to be*. He knew fully well now that Isabelle had been putting on an act. Yet still he detected a frisson of attraction between himself and Sarah, like an electric current pulsing back and forth between them.

They'd started out the best of enemies, back at Al Mina'a, but with time Range figured he'd gone from being the gun-toting mass-murderer to something close to the vigilante, and from there to the dark avenger. As for her, she'd gone from being the wide-eyed tourist guide of Al Mina'a to the gun-toting lady pirate, which was the role in which Range much preferred her. And right now, they were united in their mission to nail de Saint-Sébastien and get some answers.

Their common quest had drawn them closer. If the coming mission proved wholly successful, the people of Al Mina'a – a Puntland fishing village now mourning its dead – would be more than avenged. In fact, Range and his team would be the unsung heroes of the Puntland nation. Sarah would have to front all of this up, though, leaving the role of Range and his men forever a hidden one.

But the quid-pro-quo would be that no one was ever going to investigate the role played by six foreigners who had sailed the MV *Endeavour* into Al Mina'a and so delivered the bomb to its intended target. There were already rumours of a blood feud sworn by the relatives of the dead – the mother of all blood feuds that would last for a thousand years.

In exchange for what was coming, Sarah would ensure the blood feud was settled. For ever. There was always an alternative to paying the debt in blood, and that was for the debt to be paid in hard cash. In fact, a specific amount would be put on each of the dead men's lives. Such a payment was called 'blood money', and paying it was a common enough means to settle a feud of this sort in such parts of the world.

Range and Sarah had done their back-of-an-envelope calculations, working out the kind of figure they needed to cover the blood money. Over a final dinner of fine fish, cooked by the chef that Sabanci had insisted he provide for the duration of their stay, they'd worked through their sums. They'd try for a great deal more money, of course, but at least they'd worked out a bottom line.

They sat late on the villa balcony overlooking the Bosporus, the treacherous ribbon of water that separates northern Turkey from its southern half, so linking the Mediterranean and the Black Sea. One of the busiest and most dangerous shipping lanes in the world, the Bosporus is also a place of history, high drama and – inescapably – of romance.

The lights from the villas lining the southern side of the strait stretched into the darkness, reflected in shimmering steps of brightness that danced across the water. As the evening went on several gaily lit cruise ships slipped past, sailing westwards from the Black Sea, and it seemed as if the upper decks were almost within reach of Range and Sarah's touch. Directly across from them lay one of Istanbul's ancient palaces, a towering edifice of white-walled splendour, one that a cargo ship had accidentally crashed into a decade or so before.

The straits were so busy with shipping and the sea currents so strong that countless ships had got forced off course and smashed into the buildings that lined the waterway. With over twelve million people living in Istanbul, there was a whole lot of buildings for the busy sea traffic to avoid, not to mention the bridges that spanned the water, linking one side of the city to the other.

Not for the first time since they had landed in this magical city, Range wondered about the possibility of getting out of London and perhaps making a place like this his home. Turkey was booming, the city itself was cosmopolitan and liberal, the climate was fantastic, and the scenery breathtaking. If he could find the right woman to settle down with, he could maybe even imagine raising a family here – of the kind that he had never had as a child.

A few weeks back he would have been thinking about doing such a thing with Isabelle. Now . . .

He felt a light touch on his arm. 'Say, is that goddamn ship heading our way?' Sarah indicated a vessel out on the water. She was laughing with her eyes. ''Cause if it is, I say we get off the balcony and take cover somewhere a little more . . . comfortable.'

Range eyed the approaching vessel. 'I figure we've got a few seconds before we got to run.'

'No way. C'mon, Mr Range, let's go.' She grabbed his hand. 'That big mother-fucker is coming right for us.'

She grabbed his hand and ran laughing from the balcony. There was an instant when he thought she was making for the lounge, and he'd misread the situation, but then she turned left, and dragged him onwards towards her bedroom – not that he was resisting. She turned the handle, stepped into the dimly lit room and glanced back at him through the open doorway.

She flashed him a playful, yet challenging smile. 'So, are you comin', you big lovely bastard?'

He took a step into the room and reached for her, hungrily. There was no doubt about it, he loved the way she said that word – *bastard*.

CHAPTER TWENTY

Range stepped out of the sterile, slick efficiency of Geneva's Cointrin International Airport and scanned for any watchers. There was no easy way to do this. Somehow, he had to appear as if he was on a serious payback mission, whilst still getting himself captured. And ideally he'd get himself taken but not killed.

He ducked into a cab, making sure that Sarah had grabbed the one behind his. He'd not detected any followers yet, or that he'd been picked up by any of Jean-Pierre de Saint-Sébastien's men, but his counter-surveillance skills were rusty from lack of use, and it wasn't something they'd ever been taught much in the Regiment.

When they'd been planning this operation, O'Shea and he had both had the same thought: go for the most obvious point of all – the Hotel d'Angleterre, the establishment on the lake where de Saint-Sébastien had billeted them. But they'd figured that would be too blatant. No operator with any savvy would go back to the scene of the crime, or at least the scene where the crime had first been hatched.

He gave his taxi driver the name of a hotel – a basic, three-star place in the city centre, set some way back from the lake. It was the kind of place he'd stayed in countless times before. The front desk would be staffed by a family member, the lobby would smell of old carpet and air-freshener, and the lift would have a concertinaed cage that you had to slide open to enter. But it would do the job, and he knew that Sarah would be giving similar instructions to the driver of her cab.

Range asked the cabbie to go via a circuitous route that would take them across the French–Swiss border. The cabbie was a typically grumpy Genevan and he warned Range it was well out of his way, and that the fare would be exorbitant. Range told him that he was a first-time visitor to Geneva, and he fancied driving across the border that cut through the city limits.

In reality, it was a bit of obvious tradecraft to exhibit to anyone who might be following. Driving via a convoluted route, one that took the passenger well out of their way, would make it easier to detect any tail. It also gave Sarah a clear run into the hotel, so she could get checked in to her room ahead of him. They'd both purchased pay-as-you go mobile phones in Turkey, as had his entire team. They were pretty much untraceable, and would work fine for coordinating the mission.

The Swiss–French border was just as the cabbie had said it would be – an unremarkable affair distinguished by nothing more than a couple of signs and some bored-looking Swiss border guards who barely cast an eye over the vehicles that motored past. A lone white male riding in a cab with Geneva plates – Range's passing barely warranted a glance.

Before departing Istanbul Range had burned some serious money on his credit card. Via a secure link he'd managed to speak to The Hogan and explain the basics of what had happened, and what they were planning. At this stage no one was sure just who was funding the mission, for the old man in Geneva had been their original paymaster. He'd paid half the money up front, the other supposedly being due on delivery of a burned-out and gutted Al Mina'a.

So until Range could manage to turn this mission around and make it pay, it was self-funded. There was a B6 float he could access, but a lot of the expenses were being burned on his credit card. He'd taken Sarah into the finest of Istanbul's shopping districts and kitted her out at some of the top boutiques the city had to offer. Geneva being a truly cosmopolitan city, Sarah needn't worry about standing out – not as long as she looked as if she had the money and status to be there. And right now, after a visit to Istanbul's trendiest stores, she looked like a thousand other beautiful young professional woman who thronged the city – only better. That much at least of their deception was complete. Now Range had to sort out his own 'disguise', and grow into his new skin.

Range planned to get picked up by de Saint-Sébastien's security at the Triple-S's office, which was situated in the plush business district of Geneva. Sarah would need to be watching, which meant she'd be ensconced in one of the smart cafés that overlooked the steel- and glass-fronted Triple-S building.

Range paid off the cabbie and checked into L'Hotel du Jardin. It was a decent enough place, if soulless and dull. He paid extra and traded up to a room that had windows opening out onto the street out front. If they were onto him, he wanted them to know where he was, and for him to be able to keep tabs on them. The odd thing was that he'd yet to detect any sense of a tail.

Maybe the old man's people still had eyes on that tracking device in Manda Bay, and were watching Nairobi airport. There was only one way to find out. He'd keep taking a step closer and pushing them, and wait to see when the trap would be sprung.

He flicked open his mobile and put a call through to his teams. He'd already had confirmation that they'd armed themselves in Geneva with the weapons for the job, but the timing of this thing was still going to be crucial. Range needed to get himself picked up after school hours, and before the Old Man had returned to his residence, which was a place of state-of-the-art security, and supposedly inviolable.

The de Saint-Sébastien residence was The Kiwi's baby. It was an old French-style *manoir* – a grand town house set on the very outskirts of Geneva. It was enclosed on three sides by dark pine forest, the trees rolling on from there into the snow-capped mountains. The Kiwi and his team had had eyes-on the place ever since they'd reached Geneva. They'd made their way deep into the forest and set up a hidden observation post from where they noted the comings and goings at the de Saint-Sébastien household.

De Saint-Sébastien senior ran the residence with military precision. During the weekday, the routine of getting his young kids to school and himself to work in downtown Geneva, never seemed to vary. According to Sabanci's dossier, de Saint-Sébastien was on his second marriage, hence the two young children. And with the Triple-S line carrying the kind of debts that it was, the old man was working long hours to try to get it back onto an even keel again.

He left the house at six o'clock in the morning, and was in his office by 6.25 sharp. He worked through to six o'clock in the evening, sometimes later, before getting picked up by his chauffeur and his security team and whisked back to his residence. Range knew at what point he was going to have to try to get close to de Saint-Sébastien – close enough to rattle him and to make it all seem for real. But what he needed first was the ruse.

During his years in the SAS and while working as a private operator, Range had learned to swear by the adage of 'going local'. Whenever a white-eye operator like him was deploying on a foreign tasking, the best cover was always to mingle with the local population. More often than not there were the obvious challenges: white skin, sandy hair and blue eyes. But in Iraq, for example, they'd posed as a local crew in some truly outrageous situations – with the aid of Shemaghs and sunglasses, and not to mention the Dodge 4x4 with its garden furniture.

Here in Geneva there were only a limited number of local types Range could pass himself off as – or at least there were in the district where de Saint-Sébastien had his office. There were the suited and booted business people; there were the glitzy women who were always to be found anywhere around serious money; and there were the young immigrants of North African origin – waiting in bars, cleaning cars or delivering takeaways as a way to scratch a living.

And then there were the homeless. The advantage to Range of joining their number was the total anonymity that homelessness gave you. No one noticed those who'd fallen through life's safety net and ended up living on the streets. You could lurk in any doorway or side-street for hours on end and no one would pay you much heed. It was the perfect way to hide in plain sight.

Range practised in his room. He rehearsed getting the

hobo's street shuffle just right – the walk of a man who had lost all sense of self and whose life had fallen through the floor. He psyched himself into the down-trodden expression, the slumped shoulders. He adopted the hunched-in chest and the caved-in psyche of one who knew he would die on these streets someday soon.

Range left the hotel and headed to the nearest McDonald's. He headed inside, made for the toilet, and locked himself into a cubicle. By the time he exited the transformation was complete: he was indistinguishable from the scores of the city's inhabitants who lived there, but without any home. He carried with him a battered and ripped sports bag that only had the one handle. Inside was his change of clothes, plus a few props for the coming hobo routine.

He made his apparently bumbling and confused way down through the maze of city streets. Geneva was simple enough to navigate, for you could always take any route that led downhill and eventually end up by the water. He reached the city's lakeside and started to meander north along the esplanade that ran all around the edge of Lake Geneva.

In the centre of the lake the famous fountain – the Jet d'Eau – spurted water in a high and graceful arc, the fine white spray drifting through the air like a curtain of mist. It was showy and dramatic, and it was one of the things the city was famous for. True to his adopted nature, Range-the-hobo paid it little heed.

Occasionally, he'd bump into a passer-by, just to get used to acting out a grovelling apology. Now and then he'd try to accost someone, holding out a silent hand to beg. And he forced himself to pause at every bin and act as if he was picking through the contents hungrily, searching for a tasty morsel that Geneva's wealthy might have discarded.

As he meandered north Range thought about Sarah. She would already be in position, occupying a window seat in a smart café on Place Dorcière. Hers was a crucial role, and it was odd how quickly they had all grown to trust her. He guessed it was the shared experiences at Al Mina'a and the flight out of there. You couldn't live through something like that and fail to get the measure of a man – or a woman for that matter.

Even in the case of Randy, Range had let his suspicions go now. The TNF rule had gone out the window. The clincher had been Randy's confession that night in Manda Bay. He'd had no reason to reveal to Range the truth about who he'd been talking to on the satphone. It had been an act of spontaneous honesty – one designed to wipe the slate clean. And Range needed to be able to trust the both of them absolutely for what was now coming.

He left the lakeside and took a turn north-west, threading his way through Brunswick Gardens, a small but beautiful park that overlooked the lake. He noticed the disapproving looks on the faces of the mothers who were giving their kids some air. Even the eastern European nannies pushing the tots' prams turned their noses up at the figure who shuffled by. Range wasn't surprised.

He'd got his hobo outfit fresh from a genuine Istanbul tramp, and courtesy of Sabanci. His Turkish host hadn't even seemed surprised at the request: a genuine set of tramp's clothes, down to the footwear, to suit a man of Range's build. Range had asked Sabanci to pay the tramp off, but he had a horrible suspicion that an Istanbul hobo had been left in a ditch somewhere and stripped of all his clothes.

Still, it was the perfect disguise. It even smelled right. His nostrils were assailed by a mixed odour of stale urine, sweat, unwashed body, street dirt and maybe a bit of faeces thrown in. The long overcoat had once been light brown. It was flecked with greys and blacks, and torn and ripped in several places. His dirty grey flannel plants were hanging low on his hips, a broken belt apparently struggling to keep them from falling down. On his feet he had a scuffed and beaten pair of trainers which were missing the laces, and he topped it all off with that calling card of the world's hobo nation: a black woolly hat, pulled low over the eyes.

Catching sight of himself in the mirrored glass windows that he passed, Range had to fight the urge to laugh. His closest mates would have struggled to recognise him right now. He hadn't shaved for days. On a smart, well-groomed male his age, a four-day stubble was the height of manly cool. It made even nice girls go weak at the knees. But not on a man dressed like Range. On Range-the-hobo his four-day growth spoke of days on the streets necking cheap alcohol, eating leftovers scavenged from the trash, and sleeping rough in disused doorways and deserted urinals. Not nice.

There was a part of Range that was a natural friend to the down-trodden and the underdog, for he'd spent his childhood in their number. That part of him relished the role he was now playing.

Range ambled down Route de Meyrin, turned into Rue de la Servette, which eventually led into Place Dorcière. Range slowed as he made his way into the quaint-looking cul-de-sac. There was only one exit out of Dorcière, which suited Range's purposes just fine.

From under the low rim of his woolly hat Range scanned the street ahead of him. The de Saint-Sébastien building lay on the right, midway down the terrace. Mostly, these were the typical old and grand buildings that made up much of downtown Geneva. They were offices all of them, with most likely private apartments on the upper floors.

Geneva's architecture had survived the Second World War without harm. Supposedly neutral, the Swiss had escaped the aerial bombardments that had torn apart so many of Europe's great cities. The de Saint-Sébastien building was an anomaly on Place Dorcière in that it was a slick edifice of polished, gleaming steel and mirrored glass. Range counted six storeys, de Saint-Sébastien's personal office being on the top floor.

The building came complete with a subterranean garage, where many of the more senior Triple-S employees parked. De Saint-Sébastien's chauffeur would drive from the residence to the Triple-S building every morning, but de Saint-Sébastien himself liked to dismount on street level, leaving his man to deal with the car below. That offered the one small window of opportunity in which Range was going to try to get to him.

Opposite and to one side of the Triple-S building was the Café du Genève. From eight o'clock sharp every morning it served breakfasts for Geneva's city workers, then coffee and snacks until lunchtime. This being Geneva, lunches at the Café du Genève could last a good two hours, complete with several courses and wine. The café stayed open into the evening, serving yet more food, closing around nine o'clock – by which time the city's business district was all but deserted.

In theory Sarah was going to have a lot of eating and drinking to do at the Café du Genève. In practice, Range figured the only time he'd have to get to de Saint-Sébastien was when he left the office, at around six o'clock in the evening. Invariably the old man ate his lunch at his desk, and rarely did he leave the office for meetings; if people wanted to see Jean-Pierre de Saint-Sébastien, he was used to them coming to him.

To either side of the building entrance massive mirrored windows were set back in steel recessed frames. Range had noticed a homeless guy in London who slept in one such frame, near Range's apartment, using the windowsill as his de facto bed frame. But Range didn't think he could get away with the same here. The Triple-S building was bound to have security, and he didn't need to get himself noticed in the wrong way. Being moved along for being a dirty hobo wouldn't help.

The building next to the Triple-S edifice offered the perfect stopping point. There seemed to be two doorways leading into the place. One was used; one definitely was not – which was the doorway nearest his target. Range paused, shuffled about a bit, then plonked his butt down on the doorstep. He felt around in the beaten-up sports bag he was carrying, and pulled out a length of cardboard, fashioning himself a makeshift seat.

Range surveyed his location. He was nearest to the closed-off end of Place Dorcière; between him and the exit to the street lay the Triple-S building, and opposite lay the Café du Genève. On the café's terrace he could see an elegant figure enjoying a late lunch, alone at her table.

Steve Range, B6 operator and now sometime hobo, was in position.

CHAPTER TWENTY-ONE

That evening, Range ate alone in the hotel restaurant. He'd made his way back from the Triple-S building, sneaked into a different fast-food joint, and done the transformation in reverse. The hobo gear was stuffed into the sports bag, and Range had caught a cab back to the hotel.

His first sighting of the target had confirmed most of what he'd expected. On one level, de Saint-Sébastien's security team had all the appearances of being slick professionals, but to a man like Range it was almost always possible to find a weakness in any set of security measures.

The principal – de Saint-Sébastien – was driven to and from his residence in the same vehicle each day. It was a beautiful black 1960s vintage Mercedes, but hardly a car that blended into the wider Geneva traffic. The first rule of such a security operation should have been to place the principal in an unremarkable vehicle, and ideally one that was regularly changed.

They also should have varied the route of the journey. From his back-up team Range knew that de Saint-Sébastien's chauffeur rarely, if ever, did that. The old man was picked up from the front entrance to the office building. Wrong. Dead wrong. It would be far, far safer to collect the principal from the car park below, and accelerate at speed away from the entrance.

De Saint-Sébastien's secretary most likely signalled the chauffeur when the big boss was ready to leave his office, giving him ample time to bring the car up from below and have it waiting. To a potential assassin or kidnapper, there was nothing like signalling the target was coming.

The chauffeur was accompanied by de Saint-Sébastien's head of security, the man he had introduced to Range and O'Shea as 'Pierre'. He took the front passenger seat, but it was also his role to open the door for the principal as he exited the Triple-S building. Range had seen all this from his position slumped in the doorway. He had a vodka bottle from which he had kept taking a pull. The fact that it was filled only with water didn't make it any less convincing.

De Saint-Sébastien had a back-up vehicle – a Porsche Cayenne, which was a city slicker's 4x4 if ever there was one. Again, the back-up vehicle should have been chosen to be unremarkable, and Range would have gone for a boring sedan, maybe a Ford Mondeo or similar. If you were looking to hit a target and you could identify the security, it made it so much easier. It was far harder when you had no idea where the principal's security might be positioned.

The main issue with de Saint-Sébastien's back-up team was the positions they took up to safeguard the principal. There were three in the Cayenne: a driver and two guards. From behind his bottle Range had watched them pull their vehicle into the kerb, directly behind the chauffeur-driven Mercedes.

Both vehicles had waited outside the office, engines idling. The two guards had dismounted, leaning against the kerb side of the Cayenne and sharing a smoke and a chat. Even the driver had come to join them. It was spring in Geneva and unseasonably warm. The driver had left his window down – like an invitation to have a grenade chucked inside.

The guards should have been ready at the exit to the Triple-S building, the driver of the Cayenne poised at the wheel. They should have surrounded Jean-Pierre de Saint-Sébastien with a screen of bodies as soon as he exited and walked him to his car. They should have shovelled him inside, only mounting up their own vehicles when the principal was underway.

They were big, meaty blokes, and Range didn't doubt they were in reasonable shape. He could tell they were armed. They had their weapons – shorts – 'hidden' on their bodies, but in ways that were obvious to him. He'd heard them talking in German, so he figured they were ex-German or Swiss military, so probably quite capable.

The main problem with de Saint-Sébastien's security as a whole was 'Pierre'. As was so often the case in such situations, the head of security was overly protective and possessive of the principal. Range figured Pierre knew his own limitations, and so he kept the rest of the security team at a safe distance, lest de Saint-Sébastien realise them too – which was why the team from the Cayenne remained at their vehicle.

During the crucial walk from the office exit to the Mercedes, de Saint-Sébastien only had Pierre by his side – and that meant Range could get to him. De Saint-Sébastien was about to get the surprise of a lifetime. Range wanted him to be in a serious state of agitation by the time it came to talking, and he needed to truly shock the man.

Range didn't underestimate Jean-Pierre de Saint-Sébastien. He was going to be a hard one to crack. Even if they'd grabbed him and held a gun to his head, Range doubted if a man like de Saint-Sébastien would talk. No. You should never underestimate your enemy. De Saint-Sébastien was going to have to feel that he had won this thing. He'd have to believe that whatever words he said were never going to be repeated anywhere, that's if he was to go to the heart of the matter, which was exactly where Range needed him.

Range finished his meal, signed the chit, and headed for his room. He needed to phone around his teams who had arrived in Geneva well ahead of him and Sarah. Tomorrow was the big day. From all that he had seen today, they would go for it on the following afternoon – a Thursday. He needed to ensure there were no last-minute updates from his men – and his one female team member – before pressing the nuclear button.

Range had had to sanitise himself completely for what was coming. He'd got rid of his mobile phone before leaving the hotel; he'd taken it apart, smashed up the SIM card, and dumped it in the hotel trash. If there were to be any last-minute changes to the plan – and Range didn't expect there to be any – Sarah was to make contact with him in person. She'd stop as if concerned to help a homeless man, hand him a few coins, and slip a message to him that way.

Range's plan of attack was predicated on de Saint-Sébastien's security team's single greatest failing: their inability to provide close protection to the principal. He'd hit them at their weakest point, and put the fear of God into the old man. The way he was going to do it, had he wanted to take de Saint-Sébastien out he'd be more than capable of doing so, but that wasn't the aim of the coming hit: Range had to fail in his task, but fail convincingly.

Range heard a throaty roar from below ground. De Saint-Sébastien's black Mercedes 300 SEL sedan had a 6.3-litre V8 motor. It sure meant you could hear it coming. The classic lines of the 1960s vehicle drew Range's eye as it powered out of the subterranean parking lot – all curved and graceful gleaming paintwork, and highly polished chrome – and pulled up outside the Triple-S building.

The number plate sported the distinctive Swiss flag on the one side, a white cross on a red shield, and to the other side of the number plate was the Geneva canton's shield, a black griffon and a golden key, set over a red and yellow background. There was something vaguely Nazi about the canton shield, at least to Range's way of thinking. The whole effect – the classic lines of the black Mercedes itself; the exclusivity of the plates – smacked of a lifetime of wealth, comfort and exclusivity. Well, Arnault Kurtz's bubble of privilege was about to be burst wide open.

Range levered himself to his feet. He had the battered sports bag clutched in one hand. He let his shoulders droop and shuffled forward. Timing was everything now, as well as his ability to keep up the act, to hide in plain sight. The sports bag was deliberately unfastened. Range meandered his way past the Cayenne that had pulled to a halt. The guards had dismounted from the vehicle, but they paid little heed to the dirty hobo shuffling past.

Range wandered onwards, passing by 'Pierre', who was standing by the rear door to the Mercedes, looking important and waiting for de Saint-Sébastien to appear. He made about ten paces, before letting his bag fall. Various bits of hobo kit tumbled out of the open zip, including the precious bottle of vodka. Range paused, and stared down at the bits and pieces, as if his booze-addled mind was taking a few seconds to catch up with what he'd done.

He shuffled forward two paces, knelt and started to reclaim his few worldly possessions. Being a drunken hobo he was slow to his task. Pierre threw Range one sharp disparaging look, and shook his head disgustedly. Why wasn't there someone around to move on such a waste of a human life? Where was Geneva's city police force when you needed them?

The door to the Triple-S building sprang open and Jean-Pierre de Saint-Sébastien appeared. Pierre stepped forward to meet him. Range paused in mid task. He made a grab for the vodka bottle but scooted it in the wrong direction out of his reach. He lurched towards it, came up close to Pierre and struck. If he were doing this for real, he'd go for a blow to the head, to put the man out cold, but if he did that now Pierre could fall and hit the pavement, cracking his skull and killing himself. What he needed here was measured violence.

His hobo's shoe lashed out at Pierre's leg, landing a savage blow sideways against the knee. Range heard something crack, and as Pierre crumpled he delivered a lightning punch to the throat. It wasn't enough to kill him, but he'd be down and out for a good while now. De Saint-Sébastien had barely turned to register what was happening when Range's arm shot out and grabbed him around the neck. He dragged him down, ripped Pierre's weapon from its holster, and whipped it up until he had it held to de Saint-Sébastien's throat.

The entire manoeuvre had taken a matter of seconds. 'Hello, Mr de Saint-Sébastien,' Range snarled in the old man's ear. 'Or should I say Arnault Kurtz of old? It's Steve Range, and I've come to tell you it's payback time.'

Range felt the old man stiffen in panic, but his grip was too tight for him to be able even to scream. Range dragged him across the pavement and towards his own vehicle. He was going to use it as if to cover his back, although he knew fully well what was coming.

'Back the fuck off!' Range yelled, as the three guards from the Porsche seemed to wake up to what was happening. 'One step, and there's a bullet in his brain!'

Range watched as they realised the full extent of the calamity unfolding before their eyes. Range wasn't a Geneva hobo; he was their worst fucking nightmare. They wrestled for their weapons, but seemed more intent on taking cover behind the Cayenne than on doing anything to rescue the principal.

'Order your chauffeur out of the Merc,' Range snarled into de Saint-Sébastien's ear. 'We're going for a little drive, Mr de Saint-Sébastien. Just you and me. Just the two of us. I thought we'd have a nice cosy talk down by the lakeside.' Range forced the muzzle of the pistol deeper into the old man's throat. 'Do it!'

Range loosened the grip slightly, just enough so that de

Saint-Sébastien could utter a few strangled words in German. A figure emerged from the driver's side of the Mercedes and stepped away from the vehicle. Range gestured with the pistol, waving the driver further off to one side. Dragging the old man with him, he circled around the front of the Merc, and yanked open the offside passenger door, roughly shoving de Saint-Sébastien inside.

Then he dived into the driver's seat, dropped the clutch and deliberately stalled the vehicle. He placed the pistol on the dash, where he knew the chauffeur could see it, and started trying to restart the Mercedes. Now surely they would do it; they'd take the bait and come running for him.

'Stay the fuck where you are,' he snarled, eyeing the old man in the mirror. 'You try to run, I'll put a bullet in your brain.'

De Saint-Sébastien looked truly petrified, but there was something else in his eyes too: the defiance of a man who was prepared to run. That momentary glimpse in the rear-view mirror had given Range a fix on the guard force. They'd bundled themselves into the Cayenne and were preparing to follow. He needed to give them something extra, an irresistible come-on.

The engine started, he reached for the pistol and went as if to check he had a round chambered. Instead, he flicked the magazine release catch and watched the thirteen-rounds mag fly out of the weapon and scatter bullets across the Merc's footwell. He let out a string of curses, enough for de

Saint-Sébastien in the rear to know that something was badly wrong. He bent as if to collect up the mag and the bullets, and tensed for what was coming.

He heard the rear door release go, as the old man bolted from the vehicle. He'd realised his team wasn't coming for him and that the only person who was going to save him was himself. Range heard him screaming out in German as he ran.

He raised himself up from the footwell to see the guards piling out of the Cayenne. Ahead of him the chauffeur had finally thought to draw his own weapon. He was advancing towards Range, the pistol levelled at him through the windscreen. Range felt the driver's door yanked open. Hands reached in and dragged him out onto the road. The rear door to the Merc was swung open, and Range felt himself hauled up and thrown inside.

Bodies piled in on top of him, as he was kicked and punched down into the footwell. Range wasn't a small bloke, but the Germans had built the Mercedes 300 SEL as a motor of real luxury and class, and there was room enough down there for him.

There was a squeal of tyres and the 300 SEL tore away from the kerb. The kicks and punches redoubled now. Range covered his head with his arms, as they rained savage blows onto him. Like true professional killers, they went for the head, the kidneys and the groin, as they vented their shock, their fear and their aggression.

The blows were agonising, and Range knew they'd do some real damage if they carried on for much longer. He'd gambled on the fact that the old man would want him kept alive and conscious enough to talk, but maybe he'd misjudged things. Range told himself he'd survived a dose of nerve gas, a LPG mega-bomb, and a HIND gunship over recent days. He just had to live through this beating.

As their fear and aggression subsided a little, the driving became more subdued, and so finally did the beating. Range could hear the guards breathing heavily from all the exertion, as one talked to what he presumed was the other vehicle, in German. De Saint-Sébastien had made a run for the Cayenne, and he had to be in it with the remaining security team.

Presumably someone had thought to scoop Pierre off the pavement and bring him with them, in which case Range had that reunion to look forward to whenever they got to their destination.

No one had thought to blindfold him, though. Sure, he was down in the footwell and couldn't see much, but he still had a sense of where they were going. Patches of shadow kept flashing through the windows at regular intervals. Trees. An avenue of trees lined the road that ran along the lakeside. By the slant of the sun's rays he could tell they were heading east. He heard the hoot of a ferry out on the water. No doubt about it, they were making their way east along the lakeside road.

Thanks to Emin Sabanci's dossier compiled in Istanbul, Range had a good idea where they might be going. Amongst several properties – including a villa in Bermuda and a private island off the Italian coast – de Saint-Sébastien owned a *gartenhaus* on the banks of Lake Geneva, at Evian-les-Bains, an exclusive lakeside resort. It was used occasionally by the family when they wanted to enjoy the warmer months by the water.

It was discreet, isolated and remote, and Range didn't doubt that was where de Saint-Sébastien was taking him. It lay across the French side of the border, which might explain why the worst of the beating had stopped. The last thing de Saint-Sébastien or his security team needed was to get stopped by the French border guards, with an apparently beaten-up tramp lying hidden in their vehicle's footwell.

Range could taste the blood in his mouth. Pierre more than anyone was rejoicing in the beating. They had dragged him into the *gartenhaus*, while all the time Jean-Pierre de Saint-Sébastien stomped about yelling orders and generally berating his security team for almost getting him taken by a lone assailant – Range. The fear and shock of what had happened had seriously got to the old man, and he was beside himself with rage.

De Saint-Sébastien's security team had Range held in some kind of a utility room. They'd been kicking the living daylights out of him on the hard, tiled floor. As he curled into a foetus and took his second major beating, Range tried to focus on the fact that he had de Saint-Sébastien exactly where he wanted him. But it was cold comfort right now, for there was little sign of the savagery stopping. *Christ, much more of this and they would kill him.*

It was only on a curt word from de Saint-Sébastien that the blows finally came to an end. Range heard the old man bark out a few orders before he retired to what Range presumed was the main living quarters of the *gartenhaus*.

Range had gleaned a few things from those orders. Pierre's real name seemed to be Hans. De Saint-Sébastien appeared to be incensed at the man for what Range could only presume was the utter failure of the security measures that Hans had put in place, supposedly to safeguard his principal.

Hans hauled Range to his feet. He felt a last blow to the head. Thankfully Hans punched soft as shit, not that Range was letting on. He allowed his bloodied and bruised head to loll on his neck with his shoulders thrown down and forward, as if he was completely beaten.

'You, *scheisskopf*, get out of the clothes,' Hans snarled, his spittle spraying into Range's face. The guy was beside himself with rage. 'Out of your clothes, *arschloch*!'

Range did as he was ordered. He peeled off the tramp's overcoat, the grimy shirt and the slacks and the hobo's beaten-about trainers. He'd been wearing the shoes barefoot, and they'd left his feet dark and grimy. He was left standing in his boxers only, but with a charity wristband on the one hand and his Omega watch on the other.

Hans rifled through the clothes. He found nothing of interest. The tiny tracking device sewn into the overcoat went completely unnoticed. Leaving the clothes in a heap, Hans turned back to Range.

'Now, *scheisskopf*, you go to see Mr de Saint-Sébastien. To apologise.' He cracked Range around the head again. 'Say to Mr de Saint-Sébastien you are very sorry. You got me, *scheisskopf*?'

Range nodded mutely.

He kept his head low and eyes downcast, as he was marched in to Mr de Saint-Sébastien's presence.

CHAPTER TWENTY-TWO

Range was shoved into the room, Hans's pistol digging into the nape of his neck. De Saint-Sébastien was seated behind an ancient-looking desk, one that was polished to a mirror-like sheen. This had to be some kind of a study. It was sparsely furnished, but what little furniture there was spoke of family heirlooms passed down through the generations, in a de Saint-Sébastien family line that was distinguished by money and the power that real wealth bought.

The upbringing of this man could not have been more different from that of Steve Range. In de Saint-Sébastien's view at least, this was going to be far from a meeting of equals. But Range had his man exactly where he wanted him – believing himself to be in a position of absolute and unassailable strength. Yet it was now that Range had to be ultra careful. He had to get his act just right. He had to behave like a man who was totally beaten, but also as a man of sufficient stature to deserve a reckoning, at least in de Saint-Sébastien's eyes.

The old man swilled some liquor in a glass. Range could smell the drink on him. He saw the bottle on the table – a fine Islay single malt. He figured de Saint-Sébastien had necked a good few whiskies as soon as he'd made it to the *gartenhaus*. No doubt he'd needed it to settle his nerves, after what Range had done to him. But as with men everywhere, the drink should also have loosened de Saint-Sébastien's tongue.

He glanced up, his eyes slightly bleary and red-rimmed. 'So, Mr Range, welcome. I believed you were still in Kenya, at a Navy SEAL base. At least, I was told you were still there.' He flicked his eyes across to Hans. 'So my head of security here led me to believe. But evidently not, Mr Range, as here you are in Geneva – or should I say in Evian-les-Bains, for that is where we have brought you.'

Range nodded. He kept silent. He wanted to give the old man space to talk.

'So what brought you here, Mr Range? Of your own free will? Here to Geneva? Isabelle perhaps? *My daughter?*' De Saint-Sébastien sniggered. He sloshed the drink around the glass, before taking a longer sip. Range noticed that in spite of the drink the old man's hands were still shaking.

Range nodded to the bottle. 'I'll take some of that, if you don't mind.'

He felt a punch to the side of his head. '*Scheisskopf!* You answer Mr de Saint-Sébastien! And you say sorry . . .'

De Saint-Sébastien snapped a few angry words at his head of security, and the man subsided into silence.

'You have met Hans, I believe? By the looks of things he has been a little over-zealous in his beating. If only he were able to exert himself in the same way to safeguard my personal security. Perhaps not the bravest of men, but his record proves him to be a passable bully and an adequate killer when the need arises – isn't that right, Hans?'

The man grunted something that Range didn't catch.

De Saint-Sébastien stared at Range for a second. 'So, Mr Range, tell me, why have you come? A lone attempt to exact some kind of revenge? And revenge for what, if I might be so presumptuous to ask? You used a word when you tried to grab me: *payback*. Payback for what, Mr Range? You were sent in to wipe out Al Mina'a. In that you failed. Indeed, it should be *me* seeking payback from *you*, or wouldn't you agree?'

'I guess we see things differently,' Range muttered.

De Saint-Sébastien passed a glass of liquor across to his head of security. He nodded at Range. 'A drink for our guest.'

Range took the proffered glass. He gulped some of the fiery liquid, rolling it around his mouth so it stung painfully into the cuts and bruises he'd sustained during the beating. As he did so de Saint-Sébastien commenced talking again. Now that Range had got him started he didn't seem to want to stop.

'But it wasn't quite the failure you perhaps wanted it to be, Mr Range. Not entirely. You see a few hundred deaths, several hundred injured, and in such a horrific way, well, it is perhaps hardly surprising that the people of Puntland are up in arms. No one knows who did this, of course, and they will never know. But it has the hand of foreigners written all over it, and especially since there are survivors who saw "white men" – that's you and your crew, Mr Range – on that ship.'

De Saint-Sébastien smiled. 'There are reports of revenge attacks on foreigners already. Some have taken place against boats passing the Puntland coastline. Puntland was one of the few countries fighting piracy in the Horn of Africa. Their anti-piracy Task Force was even trained by you British, I believe. The attacks will only escalate as the word spreads. Puntland is becoming an angry and hostile place for foreigners, so your mission was in part successful. Not as successful as it might have been had thousands died. Women and children would have helped. The more the better. That always gets the locals enraged. But as far as I am concerned you did passably well.'

'To what end?' Range queried.

'And why would I choose to enlighten you, Mr Range?'

Range could see that the old bastard was dying to tell. Sooner or later he knew he would. But there was no harm in prodding him a little first. 'Better you confess your crimes to someone. You can always start with me.'

'Crimes! Those are not *crimes!*' De Saint-Sébastien snapped. 'I tell you what are the real crimes. Three decades ago I took over as chairman of Triple-S. We were one of the foremost shipping lines in the world, a multi-billion-dollar business built up over generations. We employed tens of thousands of workers, Mr Range, and most of them in Europe. Decent, hard-working men supporting families all across this fine continent. You know what has happened since? Our competitors have crewed their ships with Chinese, Turks and Africans, flagged those ships to nations of convenience – Liberia and Panama, for God's sake – and they have proceeded to do their best to evade any laws that may control them, and in the process they stole our business.

'So, Mr Range, tell me, who are the real criminals? And tell me, how do you compete against this? You have a historic family business, the Triple-S line, going to the wall, and thousands of honest, decent seamen and their families losing their livelihoods. How do you fight against it, Mr Range? Do you let your business go to the wall? Or do you fight?' De Saint-Sébastien took a long pull on his whisky. 'I tell you, Mr Range!' he spat. 'You fight. And where necessary, you fight fire with fire.

'You are a military man, Mr Range, although you do not seem to have planned your present mission with the famed efficiency or lethality of the British SAS . . .'

'I was that close to getting you,' Range cut in. 'If you hadn't noticed, your security under Hans here is a joke . . .'

Range felt the heavy butt of Hans's pistol crack across his skull. He half went down under the blow.

De Saint-Sébastien shot to his feet, his face puce with rage. '*Dummkopf!* You will leave the disciplining of Mr Range to me! Mr Range and I may not see eye-to-eye on many things, but on this point we most certainly do. If you want to stand any chance of keeping your post in my company, be careful, Hans. Very careful.'

Range felt Hans stiffen at his side. 'Yes, sir.'

De Saint-Sébastien settled back into his seat. Range felt around the area of his skull where Hans had smashed the butt into him. He winced, and his hand came away red with blood.

'Where was I?' De Saint-Sébastien mused. 'Oh yes. You are a military man, Mr Range. You are not, I think, a man of international affairs, but you will need to understand a little of that to realise why a village of Africans had to die. Once I had decided to fight fire with fire, there were no holds barred. And the most lucrative of all the schemes my rivals were involved in was the dumping of toxic waste. And I presume even for a man of your intellect, Mr Range, it would appear obvious that the lawless waters off Somalia are the ideal dumping ground.'

'Still doesn't explain why Al Mina'a had to fry,' Range interjected.

'Perhaps not.' De Saint-Sébastien took the whisky bottle and poured himself a generous slug. 'But factor in Steiner-

Lambert-Finklestein, a firm of New York attorneys, and you might start to understand. Two years ago those bastards served a writ on my company – a class-action lawsuit charging us with illegal dumping of toxic waste off Somalia. And as you may have guessed, Mr Range, the lawsuit was brought on behalf of the people of Al Mina'a – the odd barrel of low-level waste having been dragged up in their fishing nets. The lawsuit would have finished the Triple-S line. That, of course, I could not allow to happen.'

Range let out a long, low whistle. 'Like the mother of all blood feuds,' he muttered. 'But you kill the village, you kill the lawsuit . . .'

'Exactly, Mr Range.' The old man was clearly warming to his topic. 'Once you have no plaintiffs, no class action, you have no lawsuit. But of course, I needed the kill mission to be utterly and totally deniable, and those undertaking it to have not the slightest idea of the real reason why they were being sent in to wipe out an African fishing village. In that I think I succeeded remarkably well.' De Saint-Sébastien paused. Range could tell he was enjoying this.

'All of this being so, Mr Range, it should not take a genius to work out how a brutal attack on a peaceful fishing village by a foreign-operated LPG tanker would reap enormous benefits . . .'

'Profits, not benefits,' Range interjected.

'A destabilised Puntland up in arms against foreigners is an added bonus . . .' de Saint-Sébastien continued, ignoring

Range's comment. 'What New York lawyer is ever going to be willing to step foot in Puntland now? I took a massive gamble, Mr Range, but so far it has paid off. Thanks to you, Mr Range, I gambled and I won.

'I have carried a heavy burden as I have attempted to keep our ships, and those families who depend upon them, afloat. That lawsuit would have finished us all. I would have preferred the entire village fried, of course, but your mission was at least partially successful. In short, you should feel proud of yourself, Mr Range. You have safeguarded thousands of livelihoods across Europe, and at what cost? That of a few poor and ignorant African fishermen.'

'So what're the numbers?' Range asked. 'Just how much is your shipping line worth, with no lawsuit to ruin it?'

'Since your partially successful mission, we've seen our shares rising sharply as the markets sense the threat of the lawsuit receding,' de Saint-Sébastien answered. 'The total value of the Triple-S line is back up at around the 2.5 billion dollars mark, as things presently stand, which means we are getting back to the top of our game.'

'But why the need for us?' Range probed. 'Why not use Hans, or one or two of the other security guys you employ?'

'Many reasons,' de Saint-Sébastien replied. 'Deniability. The link between you and your team and the Triple-S line was an intangible one at best. Capability. You and your team were capable of such a mission. Hans and his ilk I suspect are not. Expendability. When you have lived and worked as closely as I have to your own security team, you cannot help but grow a little attached to them. Not so easy to send such men on a mission from which you know they are not going to return. Or at least, you don't expect them to return . . . You and your men, Mr Range, you have proven more than a little difficult to kill.'

'That's what we specialise in.'

'Ah yes, but not any more, eh?'

'So, a final question, if I may,' Range prompted. He necked some more of his whisky, as a truly condemned man might. 'Why the need for the initial kidnap scenario and Isabelle's little charade? Why not just call us up and offer us the job, straight? Well, not straight, but at least the bit to go waste the world's foremost pirate stronghold.'

'Because, Mr Range, you wouldn't have taken it. Who would? Sail into a supposedly impregnable pirate harbour, get yourselves and your ship seized, and all in an effort to blow the pirates to pieces. Not the most risk-free of operations, is it, Mr Range? No. We needed you to be totally emotionally committed – committed beyond all reason, you might say – hence the tiresome Isabelle-my-daughter kidnap and ransom charade to ensure your buy-in. And you have to agree, it worked perfectly, didn't it Mr Range?'

Range nodded. 'You got me suckered right enough.'

'You never suspected a thing.' De Saint-Sébastien's tone was close to gloating now. Triumphant. 'That's why I hired you and your crew. Brave to a fault you may be, but you had neither the brains nor the imagination to see through any of this. Like soldiers everywhere you follow orders blindly, and even to your doom.'

Range kept silent, doing his best to act the dumb soldier.

'You've allowed the Triple-S line to rise phoenix-like from the flames of that lawsuit,' de Saint-Sébastien continued. 'In theory, you should be due a bonus. A big one. Pity life doesn't always work out that way.'

Range shrugged. 'You win some, you lose some. So this way the Triple-S line gets to fight another day?'

'It does. However, I am afraid you, Mr Range, do not.' De Saint-Sébastien raised his glass. 'Drain the rest of your whisky, Mr Range, in a toast to Triple-S. A pity to waste the last drops of a fine single malt such as this.'

Range took a sideways glance at the pistol that Hans was holding, then down at his bound hands. He'd been forced to hold the glass and drink two-handedly. 'Yep, I guess this is the end. Unless . . .'

'Unless what?'

'What about the others on my team? You planning to hunt us all down?'

'I think I need to finish what I started, don't you?' de Saint-Sébastien mused, setting down his empty glass.

'Unless . . .' Range repeated.

'Unless what?' There was an edge of irritation creeping into the old man's voice.

Range shook his head. 'No, nothing. Not yet, anyway.'

De Saint-Sébastien turned to his head of security and issued a few curt commands in German. Range figured it was the issuing of his death warrant. So now that was done, he figured maybe it was the right moment.

'So, Mr Range, I think it is time you were leaving,' de Saint-Sébastien announced.

'Yeah, maybe it is. Unless . . .' Range glanced at the telephone sat on de Saint-Sébastien's desk. 'You see, I think your phone is about to ring.'

The old man dropped his eyes to his desk, before brushing away the suggestion with a wave of his hand.

'Playing for time, Mr Range. Not what I would have expected of you.' He rose to his feet. 'Perhaps it is best not to shake hands. So if you'll—'

Bring-bring. Bring-bring. De Saint-Sébastien stared at the phone on his desk. *Bring-bring.* He flicked his gaze across to Range, then back to the phone.

Range smiled. 'Odd, isn't it? I mean, who would know you're here, in your *gartenhaus*? Your wife maybe? Well, I guess you'd better answer.'

De Saint-Sébastien hesitated for an instant, as the phone continued with its soft ringing, then snatched it up in his hand.

'De Saint-Sébastien!'

Range heard a female voice on the other end of the line. She was jabbering away in obvious panic and in German. Although Range couldn't understand a word of what the woman was saying, he saw the colour literally drain from the old man's face. He felt the pistol jabbing harder into the base of his neck, as Hans responded to the tension and shock that was written across his employer's features.

He didn't even know the half of it yet.

The woman's voice stopped talking. A man came on the line. This time the voice was speaking English, though Range could catch only the odd word or two. The voice stopped talking. There was silence for a long second. Then de Saint-Sébastien spoke into the receiver, his voice reduced to a quiet and muted semi-whisper.

'Ja. Ja. Yes. I understand.'

The voice on the line uttered a few final words, and again de Saint-Sébastien confirmed that he understood. The line went dead. De Saint-Sébastien replaced the receiver. He sank into his chair. Range saw the old man pinch the bridge of his nose, as he tried to deal with the shock that he was experiencing. Finally, he glanced up at Range. There was a new expression in his eyes now, and it was one that looked to be very close to the edge of madness.

'So, Mr Range, I suppose you think that you have won? I suppose you think you are free to go – that Hans will cut your bonds?'

Hans tried to utter some words of protest, but the old man silenced him with a gesture.

He cracked a thin smile. 'The trouble is, Mr Range, I know that none of your men are capable of doing this. Harming an innocent mother and her children? Defenceless as they are? Despite what they say, your men do not have it in them. And that means I still have you at my mercy, as long as I am willing to take the risk. Don't you agree, Mr Range?'

'Maybe. Yeah, you're probably right.' Range shrugged. 'But Aisha . . . The woman from Al Mina'a they've got with them. Her fisherman husband killed in the explosion. Fried like the rest of them. In her grief and her anger I reckon she's capable of anything . . .' That last detail about a fisherman husband was a lie, of course, but Range figured it was a nice bit of colour to add to the scenario. 'If you don't believe me speak to your wife again. There's a Somali woman with them and she's ready to cut out your children's . . .'

A string of savage curses erupted from de Saint-Sébastien's throat. His hand shot beneath his desk and it came up holding a weapon. With the pistol covering Range and pointed bulls-eye at his head, de Saint-Sébastien spat out a string of orders. The words were in German and directed at Hans, but Range had no doubt as to what he was saying.

Hans strode across to the door and flung it open. He yelled at the rest of the security team. Figures tore about, grabbing weapons and kit, before they headed out of the front door. Range heard an engine fire up, a squeal of tyres on loose gravel, and then the Cayenne was tearing up the driveway towards the main road.

'So, this is how it is,' de Saint-Sébastien announced, his voice slick with menace. 'My security team are heading direct to the de Saint-Sébastien family residence, as you may have guessed. You will use the phone to speak to your men – plus this Somali bitch – and call them off. If not, I will start shooting. I will not kill you, at least not at first. I will shoot the parts of your body I believe will cause you most pain.' He lowered the pistol until it was levelled at Range's crotch. 'I will start with your manhood, Mr Range.'

He waved the pistol at the phone. 'Use last-number recall. Call your men off. Now!'

The last words were delivered in a crazed snarl. As if to punctuate them, the old man twitched the pistol a fraction to one side and fired. The bullet tore past barely inches from Range's crotch, the pressure wave thrown off by its passage hammering into his side.

Range took a step towards the phone. This wasn't going quite how he'd planned. Either he'd underestimated the level of the old man's insanity, or he'd overestimated de Saint-Sébastien's love for his wife and children. Right now Range needed some back-up, and fast, or it was all going to go horribly wrong.

The single pistol shot had torn apart the night silence in the forest that surrounded the *gartenhaus*. In response two figures rose from the undergrowth and began racing through the trees. They flew towards the lighted windows of de Saint-Sébastien's study like black wraiths, moving silently, but with deadly speed and intent.

As Range went to lift the phone the first of them came

crashing through the window, rolling forward in a cascade of shattered glass, and springing to his feet. The figure was dressed from head to toe in black. The hands that had punched their way through the window were shielded in tough leather aviator gloves, and even the face was obscured by a thick, black, rubberised balaclava.

As he came to his feet the figure's silenced MP5 sub-machinegun was in the shoulder, sweeping the room. It came to rest menacing the old man.

'Drop the fucking weapon!' Randy snarled. 'DROP IT! NOW!'

Range sensed Hans swinging his pistol round to open fire on Randy, but Range was quicker. His bound wrists came up in a classic Krav Maga move, a double-handed blow knocking the pistol aside. The bullet fired off harmlessly, as Range's hands gripped Hans by the windpipe, pulling the man towards him with savage force.

Range's head lashed forwards, as he used the power in his shoulders and upper torso to lend added weight to the blow. His forehead smashed into Hans's nose, and Range heard the reassuring crunch of bones breaking, as blood spurted out from where he'd stove the guy's face in. Hans went down like a sack of shit. He lay on the floor of the study, his hands clutching his broken face and screaming in agony.

A second figure came diving through the window, O'Shea coming to his feet, weapon in the aim. De Saint-Sébastien found himself staring down the barrels of two Heckler and

Koch MP5 sub-machineguns, each capable of churning out eight hundred rounds a minute. His hand wavered for an instant, and then the pistol was lowered. As he placed it on the desk, Randy strode forward and disarmed him.

With Randy keeping the old man covered, O'Shea pulled out a knife and bent to slice through the bonds that tied Range's hands.

'Thanks,' Range remarked, as he massaged some life back into them. He was stiff as hell from the beatings, plus the crack to his skull from Hans's pistol. He turned to de Saint-Sébastien. The old man was sitting stiffly behind his desk, his face like a rigid death mask.

'I guess this is goodbye,' Range remarked. 'Unless—'

'Mr Range, there is one thing you need to know,' de Saint-Sébastien cut in. 'No one, but no one does this to me or my family. I will find you.' He glanced at Randy and O'Shea. 'And your friends. I will not rest. I will track down you and your families . . .'

Range held up a hand to silence him. 'No thanks. Not another blood feud. We got a few too many of those already.'

'You started this,' the old spat. 'I will finish it when I see fit to.'

'Wrong, old man. You started it. And let me tell you, you don't know the half of it yet. And that's why it ends here.' Range turned to Randy and O'Shea. 'Let's get going.'

Under the cover of Randy and O'Shea's sub-machineguns the three of them made for the doorway.

CHAPTER TWENTY-THREE

'You got it all?' Range asked, as he settled into the rear seat of the Istanbul hire car.

Randy smiled. 'Yeah. Everything. It's perfect.'

'The quality?' Range asked.

'Dude, like your hottest ever porn movie, only a fuck sight more explosive.'

Range laughed. It hurt to do so, from all the bruising and lacerations on his body. 'O'Shea?'

O'Shea drummed a tense rhythm on the steering wheel, as he accelerated away from Evian-les-Bains. 'Buddy, we got it all, but I'll be happy when we're out of here and make it over the border.'

'But Sarah's uploaded it already, right?'

'Yeah, she should have got it via the live feed, and posted it online right away. But the old man doesn't know that yet, and until he does it doesn't buy us much safety.'

'You've warned The Kiwi?'

O'Shea nodded, keeping his eyes on the road. 'Yep, I made the call back in the woods. That's why Randy got to you a few seconds ahead of me.'

They slipped across the Italian border in the early hours. They'd headed for Rome, for no other reason than it was the pre-arranged plan to do so. Rome was a city big enough to lose yourself in, and one with great international flight connections. Range's team sensed this was all but done now, and they were keen to get back to home and family. It was just the final, final chapter that needed to be closed.

The rendezvous point was the Hotel Dei Borgognoni, in the historic old-quarter of the city. It was a more than half-decent place to stay, and Range figured they could afford it, for they were about to hit pay-dirt. It was great to be reunited with the rest of his team. The Kiwi and his crew had made it there just a short while before Range, having evacuated the de Saint-Sébastien residence at the highest possible speed.

Sarah had been first to arrive, of course. After uploading the footage she'd headed for Geneva airport and the short flight to Rome. Hers was a role that the old man had never got wise to, so it had been safe for her to leave via the airport. Apart from making a couple of calls on her mobile to warn O'Shea's team and the Kiwi's that Range was mobile in the old man's Mercedes, her only role then had been to wait at the hotel for the footage to be beamed across to her.

But the role she'd played in strategising the whole thrust of the mission over the past few days had been an absolutely pivotal one. It was all about to come to fruition now. Everyone crowded into Range's room. No one wanted to miss out on this, the final dose of revenge, and they figured they'd be getting serious bang for their bucks this time.

Range logged onto the internet, dialled up Skype and made the call. Thanks to the pressure The Kiwi had put on Mrs de Saint-Sébastien, they had the old man's every number – residence, office, mobile and more. They had his email addresses. They even had the details of all his various boltholes around the world. The Kiwi hadn't done anything even remotely beyond what was acceptable. The wife, the kids – no one had been touched. When he got the cobra look in his eyes, he didn't need to hurt anyone.

The number rang a few times, before there was a tight, clipped answer. 'Yes!'

'Mr de Saint-Sébastien, this is Steve Range.'

Silence. Then. 'I have nothing – *nothing* – more to say to you!'

'Before you cut the line, you do need to hear this.'

'Convince me!' the old man's voice snarled.

Because Range was using Skype, all those gathered in the room were able to listen in on the conversation. Range

332

was speaking into the laptop's speakers, and the old man's voice was hissing out of them, tight with rage.

'Mr de Saint-Sébastien, are you near a computer?'

'It's Friday, and I'm in my office,' the voice snapped. 'You don't think a few threats and the cowardly kidnapping of my family would stop me, do you? It's Friday, I'm in the Triple-S office, and I have work to do.'

'Sir, you need to log onto www.vimeo.com/kurtzconfession. Have you got that? And sir, the password is: almina'a. You might want to call me back when you're done watching. Or better still, I'll call you.'

Range heard the line go dead.

'D'you think he'll goddamn watch it?' Sarah asked. 'He sounds pissed as hell.'

Range smiled. 'Not as pissed as he's going to be in about, say, twenty minutes' time.'

Range was logged on to the vimeo site himself. It had a function that allowed you to view the identity of anyone who had watched a video or was watching. Range saw a second watcher's ID pop up on screen: JPdeSt.Sebastian@TripleSLine.com

That was their man. Mr de Saint-Sébastien clicked the play button. Range let the video play on his computer screen too, for there were some on his team who hadn't seen it yet. The old man's image appeared, his voice ringing out loud and clear. 'That being so, Mr Range, it should not take a genius to work out how a brutal attack on a peaceful fishing village by a foreign operated LPG tanker would reap enormous benefits . . .'

Range left the video playing, and went to grab himself a cold beer. The minute recording device embedded in his fake Omega watch had worked wonders. It consisted of a tiny camera lens and microphone, plus a transmitter that had beamed both sound and images out to O'Shea and Randy, who had secreted themselves in the thick forest surrounding the de Saint-Sébastien family's *gartenhaus*.

You could buy these camera-watches from any number of specialised spy shops around the world, complete with the receiver unit. Every major capital seemed to have one, and it certainly hadn't posed Emin Sabanci any problems getting hold of one back in Istanbul.

But Range hadn't wanted to trust to the watch alone. Say one of de Saint-Sébastien's men had taken it, as a keepsake or a souvenir off a dead man? The charity wristband had been the back-up. It had a simple listening device embedded within it. They'd have settled for sound alone if need be. But as it was, they'd got it all on perfectly usable video – a video that Mr de Saint-Sébastien had just finished watching.

Range dialled his number once more. Best to strike whilst the iron was hot. The voice that answered sounded drained and tired. Defeated almost.

'Yes, Mr Range. Very dramatic. Very clever . . .' A pause. 'What is it that you want?'

'Sir, right now you have two options. We've posted the

video on a private, password-only section of the website. It's been viewed by us, by you and no one else. But one word and it goes viral, plus it will be released to all the major news networks. The mysterious massacre of a couple of hundred fishermen in Puntland isn't headline news right now. But trust me, if we release that video it will be. That, sir, is Option One.

'Option Two is this,' Range continued. 'You do a fire sale of all the Triple-S businesses. By your own admission, even in their present state they're worth some 2.5 billion dollars. Let's say it's a dead cert you'll raise in excess of two billion. Once those two billion arrive in a numbered bank account, the details of which I will give you, that video will get destroyed. It will never be seen by anyone. At that stage your family may have lost its wealth, but at least the Triple-S line won't be vilified and disgraced forever, and your good self revealed as a mass-murderer. And as a bonus, you won't be spending the last years of your life rotting in gaol.'

There was a long pause on the other end of the line. 'So, Mr Range, we are not so different after all, you and me? This is also for you all about money.'

'Maybe, maybe not. That's not your need to know. The question is, sir, which option do you go for? And with respect, sir, in reality I don't think you really have any options. Oh, and just in case you were wondering – if anything unpleasant were to happen to me or any of my team which was in any way connected to you, that video will go live. That's part and parcel of the bargain.'

Silence again. 'I suppose, Mr Range, we have a deal. As you say, I really have no options. But, it will take me some time to find buyers for my companies, and to raise two billion.'

'Sir, you have a month. No more. Like I said, it's a fire sale. One month from now the balance in the account I will give you must be two billion dollars. That's the deal.'

'But it will mean selling them at a bargain price . . .'

'That's as may be, sir, but mass-murderers don't really have the luxury to shop around for the best buyers, do they?'

'The bank account details?'

'I'll email them to you. And sir, please don't delay. We've put software in place that will email those video clips to every foreign correspondent on all the major global TV networks the day the deadline expires. One month, and then it goes global.'

'So, buddy, was that fucker de Saint-Sébastien right?' O'Shea asked. 'Is it all about the money?'

Range glanced at Sarah. 'You want to tell him?'

'You tell him. It's your sting.'

'It's your country.'

Sarah smiled. 'Mr O'Shea, two billion dollars is more than the entire GDP of Puntland in one year. It will give my country a real fighting chance. A strong, democratic

Puntland will be a barrier against piracy and terrorism from Somalia itself. So the money is akin to reparations if you like from our Mr de Saint-Sébastien. The people of Al Mina'a can never get back those they lost in the attack, but this way we can rebuild and strengthen the nation. Putting a bitter and twisted old man behind bars wouldn't achieve that, or bring back the victims.'

O'Shea turned to Range. 'Range, you just extorted two billion dollars and you're gonna give it all away? Like I said before, buddy, you're all heart.'

Range shook his head. 'Not me, mate. Have you any idea how vindictive a blood feud sworn by every relative of every victim from Al Mina'a would prove? Put it this way – you don't want to know, and neither do your family. This way, we deliver the biggest chunk of blood money that has ever been paid, and in return we get our names out of this – for ever. For good.

'We take out our expenses first, and B6's fee for doing the job,' he continued. 'But what kind of dent will that make in two billion dollars? Not even a fleabite. That two billion, it's our get-out-of gaol-free card, and I reckon we got off fucking cheaply.'

It was three weeks later, and they had agreed to meet in Paris. Neutral territory. Range had got her new number off the old man, just one more small favour he had extorted from him.

The amount of money in the numbered Swiss bank account kept rising, as de Saint-Sébastien off-loaded his businesses to anyone who would buy. The Qataris – rich with a sovereign wealth fund swollen by petro dollars – had been particularly keen to snap up the bargains, and they had no problems raising the cash to do so. All in all, the money side of it was going very well.

She strode along the walkway that ran along the banks of the Seine. She'd lost none of her elegance and poise, Range noticed. He leaned on the railings and waited for her. They came face-to-face, and stared at each other for a long beat of silence.

Range was the first to speak: 'I hope you feel good about yourself.'

'You never called . . .'

'What d'you mean I never fucking called? Fucking matey there – *your supposed father* – told me you were dead. And at that stage I *believed* he was your fucking father!'

'Take one step back, Mr Range,' she replied, coolly. 'The number I gave you at the end of our time in Kenya – that was my real mobile number. I had been instructed to give you one that he would control. I did not. The texts we exchanged were genuine – at least on my part.'

'You trying to tell me you're the innocent party in all of this? I don't fucking think so.'

'No. I am far from being an innocent. I read the papers. I watch the news. I saw how hundreds of Puntlanders were killed. When I read of that I feared that was the . . . connection. But I needed the money. And take a look at your own actions. After rushing off to save Randy you dashed off to do de Saint-Sébastien's bidding, believing right away that I was dead. If you had called my number to check . . .'

'So, you're on the side of the angels now?'

It was time for her anger to flare. Her eyes blazed. 'No. I. Am. Not. But I did try to warn you. I would have told you. If you had called me and come to see me in Geneva, I would have told you that the whole Kenya thing was a scam. An act. Something I was paid a lot of money to do – money that I desperately needed.'

She paused to wipe away a strand of hair that had blown into her eyes. 'I am far from proud of my part in all this. He warned me if I ever spoke to anyone about it, there would be dire consequences. I had seen all his bodyguards – the men with guns that surrounded him. I was aware of his wealth and his power. But I was willing to take the risk to speak, if only you had called.'

'So, why didn't you bloody call me?'

'They told me not to. They warned me what would happen if I contacted you . . .'

'Mind telling me what you needed the money for?'

'I am a single mother, and something of an unsuccessful actress . . . I have a daughter who is dying with a very rare form of a tumour. It is benign, but because of where it is positioned it will still kill her. There is a possible cure, but

339

it is experimental and not available on the Swiss health service. It is maybe a selfish reason to have taken de Saint-Sébastien's contract, but what parent would not do all they could to save their own child? And in any case, I had no idea of the ultimate end of his deception.'

Range caught the scent of her as they walked. It brought back a flood of conflicting memories. As they wandered along the river-walk, she explained to him how the Kenya sting had been orchestrated. It hadn't been so very difficult. Like her, Amir had been paid to put on an act. He was a local Somalian ransom negotiator for real, but he was happy to work for whoever paid him. If you had the kind of money de Saint-Sébastien had, you could get anyone to do just about anything.

But she insisted that the affection that had grown between them in Kenya – that had been genuine, as had been her desire to talk to him and to warn him what was coming. They'd just never got the chance to meet and talk. They'd never got the chance for anything much to happen, she added, and there had been so many tantalising possibilities.

They paused. She turned to face him.

'Back in that beautiful hotel in Kenya, you remember how you promised me dinner?' She gazed into his eyes, her own belting out the sincerity message big time. 'Would it not be possible, Mr Range? Here in Paris they say they have the world's finest restaurants. I will treat you. Tonight? Dinner?'

They'd reached a part of the esplanade that was popular with riverside diners. Range had agreed to meet someone for lunch here. He glanced across at the restaurant, and a familiar figure stepped out from under a sunshade. She waved. Somehow, she had the look of a pirate queen about her.

Range glanced back at Isabelle.

She smiled. 'For old times' sake, will you dine with me, Mr Range?'

He stepped closer and kissed her on both checks. He looked her in the eyes. I forgive you. No more blood feuds. No more revenge. No feuds at all.

There was a long beat between them. 'It's been good to talk,' Range told her. 'But as to dinner – maybe some other time. Let's stay in touch.'

The sun beat down from a cloudless sky as he crossed the warm flagstones and headed for the restaurant. As he walked he reflected on the deal he was about to cut. It was going to be the quickest way to blow two billion dollars that he'd ever heard of. For a man who liked to think his only loyalty was to his bank balance, it had been hugely tempting to keep the money. But on balance, he reckoned he and his men had got off pretty lightly.

If it meant that the mother of all blood feuds was settled, he figured it was going to be worth every penny.

EPILOGUE

The deal that Sarah Greenfield and Steve Range sketched out over that long Paris afternoon was pretty straightforward. An anonymous donor would offer the Government of Puntland a little short of two billion dollars. The donation was to further strengthen the rule of law, civil society and democracy in the country, and to contribute more generally to the wider development of the nation.

The terms of the donation were to be negotiated via one Sarah Aisha Imam Greenfield, a US citizen born to a mother originally from Puntland. It came with several strings attached. Sarah wanted a particular emphasis to be put on ensuring girls received an education on a par with boys. Range said he was good with that.

Twenty million dollars was to be ring-fenced for the reconstruction and improvement of the Al Mina'a harbour area. The fishing fleet was also to be rebuilt, with funds set aside for the purchase of new boats and the training up of men who could take to the seas. The fishermen were also to be trained and equipped as Marine Watchmen, to keep a look out for Korean, Chinese and other trawlers illegally fishing in Puntland's waters, which would be reported to the nation's Marine Security Task Force, so the vessels could be interdicted.

A further two hundred and fifty million dollars was to be set aside as compensation for those killed in the attack on Al Mina'a. It amounted to approximately 125,000 dollars per man, a not inconsiderable amount in that part of the world. Those families who accepted the dollars were to know that this was 'blood money'. As a result of taking it, all blood feuds sworn against those who had perpetrated the attack on Al Mina'a would be settled.

A significant proportion of the money was to be ear-marked for further building up Puntland's Marine Security Task Force, and especially its anti-piracy and illegal fishing capabilities. Better equipment was to be provided to the Marine Security Task Force, including fast pursuit boats modelled on the Navy SEAL RHIBs, plus helicopters. The money was also to fund a top-quality Marine Security training package.

The company pencilled in to run that training was a British-based private security company called Blackstone Six.

DESERT FIRE
No Rules. No Loyalty. Only the Mission.

Phil Campion

Colonel Gadaffi 's youngest son, Sultan, has been kidnapped by Tuareg warriors armed to the teeth with illicit NATO weaponry.

He's being held, along with a king's ransom in gold, in a fiercely defended Libyan desert stronghold. The British government is desperate to stop Sultan sharing his father's deadliest secrets, and needs a black-ops team to seize him before it's too late.

There is only one man for the job. Steve Range.

'One of the best first-hand accounts of life in combat ever written'
ANDY McNAB

Quercus
www.quercusbooks.co.uk